More Dark Tales

Insights into the Unseen

by J.R. Armstrong-Gregson

I0693233

For Jenny

Published in June 2025 by emp3books

ISBN 978-1-910734-61-2

© J.R. Armstrong-Gregson 2025

www.emp3books.com

Also by J. R. Armstrong-Gregson:
The Roman Army over Time (an e-book)
Dark Tales from a Dorset Rectory

(writing as Gavin Armstrong)
Red Hound: the making of Cuchulainn
King over the Water
Clearances: a morality tale of the Old West

CONTENTS

FOREWORD

This collection of stories falls into two parts, the first being in effect a sequel to my earlier volume *Dark Tales from a Dorset Rectory*, and containing further incidents involving the Reverend Theophilus Hale, rector of St. Mark's, Stoke Armitage, in the later eighteenth century. The second part shifts to the other end of Britain and a more recent period, featuring tales set in twentieth-century Scotland; it is hoped that the variety, of style as much as of setting, will please at least some readers.

TRUTH

Don Tommaso smiled broadly: "And how do you like our Papistical churches, eh?" The Reverend Hale had to grin back: that day alone he, the visiting English clergyman who needed to be convinced of the antiquity and wonder of the Roman tradition, had been taken 'behind the scenes' by three earnest Italian priests to be shown the marvels of their particular parishes. In one he had been taken aside into the sacristy to be shown phials of Christ's blood, Mary's milk and some other liquid over which, perhaps fortunately, his grasp of the Italian language had failed. In another, he had been specially permitted to look behind the altar where were kept the bones of the dragon slain, allegedly, by St. George, his own national patron; in silence, he recognized the ribs of a small whale, such as he had seen on the coast of the West Country. Lastly, and most wonderful of all, an elderly Capuchin had in all seriousness shown him, kept in a crystal and silver box, the tiny skeleton of the Virgin when an infant.

"The buildings are magnificent, of course, and quite ordinary parish churches have on display works of art which surpass those in English cathedrals, and can call on first-rate musicians; but I have very mixed feelings about the faith practised in your churches. The devotion of many of the people cannot be doubted, and their attitude to the Church and the clergy is often admirable, but I cannot stomach the kind of superstition and idolatry – excuse me, my friend – with which these are so often bound up; it seems to me at times that Christianity passed by without leaving much impression on ancient ways of thought, apart from a building. And I don't only mean the peasants: some of the priests are as credulous. Worship is for God alone; praying to the dead, no matter how pious they were, seems to me no different in kind from savages offering gifts to the spirits of their ancestors."

3

Now Tommaso laughed. "I assume you refer to the cult of the saints, and like all Protestants you misunderstand. The saints are those proven to be in bliss and hence to have the favour of God and, presumably, to be in contact with Him in some way. Prayers to them, properly speaking, are not expressions of worship or requests for them to work miracles, but merely ask that they add their prayers to God to ours and advocate – is that the English word? – our causes before Him. I admit that the language used often makes it seem otherwise, as when a particular saint is spoken of as being the patron of one group of people or as being of assistance with a particular problem, but it is not part of the teaching of the Church that saints act as, as – demi-gods, in their own right. Not like the ancient pantheon. Next you will mention statues, yes? It is always so: the people pray to statues, the people worship statues, and so on. Not so: the statue, like the cross, is merely something on which to focus the thoughts; people are visual, and need visual images. You have images in glass in your churches, yes? It is the same. The prayer is to the saint represented, not the piece of stone or plaster, and, as I have said, it is actually indirectly to God Himself as the only fit object of worship. But we are Italians, we are an emotional and theatrical people, as you know, easily moved to exaggerated gestures which often mean nothing; so it is not surprising that sometimes we leave offerings before statues, drape them with garlands, process through the streets carrying them. We are a visual people, in many ways a simple people, and we are above all interested in people, and we find it easier to relate to such figures than to abstract notions of divinity."

"I understand what you say, but it is difficult for a northern Protestant to sympathise with the material nature of much of this faith. Often it seems to me that the emphasis is on praying for good fortune or for better health, rather than on the salvation of the soul; and that seems somehow primitive and limited in thinking, and disrespectful to a God who is so far above such things and who offers us things far more precious than any worldly concern. And there is so much importance attached to material relics, often patently false." He mentioned the things he had seen that day. "And since arriving in Italy I have seen a whole charnel house of bones of saints and apostles which should be lying in a graveyard if they were properly respected, and not held up for public view. I won't even mention entire mummified saints. And then there are the objects: bits of sail from St. Peter's fishing boat and St. Paul's ship; nails from the true cross and Noah's ark; thorns from Christ's crown and the burning bush. It is as though throughout Biblical times squads of men were engaged in gathering up and hording every discarded scrap in case it turned out to have holy connections. It is largely because of the veneration of such things, and the financial profit some make from them, that our English church broke from Rome in despair over two centuries ago. The humblest follower of Christ seems to have left behind more physical evidence of his existence than a half a dozen kings of England living a thousand years later!"

Don Tommaso shrugged. "If such a thing helps strengthen the faith of even one soul, where is the harm? The faith of St. Thomas is adequate, even if not perfect like that of those who could believe without the evidence of Christ's physical presence. Which of us is perfect, eh?"

"It is not honest to pass such things off as genuine, especially not if we want true faith to depend on them. And faith is of the spirit, not bound up in gold reliquaries."

"You are so – austere is the word, yes? But look, the sun is going down behind the hills, there is good Chianti in the jug, and God smiles on us. Surely that is enough to tell us that the world is not so bad, eh?"

It was Hale's turn to shrug. He knew his host could not be angered, but it seemed churlish to continue to disagree so vehemently with him. He had been puzzled since arriving in Italy: the people, even the poorest, were jolly and life-affirming, forever singing, and he found them almost invariably welcoming and open and, where possible, kind and generous. And yet this was the heart of the Papistical religion, supposedly the seat of ecclesiastical tyranny and religious oppression. He thought of the Protestant centres he had seen on the way – in Holland, in Geneva – how grim and closed and intolerant they seemed by comparison. It was perhaps because he found this anomaly so disconcerting that he fought so hard to maintain his stance.

He was, in truth, delighted by Italy, and considered himself greatly blessed in having had the opportunity to visit it at some length. His background had not been such that he could have dreamt of undertaking anything like the fashionable Grand Tour in youth and his resources now would scarcely have supported even a short visit, had his pastoral duties allowed it, and so this trip was a complete bonus, perhaps a sign of divine bounty which he hardly deserved. More immediately, it was the gift of the bishop – or rather, from the bishop's point of view, it was a diocesan duty. The problem was that Bishop Sackington-Lyle did not feel capable of travelling to Rome alone, or with only a servant: he was not very well travelled, was not very practical and was not as fond of solitude as some of his profession. His chaplain was too old and frail for the trip, and his secretary had several small children and another due to arrive imminently; the bishop's wife had been dead two years and they had had no family. He had long wanted to visit Rome and Tuscany, and had built up a series of contacts to that end; furthermore, he felt that in a few years he would be too old to enjoy it. He had looked around his little kingdom for a champion to accompany him on the quest – and had singled out the quite young but serious-minded Reverend Hale, respected for his energy and zeal, as lacking in commitments other than professional ones as his lordship, and well-known for his interest in the Classical world, extending to post-Classical Italy. In order to read Dante, he had taught himself Italian, which would be of enormous value, and he remembered far more French than did the bishop. Hale agreed to the plan at once, a locum was appointed to Stoke Armitage, and within two months bishop and rector were on their way south.

Their route was cross-country, as the bishop could not abide ships: the smell of the sea made him nauseous; the thought of being in a wooden box on the deep gave him the terrors; the motion of the boat made him extremely ill. The crossing to Calais was enough of a nightmare; the rest of the journey was across Europe by land, staying much of the time in accommodation provided by friends, acquaintances and contacts of the bishop. Sometimes they were entertained royally; sometimes the bishop was given the spare bed for the night and Hale had to sleep in the attic or stable as though he had been his valet. But first they had travelled north, for the bishop wanted to see parts of the Low Countries while he had the opportunity – though he would not contemplate the longer sea crossing to Holland. Then they turned south, called in briefly at Paris, then made their way as quickly as they could down through France and over the Alps to emerge into the sunlit plains of northern Italy; then south again, to spend time in Florence, Siena, Lucca, Pisa, before pressing on to the glories of Rome itself. Fortunately, the two men got on extremely well: they shared a love of the Classics, found much in common in their tastes in art and music, and generally shared opinions sufficiently to avoid any falling out without being boringly similar. Hale responded much more to the beauties of nature, and would have lingered in places which the bishop saw as mere dividers between one city and the next, but his senses were so filled every day with new sights, smells and sounds, bright colours and dazzling light that it hardly mattered that scenes passed so rapidly.

It was on their way back from Rome that the bishop had his accident, falling down the steps outside the church of San Miniato, having climbed the hill at the edge of Florence in blistering heat to reach it. Nothing was broken, but one leg was so badly twisted and the blow to his head so severe that he was advised several days strict bed-rest, to avoid the risk of permanent injury. The British consul in Florence, a former naval officer from the West Country, was happy to continue to accommodate him – they had been there as guests for two days already – but he was unfortunately unable to extend this to Hale after that night, as he was expecting the Duke of Evesham's party for the rest of the week and every room was needed. And so Hale had been passed on to Don Tommaso, a clergyman who was a close friend of the consul and spoke much better English than Hale spoke Italian, for a few days. The rector would come into town each day to visit the bishop, of course, but otherwise, for the first time in weeks, he was basically free to do as he wished.

Don Tommaso was the parish priest of San Stefano al Monte, a village on top of a hill overlooking the valley of the Arno and with a view of Florence which just allowed one to distinguish the great dome of the cathedral. His action in taking in the homeless English priest was, in truth, not purely generosity nor even an act of friendship towards the harassed consul: he was a great admirer of England, and seized the chance to practise his English, which was excellent, as he had spent two years at Oxford after graduating – though exactly what he had studied there was never apparent. (Time and money were not issues; he came from an ancient and noble family, and could probably have been a bishop if he had wanted, with a word here and a favour called in there. He preferred to sit on his hill and admire the view.) He loved the English countryside, the literature and the character of the people – but not the food, the weather or the religion. As the religion was almost the only thing Hale found fault with in Italy, religion became the main topic of their conversation; the fact that it perhaps sounded rather acrimonious should not hide the fact that it was the one area for sparring amidst an almost solid concurrence of ideas. As they sat, silent for a moment amidst the huge potted azaleas which surrounded the terrace behind the priest's house, looking down the darkening valley towards the first lights of the city, Hale felt a sense of peace and harmony – and yes, almost of belonging – as strong as any he had ever felt.

"To some extent I agree with you," said the Italian, in conciliatory mood. "Centuries of Hellenistic culture, experience of the most sophisticated ideas from all over the civilised world, a millennium and a half of Christianity have scarcely affected the mental and spiritual world of some of our more remote peasants; they still look for nothing more than a tutelary deity to protect the fertility of their beasts and their fields and to ward off the evil eye. For them, perhaps, Christ is just first amongst the household gods, and the saints are the modern version of the spirits which the ancients remembered as having been imagined to dwell in every river, tree and rock. For them, a god is easily made if one needs one, and the relic is a magical talisman. But faith is faith, and each man has his own kind, at whatever level he can grasp it, in just the same way as one man might see in your Shakespeare's *Hamlet* an acute study of divided loyalties, of clashing ideologies, of, of, inner," the word 'psychological' not being available to him, "of internal pressures leading to physical inertia and mental collapse, whereas another might see it as an overlong story of revenge with a comical gravedigger and an exciting swordfight at the end.

"If a saint does not – what do you say in English? Corrode? Corrupted? If the body is not corrupted after death, it may be a sign of divine favour, as Hector's body was protected while kept by Achilles. Such things do happen. What if that inspires faith in the power of God, in the people? Can that be bad? Faith dependent on a material sign need not be misdirected or in vain. I will tell you a story about faith. About a hundred years ago, in a forest not far from here, a young nobleman called Lorenzo was out hunting with a servant. In those days muskets were clumsy and unreliable things, fired by means of a burning match, and he preferred the quiet efficiency and accuracy of the crossbow. They had had little luck all day, but late in the afternoon they found themselves stalking a group of deer westwards through the woods. Suddenly, a magnificent stag walked out of the trees into a glade in front of them and stood still, presenting an easy side-on target to the huntsman. He raised his crossbow and aimed at the side of the chest, but stopped when his servant caught his arm and hissed very quietly. He lowered the weapon and looked up: as the creature turned in the direction of the faint noise it had detected, the low sun burst through a gap in the foliage directly behind its head and shone through its horns – one of which stuck straight up with large tines at right angles: in short, it formed a perfect cross. For a moment, Lorenzo was blinded by the image of a cross against the disc of the sun; when he recovered himself, he vowed to follow the stag, which was already moving off briskly, wherever the sign might lead him.

"They made their way deeper and deeper into the forest, through bushes and brambles, trying their best to follow the trail of the deer as the sun set ahead of them. Eventually, they lost the trail entirely, and indeed realised that they were themselves quite lost in an unfamiliar, dense part of the forest, in the dark. They had scouted around for some time and were about to give up and look for a safe spot in which to sleep, when Lorenzo spotted a light amongst the trees too low down to be a star. They pushed their way through thick undergrowth, and eventually came to a clearing in which stood a tower with lights at the windows. They approached unobserved, and cautiously mounted the stairs which led up to the great doorway. Carved above the door was the badge of the owner, which they could see clearly by moonlight and the glow from a window above: it was the head of a stag turned towards them, with a cross growing on it between the antlers. Encouraged, they struck the door and were admitted. In brief, the lord of the tower invited them to supper and to stay the night, or, when he learnt who they were, longer if they wanted. Lorenzo met his daughter, and sent the servant home next day to explain what was happening, while himself staying on to woo the girl. They fell in love, married, and had beautiful children. And all because of Lorenzo's faith in a sign which he could have dismissed as a sport of nature or a trick of the light."

"A pretty story!" said Hale, "but legends and folk-tales are for our comfort and indulgence and are not to be treated as holy writ."

"Perhaps; but Lorenzo was my great-grandfather and the girl in the tower my great-grandmother. I first heard the story from my grandfather when I was a small boy. Our family still owns the tower in the forest."

Reverend Hale did not sleep well that night, wishing that he had not categorised his host's story as a fairy-tale before hearing its origin; Don Tommaso did not seem offended, but Hale saw his own words as being highly inappropriate, especially given the hospitality he was enjoying. Next morning, when the Italian returned from saying mass, Hale asked him if it might be possible to him to visit the tower in the forest – not that he doubted the story, he added hastily, but that he was interested in such unusual happenings and co-incidences and would like to see the actual place involved. Don Tommaso was pleased to say yes, and suggested that it might most conveniently be done by means of a detour on their way back from visiting the English bishop in

Florence, which Hale had promised to do after mid-day. Hale protested that he did not expect the priest to escort him, and, though he would value his company greatly, he certainly did not wish him to spend his valuable time in accompanying him to the city. Don Tommaso insisted: it would be pleasanter, and safer, to go together, and there would be no danger of his straying off the road; he had some business to attend to in Florence while Hale was busy with his patron; and in any case, finding the tower without a guide, even with directions, would not be easy. And so it was that in the afternoon, after Hale had found the bishop to be irritable at his incapacity but improving and well-cared for by the consulate staff, the two priests of different faiths were riding briskly out of the far side of the city and taking a great loop round into a wooded area several miles out. Though it was Autumn, the road was dusty, and it was much warmer than it would have been in England – more like Summer.

"The forest is not as large or as dense as it was when great-grandfather Lorenzo was young, but it is still quite extensive and the tower is remote and well-hidden."

They turned off the road onto a path through the trees, and began to go down into a little valley. Although some of the trees were turning brown and leaves were beginning to fall, they gave welcome shelter from the sun, as well as delighting Hale with their variety. At the bottom, where it was cooler still and the birds sang in appreciation, they followed a stream for a while, then suddenly rode into a clearing in the middle of which stood a squat, almost square, ancient tower, with a few small wooden outbuildings huddled round it; Hale had seen no sign of its presence in advance. He was not yet very familiar with the styles of old civil architecture in the country, but he guessed that this rugged, solid, quite plain structure, built to survive a turbulent age, was probably of approximately fourteenth-century date. The ground floor had few windows, and those small, high and heavily barred; he assumed that that part was used for storage, or perhaps sheltering animals. An open staircase ran at right angles to the wall, up to the main entrance, a single large rectangular doorway set in an arched surround; in the tympanum, or semi-circular space above the door, was the image of the stag's head bearing the cross, which the smiling Tommaso pointed out. The windows of that floor and the floor above were larger but divided into slender sections by stone mullions. On top were battlements, with a small structure in one corner of the roof which was presumably the top of a spiral staircase which gave access to that level. A short, bare flagpole was attached to it. Had it not been for the pretty story and the connection with his host, Hale would have described it as grim; in England, Cromwellian cannon would probably have reduced, or elevated, it long ago to a picturesque, ivy-clad, romantic ruin.

"I should explain that the tower is mostly left empty these days. In my father's time, and perhaps before, it was really only used as a hunting lodge, but my brother, who is the landowner, does not hunt much. The building is maintained; a mason comes out every Spring to look at Winter damage, and then a team of cleaners, decorators and builders follows for a day or two or however long is needed to put it to rights. Then it is locked up again, often for another year. A waste, really, but that is my brother's business."

He rode up to one of the outhouses and reached into the corner of the eaves; he extracted a leather bag, which turned out to contain keys wrapped in oily rags to preserve them. They tied up their horses at a wooden stable and went up the stairs; Tommaso turned the huge key with some effort and pushed the heavy oak door open. As they stepped in, the musty smell which pervaded the tower assailed them at once. Damp, dust and cold had waged a long war here against the fillers-in of cracks, painters-over of stains and wipers-off of mould, and at his point in the cycle the natural elements were definitely winning.

13

"Sandro leaves enough equipment in the kitchen for a meal to be prepared and eaten should he choose to visit, and obviously the old furniture is still here, unused, but no linen or hangings are left here because of the dampness."

The first floor was divided into unequal halves, the smaller containing antique kitchen, pantry and scullery, and the other containing a single huge room with a mighty fireplace and the staircase in the corner. A high table with chairs around it headed two sets of trestle tables and benches running at right angles to it. A long sideboard was the other main item of furniture, and a dozen portraits hung on the walls; Tommaso pointed some of them out. "Great-grandfather Renzo, of the story; Beatrice, his bride; his heir Sandro with his wife Lucia; our father; our mother. That is my brother, also Sandro. Those are all copies of paintings in the family seat; these over here are originals: Gianfrancesco, Lorenzo's father-in-law; his mother-in-law; and possibly Gianfrancesco's father. The others I don't know." Hale noted differences in style between the older portraits and those of Tommaso's family, but dwelt on the images of the characters in the story. The painting of Lorenzo had clearly been done many years after the romantic events of his youth, but even so Hale was surprised by the arrogance and hardness of the character portrayed; there was something in particular about the eyes and mouth which he did not like, something which, had he been pushed for a word, he might have called cruelty or ruthlessness. This was in sharp contrast to the smiling openness of Gianfrancesco and the vulnerable beauty of his daughter, whose unexpected underlying sadness the painter had been too honest to conceal. Something else troubled, or at least intrigued, Hale about the portraits; eventually he identified it as the ages of the sitters. Whereas Beatrice had been painted at no more than twenty, the image of Lorenzo was of a man twice that age. Surely there was not such disparity of age between the two young lovers

14

of the story? Yet, if anything, one might have expected the master's picture to have been done first. Perhaps this painting replaced one done in youth. Hale did not want to appear difficult by questioning his host.

On the second floor, the smell was even worse, perhaps because of the greater number of wooden pieces and the closed doors. Four rooms were equipped with four-posters, bare down to the straw mattresses, and armoires and one had four small truckle beds for servants. A couple of other small rooms were empty. Everywhere, the walls were bare stone, levelled and mortared but still hard and cold. "You will note that in all the main rooms there are fittings for tapestries to cover most of the walls; unfortunately, many are rotted away and the rest are preserved by being used at the castle."

The brief tour completed, they rode back up the little valley and out of the forest to rejoin the road back to San Stefano. Hale remembered to thank his host, but otherwise he was deep in thought and said little on the way back, until Tommaso felt he had to ask if all was well with him. It was the images of the two lovers which vexed him – so unlike what he had expected; the secret sorrow of the girl in particular troubled him, and he could not shake off the memory of two large and pleading eyes almost at the point of tears. He must have dreamt of her that night, for the same memory, though animated, was still with him when he woke.

Don Tommaso had already made his apologies about neglecting his guest on that day. It was his day for going to a distant chapel to say mass after the service at San Stefano, followed by lunch with the local landowner out there. He made it his practice to call on certain elderly and sick parishioners on the way back, and would not return until late afternoon. Theophilus was welcome to accompany him, except for his having to visit the bishop, though it would be quite tedious. Hale thanked him, but said that the midday trip into Florence probably made co-ordinating their plans too complicated, and he would use the time in looking at some more of the monuments of the city. In fact, Hale had already decided that he had to revisit the tower, though he could not bring himself to tell his host and it would amount to trespassing; he had no reason for making the visit, not even for himself. He simply felt compelled to go.

Hale left as soon as his host had set off; he called on the bishop early and departed as soon as he felt it possible to go without appearing to be in unseemly haste to leave. The bishop was even more irritable and frustrated, perhaps because his movements now seemed freer, and his physician indicated that only another day's rest would be needed before he could resume his journey. Hale retraced the ride of the day before, briskly, though he hardly needed to think about the route – he seemed drawn straight to the tower. On arrival, he recovered the keys and let himself in. It seemed even more desolate and neglected than when there had been two of them in it; his footsteps and the sounds of doors reverberated and echoed in the almost empty rooms. He made his way straight to the two significant portraits: he had been right – that of Lorenzo showed a petty tyrant capable of malice and that of Beatrice showed a frail victim; the implication about their relationship was obvious. Had its romantic beginning descended to such a level so soon, given that her portrait had to have been done only three or four years later? The sadness of it, and the implied tendency of romantic comedy to slide into tragedy – the Italian story of Romeo and Juliet came into his mind – moved him deeply. But he could not really understand why he had felt it so urgent that he should return to this place, in effect deceiving both his bishop and his host to do so; surely not just to confirm what he already knew about the paintings? He looked again at the portrait of the young woman, and wondered which had been her chamber, in this rather brutal place. He made his way upstairs, and looked in at each room. Yes, it had to be this one – not the biggest, which would have been the master's, but probably the lightest, since it was in a corner and had decent-sized windows in two walls, one, looking out over the front of the tower, with a window seat. The bed, which presumably dated back so far, was also of more delicate build and lighter wood than the others, with a rudimentary vine pattern on the posts. Yes, this was surely her room, at least until Lorenzo arrived. What happened then? Presumably he took her back to his family's castle, and on Gianfrancesco's death inherited the tower; there had been no mention of any brothers. He sat in the window seat and looked out – but it was no longer a sunny afternoon: it was night, though only minutes had passed, and the darkness made the trees seem even denser and nearer; no, they were in fact denser and nearer.

Hale, too fascinated to be much alarmed, was riveted by the appearance of two figures in old-fashioned clothing down below, making their way out of the trees towards the door: when they got close enough for the light from the tower to combine with moonlight and starlight, he recognised the leader: it was the man Lorenzo, crossbow over his shoulder, with his servant following. But this was not the naïve youth of the story: this was the Lorenzo of the portrait, a muscular man in his mid-thirties, with curly black hair and a bushy beard, cursing his exhausted man to keep up. Lost he may have been, but he seemed to know now where he was and he leapt up the steps confidently and hammered insistently on the door. The noise made Hale jump slightly, and sunlight flooded into the room.

Shaking himself awake, he swiftly left the strange window and clattered down the staircase into the hall, where there was at least the comfort of the door out of the building. His eye again caught the portrait of Beatrice, and he paused to sit on one of the chairs of the high table in order to study it once more. What secrets lay behind that pale wide forehead, already slightly furrowed? What had those great eyes seen to make them so moist? The pearls and the dress of purple velvet and white lace could not conceal these things. But the purple dress had been replaced by a plain white one, the pearls by a simple cross, and the chestnut hair was loose and free. She could not be more than fifteen, but she recognized and understood the leer that passed across Lorenzo's face as he took and kissed her hand, and she backed off in fear. Her father, only a few years older than the visitor, was too honest and trusting a soul to see anything, and was too busy laughing at the honour done to his house by the lord's son. He handed Lorenzo a goblet of wine as large as his own and they drank together in the glare of the fire behind Hale and the many candles around the room, where several of Gianfrancesco's friends and retainers were eating late. Hale noticed that Gianfrancesco closed his eyes in appreciation of the wine, but the other watched his host over the rim of his cup as keenly as a hawk.

Now Hale was seriously worried. Was this a series of visions of the past? Was this what he had come here for? Or was it merely his own imagination running away with itself, trying to recast the story just on the assumed evidence of the paintings? He sat for a moment with his eyes screwed up, banishing the scene from his mind, but even so he could still hear the chatter in the room and the clinking of goblets. A voice made its way through his defences, a quite deep but crisp Italian voice, marked by determination and steadiness rather than by the vociferousness and rapidity typical of the language, which was now of an archaic cast. As far as he could make it out, it said something like, "Signor Gianfrancesco, I admire your house and am sorry that I have not visited you sooner. I understand from my father that your family live here inside our lands as though this portion of them were your own? Being free to fortify this house, hunt our deer and fell our trees? That it is a customary arrangement agreed by our grandfathers, with no force in law and no documentary evidence to support it?"

And a lighter voice, not accustomed to serious talking and finding it difficult to respond to this interrogation without making a joke of it, replied something like: "Yes, your honour. My grandfather was a man at arms in your grandfather's service and saved his life in battle against the Milanese. In gratitude, he graciously permitted my grandfather to settle in this redundant bastion and treat this end of the forest as his own – within reason, of course; with due regard for the interests and honour of your family…"

The vision had faded, and Hale sprang up and made as swiftly as he could for the door; scarcely remembering to lock it behind him, he staggered down the steps, mounted his horse, thrust the keys back into their high place of concealment and galloped away until the trees slowed his horse. He was perfectly composed by the time he returned to San Stefano, still just ahead of the priest.

"So what new did you see in the city today?"

"Oh, I think I can say that I have seen all the principal sights now, and rather more than my lord the bishop has! His physician says he needs only one more day of rest, so I would be a burden to you for perhaps two more nights, if that is acceptable to you?"

"Of course. I would it were longer; it gives us only tomorrow to explore somewhere together. Not even that: I assume you will be returning to his lordship at the usual time tomorrow, and perhaps going back later to help him pack, so what would you like to do tomorrow afternoon?"

Hale himself was surprised at what he said without thinking; "I would very much like to see again the tower in the forest."

"Eh? I can't see what fascination that has for you. You saw all there was to see, in less than a quarter of an hour."

"But the ride out there is so pretty, and I will soon be travelling on dusty roads for weeks, with the bishop refusing to stop to look at any trees or lakes or mountains! In any case, the ride out fits in very well with my requirement to visit Florence. If you don't mind, that is."

Don Tommaso did not object, but he did find the request very odd, and thought that perhaps Hale simply did not know of anywhere else to go. Several times that evening he made alternative suggestions as to how they could spend those hours: a visit to the cathedral and ancient ruins at Fiesole, perhaps. Hale, however, grew in determination: he had no idea why he wanted to go back again, but somehow he felt that he would never be at peace until he had done it – and this could be the last chance of his life. He had, indeed, a strong desire to know what happened next in the story of Lorenzo and Beatrice, if that should be granted to him, but why he should be seeing what he saw, and what manner of things his visions were, he was not at that time sufficiently dispassionate even to speculate on. He certainly felt he could not confide in Don Tommaso, who was personally so close to the story. He slept little that night, in anticipation of returning to the tower again and what he might learn this time – though why he should feel so excited, so involved, he could not have said.

In the heat of the next day, Don Tommaso met Hale on the road outside Florence after his visit to the bishop, and together they rode into the forest. Hale tried his best to appear unexcited and told his host what they had discussed: how much better the bishop was feeling and how he was anxious to be up, how they were going to pack up in the morning and leave by coach for the north in the afternoon, how he would like to spend a last night at

San Stefano but would need to leave early, borrowing Don Tommaso's spare horse again. But the Italian was not deceived, and at one point asked him if was feeling all right. In truth, Hale's excitement was now more than tinged with apprehension, and with the image of the sorrowful Beatrice in his mind he now saw the forest as a dark and forbidding place, and when they reached the valley bottom the lack of heat was as a chill. Indeed, it was not just his thoughts colouring the landscape: dark clouds were moving down from the north, it was suddenly colder and a wind was getting up, swaying the trees and making them shed leaves as easily as a child sheds tears. The birdsong had stopped.

They were still a quarter of an hour from the tower when the storm burst and the wind suddenly doubled and brought with it a torrent of rain. "Sometimes we have English weather here, but not all the time, as you do!" Tommaso led them to a convenient temporary shelter: a rock overhang in a high part of the stream bank, just big enough for two or three horses to stand inside with their dismounted riders. At the back of the little cave, with the animals held in front of them, they were completely sheltered, and they stared out in silence at the downpour.

It was no longer raining. Lorenzo and Gianfrancesco were hunting with crossbows in the forest not far from the tower, with two servants in attendance. They were stalking a small herd of deer, very cautiously, with Gianfrancesco well in the lead; Lorenzo was deliberately hanging back to whisper to the others and pass them small leather pouches. They reached a clearing, into which a stag was boldly making its way out of the trees, in search of the longer grass. Gianfrancesco, standing three or four yards ahead and to the side of the others, raised his weapon slowly so as not to alarm it, and carefully took aim. The servants both looked to Lorenzo, who waved them away; they turned their backs and silently disappeared into the undergrowth. The stag turned in the direction of the faint movement it had detected; the

21

low sun burst through a gap in the foliage directly behind its head and shone through its horns – one of which stuck straight up with large tines at right angles: in short, it formed a perfect cross.

Gianfrancesco paused, and slowly lowered his crossbow, staring astonished at the creature; at the same time, Lorenzo raised his weapon and fired – straight into Gianfrancesco's back. The stag bounded off as the dead man crashed into the bushes and his killer started shouting for help. The two servants returned and Lorenzo rapidly told them a story of how he and his host had both been aiming for a stag and he had misfired disastrously; he pointed out the denseness of the undergrowth and the low sun in his eyes, and made it clear that they had both actually seen all this, to which they nodded assent. Only then did they go to where their master lay.

"It is no longer raining; shall we move on?" Tommaso had obviously said this several times before Hale first heard him. "Are you all right, my friend? You seem almost asleep. Is the ride too much for you?" Hale protested his fitness and apologized, offering the cumulative experiences of the past few weeks as the reason for his tiredness. They led their horses out and mounted again. Hale was struggling with what he had seen, and with the question of whether he should tell Tommaso. But no – he had his version, which everyone else had, and it made them joyful and optimistic; it added romance and mystery to his family's history. What could be gained by questioning it and putting in its place this sordid version, which turned his heroic great-grandfather into a treacherous murderer, if not worse? For that, Hale guessed, he would have to wait for the tower. And indeed, when they rode up to the tower, Hale halted below the window he knew to contain Beatrice's seat. Voices were raised; a tearful Beatrice was beating on the inside of her locked door; Lorenzo, twice her size, dragged her back, laughing at her attempts to punch and kick at him, lifted her round the middle and threw her onto the bed – the one Hale had seen already – and straddled her, on his knees. She lifted her head to spit at him and he gave her a mighty slap across the face which caused her whole upper body to lurch to one side. Hale felt himself lurch sickeningly, the side of his head stinging….

Don Tommaso was pouring water onto his head from the bottle he kept on his saddle, and rubbing his face and neck with a handkerchief. His head hurt badly and the whole right hand side of his body felt sore and bruised. Slowly, he realized he was sitting on the wet ground, propped against a tree at the edge of the clearing with the tower. Their horses were wandering across the grass, intermittently grazing. "You English are always falling over. In England, it is with the drink, but here you do not even need that!" He had simply slipped from his horse, after snoring for a moment as though asleep, Tommaso said. Perhaps they should go home: he obviously needed some rest before the exertions of the next day, and to recover from his fall. Hale, too stunned by his accident and too appalled by what he had seen, could not speak beyond a few grunts of agreement and reassurance. He was helped back into the saddle, though Tommaso took the precaution of keeping their horses close enough together that he could catch Hale if necessary, and guiding both animals. They rode off, and Hale did not even look back at the tower.

The rest of the day was awkward. Hale felt both sore and foolish from his fall, and he continued to be deeply moved by the events he had witnessed; he was still also struggling with the question of whether he should tell Tommaso what he had seen, in the interests of truth. But how did he know it was the truth? And what would knowing a depressing truth gain anyone? He knew this truth, and it had simply made him miserable. Without telling what he had seen, he could not sensibly or honestly account to his host for his movements and his mood. These internal struggles all but prevented him from speaking, and eventually he had to apologise to the priest for his apparent rudeness. As well as offering tiredness and the heat of the day as reasons for his condition, he did go so far as to offer this as an excuse, over dinner: "I have been much vexed about the subject on which we touched the other night: the value of aids to faith, the dividing line between faith and superstition, and so forth. I am afraid that years of parish life have rendered me incapable of serious theological thought without much painful effort! I have come to the conclusion that I am perhaps too harsh in my judgement. If stories and relics and statutes can inspire and induce faith and prayer, then so be it, especially where other means are scarce. And I see no reason why almost equally suspect scientific methods and explanations should be used to upset such a situation in which only good is being produced. As you say, which of us is perfect, which of us knows all?" And that night he stretched his faith even further by praying for the soul of Beatrice.

But even if their residual desire for justice, long since almost entirely dispelled, was not satisfied, somewhere the spirits of Beatrice and Gianfrancesco, though already at peace, rested a little easier for knowing that the truth was finally known by at least one good man. For the rest, they were content that their descendants should live warmed by the romantic yarn and be ignorant of the horrors behind it.

THE BARROW

Lord Thorning of Thorningley Castle has already featured in these accounts of unusual incidents in the life of the Reverend Hale, rector of Stoke Armitage [1], and it will not surprise the reader to find him again engaged in antiquarian pursuits – though on this occasion the antiquity was much greater than the Middle Ages which usually held his interest. It was Dr. Herbert Norrington of St. Clement's College, Oxford, who had first rediscovered, in a patch of rough ground in the fields around Lower Thornton, a significance which had been lost perhaps two or even three thousand years before, and rediscovered then only by accident. Dr. Norrington's work is little known now, partly because his later writings tended towards a kind of romantic and imaginative speculation which finds little favour in modern scientific circles, but in his day he was celebrated for his vivid recreation of past cultures and his belief in the worth of investigation literally on the ground rather than entirely through the written record, a quite revolutionary approach at the time; his *In the Footsteps of King Arthur* was perhaps his most widely-read book. It should be understood that the idea of practical archaeology by scholars rather than grave-robbers, digging on ancient sites and opening up monuments in a spirit of scientific discovery, was then still quite a new one – the study of antiquities generally being limited at this period to the study of ancient texts and works of art, and hence to the strictly historical period.

It was on his return journey after visiting Somerset, Tintagel and King Mark's Cornwall to research the settings of the story of the once and future king that Dr. Norrington passed through the area

---

[1] See "Root and Branch" in *Dark Tales from a Dorset Rectory*.

around Stoke Armitage in Dorset and stopped to inspect the megalith known as the Lone Stone, atop of Lone Stone Hill, to which allusion has been made elsewhere [2].

A particular interest of his was our ancestors' use of landmarks and the positioning of monuments in relation to landscape and even to the stars, and so after examining and measuring the stone he strolled around it looking outwards, to see if it offered any significant viewpoints. In one direction, he could see the tower of St. Mark's, surrounded by four tall yew trees marking the circumference of its circular churchyard; although the shape of the precinct brought immediately to mind the thought that it might represent a pre-Christian ritual enclosure, there was nothing particularly unusual in this – the church could be seen from any high place in the vicinity. However, when he walked round to the other side of the stone and looked out, he saw with delight and excitement a distinct ancient feature in the exactly opposite direction, so that a perfectly straight line could be drawn between it and the equally ancient site occupied by the church so as to pass through the point marked by the monument where he stood.

This second feature would scarcely have been recognized as such by the untrained eye, but it was clear enough to Dr. Norrington, especially from this elevated position, that it was a cluster of three barrows or tumuli, ancient man-made earth mounds, probably covering burials and arranged in a line receding away from him. They were so overgrown as to be almost invisible from the ground, but when viewed from the hill the clump of wilderness and trees in the midst of cultivated fields and neat hedgerows drew attention to itself, and whereas the local people simply saw a patch of uneven and unusable waste

---

[2] See "Limits", *ibid.*

ground the scholar could discern the monuments of people long dead and forgotten. He immediately decided to delay his return by a day, descended the hill, hastily found lodgings for the night at the Thorning Arms in Lower Thornton, a little further on, and then made his way down a quiet lane towards the tree-covered mounds, which to him were quite obvious on the horizon.

They stood in between two fields, and served in effect as an enlarged part of the hedge dividing them, a kind of salient. They had clearly not been lowered or damaged by ploughing, and had probably not been touched at all for generations, since on one side of them there was a rough wooden fence, much mended, intended to keep the cattle grazing there from straying over into the adjoining field, given over to some root vegetable which Dr. Norrington would recognize only on his plate; on that side, the base of the mounds was protected by an old stone wall. The two fields turned out to belong to different farms, and so the barrows occupied a kind of no-man's land, a fact which had probably helped preserve them from agricultural disturbance. There were three mounds, in a line pointing to distant Lone Stone Hill, the central one being perhaps half as big again as the other two; it was perhaps a hundred feet long and half as wide in the middle, with a slight taper towards the ends, and it was about five yards high along its rounded central ridge. The mounds were covered with long, coarse grass and the ground between and immediately around them was rough, stony and filled with brambles and nettles; tall, thin coniferous trees and overgrown shrubs had taken root all over the site, so that it had lost any appearance of being an artificial construction – though to Dr. Norrington it was as plainly the work of a human architect as was the tower of St. Mark's over the hill.

He swiftly saw that it would be easier to gain access to the mounds through the field occupied by cows, rather than over the planted field, so he sought out the farmhouse with a milking parlour, back down the lane towards the inn, and asked to see the farmer. For some time, the two men were equally puzzled: Norrington was confused by the farmer's aggressive queries as to whether he had been sent by a Lord Thorning and whether he had come about taxes or the rent, while Mr. Ford could not understand why this stranger, who claimed to be a doctor and from a university – the nature of which he did not really understand – should be asking him foolish questions about a worthless patch of scrub at the edge of his land. Eventually, Ford understood that his visitor was not an agent of authority but, for some obscure reason, had a disinterested curiosity about the history of the property; his manner relaxed, and he allowed the scholar over the threshold of his house.

"No, I fear I cannot help you much. The only thing I know about them hillocks is that, to my knowledge, they be outside of my tenancy and, I believe, outside of my neighbour's too. But they be useful, in that they divide us, you see, without any possibility of disputes about bounds, which in my experience be the main source of trouble between folk – and I would not want trouble with Jenkins, not on any account. A cordon sanitary, I believe you educated men would call it, in French. No, I know nothing about the history of the place and have heard little of local tales, for I be new here, not from these parts at all."

"Ah. How long have you farmed here then?"

"Seven years, and so far I have hardly had time to draw breath, let alone gossip with the neighbours."

"I see. If they do not belong to you and do not belong to your neighbour, who would own them?"

"The hillocks? They be part of the estate, like all the land around here. You understand, both I and my neighbour Jenkins be tenants of the estate and do not own our farms."

"And this Lord –Thorning, was it?"

"Aye."

" – that you mentioned, he would be the owner, would he?"

"Aye, he be our landlord. He lives at the castle, a mile or two down this road."

"Would I be able to see him, do you think?"

"As far as I know, the Thornings be away at Bath at this moment, visiting, as such folks do; they have been away for a week, but it will probably be only another week before they are back, for they bain't over-sociable, if you take my meaning, especially Lady Thorning. They have had what you might call a somewhat tragic life, though nothing compared to what the likes of us must endure every day." Ford evidently had little notion of what kind of life Dr. Norrington might lead in the Senior Common Room at St. Clement's. "But if you have any questions about them hillocks, you might try Jenkins, if he'll speak to you; his family have been tenants there for at least three generations, I'm told, and he might know something."

Norrington decided that, given what he had been told about their ownership, it would be inappropriate to ask for permission to go on the mounds, so he thanked the farmer and made his way along the lane and up a track to the next farmhouse, contenting himself with learning what he could at a distance. He was stopped a few yards from the front door by a ferocious dog, which would surely have attacked him had it not been for the length of chain which secured it to a ring in the wall. The dog was alternating between straining at the furthest extremity which it could reach and dancing from side to side, and the scholar was contemplating whether retreating might be the best option open to him, when the incessant barking brought a large, bearded man to the open door of an adjoining barn. He shouted across, without any attempt to call off the dog:

"What d'ye want? What be you doing on my land?"

Norrington, understanding now why Ford did not wish to antagonise this man, did his best to make himself understood across the farmyard, over the terrible noise. He tried the ploy of using the man's name, but, recalling the suspicions he had encountered next door, followed it up by shouting that he was not from Lord Thorning and was not in the business of collecting either rent or taxes. He announced himself as a scholar passing by, interested in the history of the area and hoping for a word with the farmer, on the recommendation of Mr. Ford. At this, Jenkins made a face and gave one shake of his head, but he strode across the yard with a reluctant air; he raised his fist and bellowed, "Back, Demon!", and the dog whimpered and slunk back to take up its post, sitting by the door. The farmer stood between Norrington and the house, hands on hips: "Well?" Off-putting as his reception from Ford had been, it was clear that he was the soul of hospitality compared to this man, so Norrington explained as briefly and as simply as he could who he was and what his interest in the property was.

"Those," he recalled Ford's word, "hillocks over there, amongst the trees between your field and Mr. Ford's –"

"What of them?

"Well, I wondered if you knew anything about them," Norrington concluded lamely. Jenkins stared at him impassively, either unaware of the embarrassment his silence caused or else deliberately trying to unsettle his visitor by it. "You see," continued the scholar eventually, "I believe them to be man-made tumuli, ancient monuments, in fact. Old burial mounds," he ended apologetically. Another painful silence; at last, "And I was wondering if you knew of a similar story – or anything at all about them, perhaps."

This time the silence was shorter, and marked by something of a change in the farmer's manner. He looked thoughtful, and shifted his stare to the side, not at anything in particular, but in the general direction of the barrows.

"All I knows about 'em is what my father told me when I were a young lad, and what he said his father had told him. He said that on no account should I ever venture off our land onto 'em; he said that that wall had been put there as a boundary as to where we could go and where we couldn't, and that I should leave the trees and the mounds alone. Which I have done ever since, and intend to do in future. That's all I knows."

"Ah, that must have been because your leasehold, as I understand it, does not include that piece of land – or so I am told – not that it is any business of mine, of course. But are there any local traditions or stories about the mounds? I am sorry to detain you"

Norrington could see that the farmer was becoming agitated again, which he ascribed to his being kept from his work. Jenkins briefly spread his hands and gave a kind of shrug.

"I pays no heed to the foolish things folk might say. Them mounds, as you call 'em, are none of my business, and that's fine by me. That's all I have to say."

His hands were back on his hips and he was staring at the scholar blankly again; a breeze sprang up, ruffling the man's hair in a vaguely threatening manner, reinforced by the whispering of leaves on the hedges. Norrington sensed that he was expected to leave it at that, so thanked the farmer briefly for his help and withdrew back down the track to the road. As he went, he heard the dog resume barking, this time unchecked, and wondered whether the farmer had actually provoked it; he quickened his step, half-expecting the unchained animal to come bounding down the path behind him, but he regained the lane without incident and made his way back towards the Thorning Arms, pausing for a while to look over the hedge again at the strip of slightly elevated land on which the three barrows stood.

The sun was beginning to sink into the west, behind Ford's farm, and clouds were gathering, driven overhead by the wind, which had stiffened rapidly and began to blow quite strongly as Norrington stood there. The numerous but quite thinly-spread trees and shrubs on and around the mounds bent and rocked, the breeze being unbroken by any other significant hills or woods nearby, and the sound of the branches rubbing and creaking and the whistling of the wind through the foliage blended oddly with the distant hysterical barking of the dog. The long shadows cast by the trees over the mounds and out across where Norrington was standing danced and swayed too, in a manner which struck him as almost hypnotic, and, having come out without his coat, he felt a sudden chill. It was only a late afternoon in early September, but here was clearly a harbinger of the rigours of Autumn. With a last glance at the mounds, the top of the higher central one being visible through the trees above the slope of the nearest, he shivered and hurried along the lane the half-mile to the inn.

Despite – perhaps because of – the negative reception he had received at the two farms, the memory of the mounds at Lower Thornton stayed vividly with Dr. Norrington as he travelled back to Oxford, began to write up the Cornish chapter of *In the Footsteps of King Arthur* and commenced the lecturing and tutoring commitment of the new term. He had quickly resolved to contact Thorning, the owner of the site, to inquire if he knew more of its past than his tenants did, and to ask permission to gain access to it at a later date. The effort of actually wording the letter satisfactorily took him much longer: he was afraid that the hostility to strangers and general unhelpfulness which he had experienced in Lower Thornton might extend to all levels of society and he did not wish to alienate the landowner by appearing inquisitive or demanding. He need not have worried: although his letter was not despatched westwards to Thorningley Castle until almost the end of October, he had a reply from his lordship by the middle of November, and it was wholly positive.

Lord Thorning began by expressing regret that he had been absent when Norrington – one of whose books he had read with pleasure – had been in the vicinity, and offering hospitality at the castle when he should be in the area again. He went on to indicate his own interest in antiquities, his sympathetic understanding of the scholar's curiosity and his delight that he had discovered something worthy of his attention on the Thorning estate. Becoming more specific, he said that he had long been aware of the peculiar nature of the mounds, and had inspected and surveyed them some years before when he had just left the army and the adjoining farm was briefly untenanted. (Norrington surmised that this was before Ford's arrival.) He too was convinced that they were artificial, and of great age, such that trees had grown up on them after their original purpose had been forgotten. He had himself wondered whether they represented an original Norman castle abandoned when Thorningley had been founded, but he had found no precedent for a three-fold structure in place of the usual single motte, or castle mound, and in any case they lacked the flat top required for a crowning structure of tower or stockade. He was excited at the news that they could be far older, indeed perhaps pre-Roman (Norrington had been cautious in initially suggesting a date), and would be pleased to allow Norrington, and any of his colleagues from Oxford, to examine them at greater length. As they appeared to be included in neither of the adjoining tenancies, there was no danger of such activity interfering with farming operations.

Greatly heartened by this response but still thinking that it would be wise to be cautious in his approach, Norrington wrote again merely thanking his lordship for his encouragement and the generosity of his offer. It was the end of term before he put together a longer document, outlining the nature of barrows, his idea of what the Lower Thornton site might represent, and the connection which he had seen between it, the Lone Stone and the churchyard at Stoke Armitage. He dropped into the account, which covered five sheets of foolscap, including some sketches, a couple of references to excavations of barrows and what might be found within them – for this was his ultimate aim: to get Lord Thorning's permission to conduct a dig to open the barrows, or at least the central one. As I have already said, archaeology as we know it was barely in its infancy at this time; however, there had already been some digs by landowners at recognised burial sites and fortifications, a practice which was in time to become quite fashionable. Lord Thorning was already aware of such occurrences from some notices in the press, and was excited by the idea that a significant discovery might be made on his land. In truth, such excavations were basically still only about finding artefacts, rather than interpreting the sites, and were often carried out by treasure-hunters, but Norrington's motivation was rather more academic; in the ensuing communications, his concern that the dig should be conducted with some scientific rigour accorded to a remarkable degree with Thorning's view of it as a quasi-military exercise.

The response from Thorningley arrived at St. Clement's on the last day of the year, and was a belated Christmas present for Norrington, for it seemed to take it for granted that a dig at Lower Thornton would take place during the following Spring or Summer. Thorning offered to accommodate the scholar and an assistant at the castle and to provide two or three labourers, with suitable tools, to do the digging and carting; he suggested that probably three weeks would be an appropriate length of engagement for them. This was far better than Norrington had expected, as he had only hoped for free access to the site, and he made the most of his lordship's generosity. It was agreed that he would come alone for a few days during the Easter vacation, to survey the site and plan with Thorning what form the dig would take, and that then work would be done in earnest in the Long Vac – in late June and early July, when the demands of agricultural work on the labourers would not be as great as they would be at harvesttime.

And so on an unseasonably cold and blustery day in April Norrington finally arrived at Thorningley Castle and was greeted by Lord Thorning; the two men knew each other quite well, at least as regards their intellectual concerns and methods, from their letters over the preceding months, and neither was disappointed when they met. After he had introduced his guest to Lady Thorning, who put in a brief and almost silent appearance for form's sake, his lordship suggested a glass of something to keep out the cold and then a quick visit to the mounds before the light began to fail. The carriage drew up in the lane at the point where Norrington had last stood and looked at the site, and it was immediately clear that Thorning had already made some changes to facilitate their future work. Firstly, a short section of the hedge lining the lane had been removed and a gate had been inserted – or rather a full-sized door in a frame of stout timbers, secured by a heavy padlock. When Thorning had opened this and they had passed through it, it became obvious that he had had the hedge separating the fields grubbed up for the fifteen yards or so that led to the base of the nearest mound, and replaced by a gravelled path wide enough for a man to push a handcart along. On either side of this path was a new, raw wooden fence, connecting on Ford's side with the existing fence and on Jenkins' side with the stone wall.

"This gives us easy access to the mounds without us getting in the way of either of my tenants, " he explained. "If we had chosen one side for our access and operations, the man concerned would have been full of complaints and discontent about the disturbance, and I would rather avoid that, even if it is all my land. This way neither loses out – this little causeway really takes up no more room than the bank and hedge did."

There had been some preparatory work done on the mounds too: the trees had not been touched, but the thicker brambles and nettles had been cleared away or cut down, and the long grass had been mown.

"Just to make it easier to see what's what, you know. We haven't cut any trees down, in case it disturbed the ground – roots and what have you. And we haven't laid a finger on any of the stones, though I doubt they are more than just stones. I hope that's all right."

Norrington assured him that no damage could have been done, and thanked him for his efforts to make the job easier, but then he noticed Jenkins, standing right up against the new fence, where it bent a little to join the stone wall. He was watching them, with a sour expression, and when he saw that Norrington had observed him he scowled at him in recognition. Lord Thorning noticed too: "Good afternoon, Jenkins."

"Arternoon, y'r ludship." He muttered the conventional words in a way which made them almost unintelligible.

"I trust we are not impeding your work, or encroaching on your tenancy, by walking here on my land?"

"No, y'r ludship."

"Good. I would be distressed to think that we might be preventing you from getting on with your business."

The man finally took the hint, and with an ill grace turned around and stalked off.

"A surly and rebellious one that," murmured Thorning to Norrington; "we would soon have knocked that out of him in the regiment. A strange one, too: he's been hovering around ever since we started work here, as though he had any inkling of what is going on. I suppose that he thinks it is a plot to steal some of his farm – not that it is his farm, though you'd think he owned it, the way he talks to me. No sense of respect, no regard for rank. But he looks after the land well enough and pays his rent, so I can't really turn him out, especially as his people have been there for the best part of a hundred years."

The two men measured the three mounds as accurately as they could, using a rope and yardstick which Norrington had brought, and the scholar made several rough sketches of the site and a more carefully-drawn plan, showing the main trees and indicating the relative position of the Lone Stone, just visible on its hill on the eastern horizon. His lordship walked around the site meanwhile, looking at the mounds from every angle and growing a little restive. At length, they withdrew; as the carriage pulled away, Norrington, looking back, thought he caught a glimpse of Jenkins watching them over the hedge. He said nothing.

That evening, the two researchers made their plans for the coming dig. Norrington made the quite obvious point that if there was anything of significance under the barrows it would most likely be under the larger, middle one, and placed quite centrally. If it were a burial, the body, or urn, would have been placed on the ground, possibly inside a chamber or cairn, and then covered over, or else buried before the mound was raised over it. If the latter, they would not have gone to the trouble of burying it very deeply, knowing that it was going to be underneath the barrow in any case. The scheme they hatched therefore was to remove a two and a half yard square of turf and topsoil from the base of the long side of the barrow, at its midpoint, and examine the structure of the mound. They would then drive a tunnel at ground level, eight or nine yards long, into the mound, to reach its central point, shoring up the hole with props and planks as miners do. If they did not find anything there, then they would dig down a little way to see if there was anything beneath. Because it was less wooded on Jenkins' side of the site and there was more room between the mound and his wall than there was between it and Ford's fence, it was decided that the tunnel would go in from that side.

Shortly before Norrington departed for Oxford the next day, Lord Thorning happened to comment that it was strange that no-one seemed to have recognised the barrows for what they were before he came to the area. This prompted the scholar to repeat his old question, as to whether his host knew of any old stories or folklore concerning them.

"No, but I have not lived here all my life; I have been here permanently, as you might say, for only the last decade or so, so I have rather missed out on local gossip and so forth. I spent most of the twenty years before that in Ireland and Canada with the regiment, and as a boy, when I suppose one picks up most of that sort of stuff, local traditions and stories and such, I was away at boarding school."

"Have your children not heard and repeated anything of that kind?"

Lord Thorning was silent, for a long time, and Norrington, sensing some tragedy or misfortune, did not press it.

June came, and with it the Long Vac, and Dr. Norrington and his student James Bradshaw, who had just completed the Final Examinations for Greats with distinction, arrived at Thorningley Castle. Under Norrington's influence, Bradshaw had developed a great interest in British antiquities and was planning to spend the summer researching the subject before commencing theological studies to enter the Church. He planned to assist his tutor on this excavation, then visit Stonehenge and Avebury, taking in Silbury Hill and the barrows of Salisbury Plain, before travelling to Glastonbury and finally Cornwall. Norrington introduced him to Lord Thorning and the two scholars settled into the rooms allocated to them for their stay. Later, the three men took the carriage down to the site, for the young man to get his first look at the mounds of which he had heard so much from his mentor. First, they paused in the lane, to take in the view of the trees and their long evening shadows, then went through the new gate and along the path. Bradshaw said nothing to give away his feelings, but he was enchanted by the site, its remoteness and mystery even in the midst of everyday life, its merging of the anciently man-made and the currently natural, its potential for endless investigation and speculation without any possibility of ever understanding the real truth about it. He blocked out the crude gravel path and the intrusive raw wood of the new fence and concentrated on the timeless emblems of ubiquitous mortality, man's heroic and doomed quest for immortality, nature's inextinguishable power to reclaim. He felt an elation, a seemingly-literal rising or swelling of his heart, a lightness in his step as though he could launch himself into the air to settle on top of the highest barrow. Here, he felt, he was finally going to be in touch, physically rather than through books, with the soil and with the past; he was going to venture into the earth to visit a place seen by no living soul for millennia and last looked on by a man from a different culture, speaking a different language and worshipping different gods but sharing the same experience which he was about to have. It was like exploring an unknown land and inhabiting another body, at the same time.

The following morning, the work began. After morning service at St. John's, Higher Thornton, Lord Thorning, accompanied by Lady Thorning on one of her rare local public appearances, Dr. Norrington and the vicar, a pale and diffident man called Roach, proceeded by carriage to the site; Bradshaw sat up with the coachman, and far behind them came a gardener from the castle with a small waggon on which were a handcart and a number of stout wooden posts and planks, in sizes ranging from two to three yards. A number of what passed for dignitaries in that remote country were gathering around the mounds, by invitation, to witness the opening of the barrow: General Randall of Randall Court, with whom Lord Thorning had served in the army; Morton, a prominent local gentleman farmer with whom he hunted; Baines, the old schoolmaster of Stoke Armitage, who had written a history of the area (though without mentioning pre-history); the Reverend Theophilus Hale, the rector of St. Mark's, with whom the Thornings had an old association. Some of the retainers from the castle and a few of the estate tenants, including the Fords in their Sunday best, completed the party; as he walked down the path, Norrington again noted Farmer Jenkins, lurking in the far corner of the neighbouring field, watching proceedings from a distance despite the invitation to attend which had been extended equally to him and his neighbour Ford.

At the nominated spot on the side of the barrow, two sticks had been driven into the turf, about eight feet up the steep slope and a similar distance apart; these marked the upper corners of the patch which was to be dug. A small wooden platform with a couple of steps leading up to it had been erected in front of this. A workman stood at either side, and one handed Lord Thorning a bright new spade. When Reverend Roach had said a few prayers for the success of the venture, his lordship mounted the dais and, unhandily though he had practised it, wielded the spade so as to cut a slight furrow between the sticks. Climbing down, he did the same with downward strokes from each stick to the ground. There was a round of applause from the gathering, and the symbolic opening of the mound was complete. Leaving the two workmen to cut out the turf within the square so delineated, the rest of the assembly made its way in a variety of vehicles to the castle, where lunch was provided in the Great Hall for the main guests and in a marquee on the lawn for the tenants and hangers-on.

Later that afternoon, the two Oxford men and his lordship returned to the site. They found that the turf had been removed from the square on the side of the mound, and soil to the depth of nearly two feet, which was being carted round to the south side of the barrow and deposited in a pile between it and the smaller tumulus. There was nothing remarkable to be seen so far – only earth. Thorning went back to the castle, leaving Norrington to do some more detailed sketching, while Bradshaw took a turn with the men in digging and carting, for it was quite hard work to dig horizontally into ground which had never been turned over before, or at least not for several millennia, and was riddled with roots and stones. By the end of the day, when Thorning returned to collect his colleagues and pay the workmen, the entrance to the tunnel was a yard and a half deep and the first two pairs of pit props were in place to hold up planking which would retain the earth above. Henceforth, because of the confined nature of the space in which they would be working, progress would inevitably be slower; it was to be expected that the tunnel would taper somewhat as it advanced, so that by the time they reached the centre spot the end of it would be about the size of an ordinary doorway.

An informal rota was established, by which there would always be 'someone from the castle' to supervise the men and watch for finds, or at least for significant changes in the mound. Bradshaw, being the youngest and most active, drew two shifts against the one of the others, but he did not mind in the least. After breakfast, Thorning would ride down to make sure that the men turned up and started their task in the required way. Mid-morning, Bradshaw would walk down to relieve him, and stay until the men stopped for their meal, when he would return to the castle to eat and report on progress. He would then return to the mound while Norrington took his afternoon nap and Thorning attended to business. The tutor would go along in the carriage in the course of the afternoon and send his student back in it; finally, Thorning would return in the carriage to collect him and pay off the men for the day. While at the mound, the older men generally passed the time reading or sketching, while Bradshaw tended to take exercise by helping with the excavating; back at Thorningley, the time was generally spent reading in his lordship's extensive library.

By the close of the third day, the tunnel was almost ten feet long, and some of the initial excitement had cooled as routine took over; by the close of the fifth, with the sixth pair of props in place, tension was rising again as Norrington's measuring revealed that they were over six yards in, and only a couple of days' digging from the midpoint. However, the next day was the Sabbath, and work had to stop. That afternoon, the three men found themselves unable to relax: Norrington was trying to read but found himself going over the same page repeatedly or staring at the same passage for four or five minutes; Bradshaw was pacing around the castle restlessly; Thorning went up on the roof, out in the grounds, down to the stables, until he finally declared that he thought he had better check up on the mound, and the others swiftly volunteered to accompany him. Tacitly, they agreed to walk, to pass the time and use up some nervous energy, though more slowly than the young man and the old soldier would normally stride out, for Norrington's sake. They arrived at the gate in the hedge in silence, and opened it just in time to see the extraordinary sight of Farmer Jenkins kneeling in his field-edge, close to the stone wall, facing the opened side of the central mound: he would have just been able to see the top of the tunnel from his position. But more extraordinary than his attitude was what he was doing, for he was holding a small wooden cross up in front of his face, both hands clutching the lowest limb, and he was speaking aloud, though they could not make out the words. His face was scrunched up and his eyes were closed, as if he was making a great physical effort, and it was clear that he was praying most earnestly – and he not a churchgoer beyond what was needed to prevent him from being fined for dissent. He became aware of their arrival, and hastily got to his feet and hurried away round the far edge of the field without looking towards them or acknowledging them in any way.

"Extraordinary fellow, that, " said his landlord. "Never know what he'll do next."

They were each drawn to enter the tunnel and feel the earth walls. There was no indication that it had been interfered with, but Jenkins' behaviour preyed on Thorning's mind and he declared that, now that they were close to the point where a discovery might be made, he would henceforth have a watch set over the site when it was not being worked on: a footman from the castle would spend the night there in his old campaign tent. The next day, a little after lunch, Thorning was organising the packing of the tent and its equipment into the carriage, in preparation for Norrington driving down to take his turn at the mounds, when Tom, one of the workmen, ran down the carriageway of the castle, waving his arms. Thorning shouted to him, demanding to know why he had left his post, and whether there had been an accident; the man slowed to a walk as he regained his breath.

"Sir, t'other gentleman says as how you and t'other gentleman has to come at once, sir. Those be his words, not mine, beggin' y'r pardon. He says you must come."

"But why, man? What has happened?"

"I don't rightly know, sir, but t'other gentleman is beside himself, as they say, as we've found stones in the earth. I don't rightly know what it all means, sir, as they just look like stones to me."

His lordship had an idea what it might mean, and quickly went to rouse Norrington. They set off at once, with the breathless Tom, and hurried up to the barrow. They found his workmate sitting listlessly on the pile of dug soil, and peering into the tunnel they could just make out Bradshaw at the far end, scraping at the earth with a trowel in one hand and a double candle in the other. Thorning allowed Norrington in ahead of him: the scholar saw what Tom had seen as stones, but which he could see as a wall of piled boulders, chosen to be of a similar, manageable size. His student had stopped the digging as soon as a spade had struck a hard object, and had then resorted to more careful removal of the soil so as not to damage or miss anything which might be there. He had cleared a patch in the vertical wall of earth at the end of the tunnel, level with his head and chest, perhaps two feet high and wide, and a few inches deep; this had exposed four large stones and the edges of others around them, close-packed. Already a slight convex curve was evident, suggesting that this was the outer edge of a rounded structure, and Norrington immediately expressed his belief that this was the wall of a small burial chamber in the heart of the mound. The two withdrew so that Thorning could have a look, and Norrington immediately consulted his plans and went to work with his rope and yardstick again; assuming the chamber was indeed circular and was

44

centred on the middle of the mound, it would be about four yards in diameter, including the thickness of the walls – quite enough to lay a body in. But then excitement turned to anxiety: how were they to enter the chamber, without destroying it? For they had clearly not arrived at its entrance, and finding that might involve digging right round the outside of the chamber, at least as much work as they had already done, given the increased difficulty, and running the danger of collapsing the whole tumulus on top of them.

But then Norrington took heart and encouraged the others by pointing out that in such ancient structures the entrance, like that of an igloo or the tent of a native American, is often very low and close to the ground, requiring a stooping or crawling posture. If they were extremely lucky, the entrance might merely be below the section that had been uncovered already; if not, they would need to excavate in the same way on the opposite side of the mound to find it. Their luck held: as Bradshaw and Norrington huddled together at the end of the tunnel to scratch the earth off the stones, with Thorning peering over their shoulders and holding candles aloft, they revealed a long slab laid in the manner of a lintel, and two upright boulders resting on the ground forming the jambs to it. These three stones enclosed an opening about a yard square – or it would have been an opening, had it not been sealed by means of a thick sheet or thin slab of slate forced into it like a door without hinges. At several places, it fitted the frame tightly; at others, there were gaps, presumably where the hammering which had forced it into place had broken fragments of it off. It soon became clear that, because of the way it was wedged in, it was quite impossible to push it inwards, while there was no way of getting a grip which would allow it to be pulled out. It seemed as though it would have to be smashed open, quite possibly destroying something on the other side of it and possibly dislodging the whole wall, with potentially serious consequences.

Fortunately, Thorning came up with a solution which avoided this drastic step: hooks would be inserted through the occasional gaps around the edge of the slab, connected to cords which would be tightly gathered together and attached to the end of a rope, which could be pulled on to drag the cover free. To achieve a steady pull close to the ground, he suggested a turning beam mounted at the tunnel mouth, around which the rope would be coiled, as a windlass draws up the bucket in a well. The others approved of this enthusiastically, and they returned to Thorningley to get it constructed, while the men erected the tent and cleared the spoil from the tunnel.

Had he understood – perhaps if he had been in Lord Thorning's service for longer than a few weeks – George the footman would have realised that being given this sentry duty at the barrow was a mark of his employer's confidence in him: it meant that he was seen as a servant with some soldierly quality in him. As it was, he was left wondering what he had done wrong so as to be banished from the castle to this place every night for, he was told, "a week or two". The old tent, set up in the lee of the smaller mound to the side of the excavation with its flap facing towards the tunnel, had been kept dry and in decent repair and aired regularly over the years to prevent mildew, and was perfectly adequate for summertime, but avoiding this sort of thing had been the very reason why George had entered domestic service rather than the army. The tent contained a camp bed, a folding chair and table, a folding washstand and a kind of flimsy wardrobe made of poles and canvas; he had declined the mosquito net. A pile of blankets and pillows, a valise containing clothes, a box of candles to supplement the one stored inside the tunnel for the diggers, a couple of pitchers of water and a hamper of extra provisions should he feel hungry away from the castle kitchen completed the arrangements. Outside, a rough hearth of stones had been made on a patch of cleared ground in front of the opening: over it stood a tripod arrangement with a small metal cooking pot suspended from it in which water could be heated, and there was a small stack of kindling and another of larger sticks. Not even the thought of an adventurous night sitting at his own campfire could relieve George's gloom as the carriage pulled away and the sun sank behind the central mound.

Early the following morning, before the paid workers had arrived, the carriage returned, closely followed by the cart, bearing the windlass mechanism, rope and hooks for extracting the slate slab. Lord Thorning and his colleagues were surprised to see that all the firewood had been burnt already, and the grass and shrubs for some distance around were burnt and blackened; had one of the trees been a fraction closer that too would probably have ignited and set the whole clump ablaze. The box which had contained a good supply of candles was discarded, empty, outside the tent. They were even more surprised when they pulled back the tent flap and saw George sitting on the bed and Farmer Jenkins on the seat. Both men were in a state neither alert nor asleep, but dazed as if they had been awake and uncomfortable all night and were only now just on the pointing of nodding off.

"What is the meaning of this?" thundered Lord Thorning, after a moment's shocked silence. "George, man, what is going on here? Stand up and explain yourself immediately!" He had had to deal with a situation like this more than once in the regiment. He recalled a particularly painful incident involving a sergeant and drummer-boy; what was worse, the sergeant had been married, with a baby at home.

The footman said nothing, but slowly rose to his feet as though in a trance. The farmer rose and spoke with unaccustomed eloquence and an uncharacteristically conciliatory tone. A wooden cross slipped from his lap onto the ground.

"Now y'r ludship, there's nothing untoward here at all. It's just that some folks don't cope too well alone in the dark, and young George here, well, he found out last night that he be one of 'em folk. He needed someone to be with him until it were light. I just sat with him. I would have gone before now, when the sun were up, but I must have dozed off."

Thorning looked sharply from one to the other and back again, chewing his lip as though unsure how to proceed. The two Oxford men managed to retreat without appearing to move; this was nothing to do with them.

"Is this true, George? Were you frightened of the dark, man? In my service and afraid of the dark?"

"Now y'r ludship, the lad's done nothing wrong, and he be no coward." Thorning glowered at his tenant, but he continued. "In fact, when I offered to take him back to my house to shelter for the night, he refused – said his orders were to stay on watch here and he would not desert his post. And he didn't, though he were frightened out of his wits."

Thorning weakened a little on hearing his own words repeated. In a low and detached voice, George finally joined in, without looking up: "Must not desert my post. Must stay here till morning for his lordship, no matter what."

Thorning resumed his harsher questioning manner, this time directly to the farmer: "So what brought you here? Why were you on estate land in the first place? "

"It were about ten by the clock when I first noticed the fire; I had seen the tent going up so I thought nothing of it. Then when I were doing my final rounds about an hour later I saw that it had grown into a great bonfire, and I came to see what were going on, in case it had been left and had got out of control. I climbed over the wall for the first time in my life, and I found George here, putting wood on the fire and lighting candles all over to keep the darkness away. He were in a terrible state, so I stayed with him. He sat in the tent, but insisted that I kept the fire going outside all night, so I had to help."

"Well, if that's the case, then I must be grateful to you for looking out for danger to the property and then for taking care of this man. But as for you," this to the footman, "I shall have to think carefully about whether I care to have in my service a man who is so frightened of the dark that he needs a nursemaid to hold his hand. Now get back to the house and smarten yourself up, and I do not expect to catch you napping later, do you hear?"

The footman mumbled something as he almost pushed past his employer; he glanced briefly at the scholars as he walked past them and the waiting workmen, slightly unsteadily and bowed in the shoulders: "Must not desert my post."

Though plainly not welcome, the tenant hung back briefly to speak for the young man again; Thorning did not lose his temper, though clearly angry, for he realised that it was without precedent for Jenkins to show such compassion and concern for anyone, and hence that the night must have been truly traumatic.

"Begging y'r pardon for speaking out of turn, y'r ludship, but it really bain't the lad's fault. I were here and I knows what it were like in this place after dark, what with the trees and the great shape of yond piles – the shadows was something to behold, and the more fire he made the more they leapt about and grew and shrank like living things, in a manner of speaking. And a wind got up and made such a howling, and the shadows waved about even more, and the mouth of that damned hole," he waved a hand defensively towards the excavation, "it went in and out and in and out with the light and the dark; it would have made me scuttle back to the shelter of my bed, indeed it would, had it not been for the lad here to look out for, and him so determined not to let you down despite everything."

"As I said, I am grateful to you for your assistance, but I do not wish to hear such foolishness and it does the lad no good for you to plead such stuff in his defence. Now good day to you, Jenkins."

The farmer made a kind of dismissive gesture with his head and closed eyes, and, stooping for a moment to pick up his cross, began to make his way back to his farm; then he stopped, paused for a moment, and turned back. He ignored Thorning, who was examining the tent for any scorch-marks, and the frowning Norrington, and walked up to Bradshaw, whom he had often watched as he worked on the mound. He thrust the cross at him quite aggressively, in a way which made him take hold of it, saying, "Keep this with you." He turned again, and to Thorning's back he said, "If I was you, I'd have the clergyman here when you go in that there place."

"You again. And for what reason do you imagine Mr. Roach would want to be here?"

"Nay, not Roach. I mean Mr. Hale, him from Stoke Armitage. He needs to be here. That there place be not right. I were told by my father not to disturb it, and perhaps you shouldn't either – begging y'r pardon, sir."

"If I need the advice of my tenants on how to deal with my property, which I do not, I shall ask them for it. Until that time, I would be obliged if you would keep your opinions to yourself." The barely-suppressed rage in Thorning's tone was quite at odds with the correctness of his expression. With that, the farmer vaulted heavily over the wall and strode around the far edge of the field. Thorning turned to his colleagues. "My apologies, gentlemen." He waved for the waiting men to approach with the windlass. "It just so happens that I have actually invited the Reverend Hale to be with us when we open the chamber, not because of Jenkins' rantings but because he has an interest in such things – I hope you don't mind? Good. Also Mr. Baines, as he is the local historian, though I have warned him that he is not to write anything about it until you have – is the correct word 'published'? – your own account to your satisfaction."

The axle and supports of the windlass had been set up and the hooks put in place and wedged in with pieces of wood when the rector and the schoolmaster arrived, riding together. The cords from the hooks were gathered and tied to a ring, to which was also tied the thicker rope which was to pull on them; the other end of this was wound onto the axle. The two diggers had been given the day off, so a gardener and the odd job man from the castle who had fashioned the device had the task of turning the handles of the windlass. On one side of them stood Baines and Hale, and the other side the Oxford men and his lordship, forming a semicircle around the entrance to the tunnel; several of them carried lanterns, already lit. When all had settled, Thorning ordered a turn of the handles; the rope tautened; a second turn, and it twanged with the tension; a third turn – no; the men pushed and strained; then a sudden bang, and part of the rope shot out of the tunnel and slackened, falling to the ground. The handles swung round a half-turn, almost throwing the two men off-balance.

Thorning moved to the entrance and lifted his lantern; yes, he could see the slate on the floor of the tunnel, three or four feet from the chamber-entrance, where there was now a profoundly black hole. He was conscious of a strange smell, a musty, earthy smell, much stronger than the earthiness of the hole, to which he had grown accustomed. "We – ." He hesitated; he had been going to lead the way at once into this place in which man had not set foot for so many centuries, just as he had once led his men into battle, but something made him hold back. "We had better give it a few minutes, for the bad air to come out." The two scholars, who had rushed forward eagerly to join him, also found themselves hovering on the brink, with a strange feeling, even before his lordship's warning, that they should proceed no further. Bradshaw struggled to understand why he felt prevented from advancing; it was nothing conscious or reasoned – it was a deep instinct; but to what was it reacting? It could only be the smell: what was it?

Seconds turned to minutes as the three men hesitated at the beginning of the tunnel – so long that the others present began to wonder if something was wrong; they moved forward a little and strained to look past them into the opening.

"Did it work?" asked Baines; "Is the chamber open?"

"Yes, oh yes," said Thorning, making light of the situation, but being at a loss to add any explanation for his delay.

After a while, Hale did what he could to break the deadlock: "Can you see anything?"

"No, not really, no."

"Well, are you ready to go in?" This from a puzzled and frustrated Baines.

"Yes – yes; I suppose so. That's what we are here for." With an assertion of purpose, Thorning strode forward into the tunnel, with his lantern held aloft; Norrington followed, with Bradshaw keeping a couple of paces behind. Baines and Hale stayed at the tunnel-mouth, standing on each side and peering round the jambs so as not to block out the sunlight. At the end of the tunnel, Thorning took off his hat and handed it to Norrington, then with a sudden determined movement crouched down, thrust his light out in front of him and awkwardly shuffled his way through the opening, his free hand on the ground to support him. As he himself blocked out the light of the lantern, he seemed to disappear completely into the blackness, leaving his anxious colleagues staring at the space where he had been. Then light could be seen inside the chamber, indicating that his lordship had moved around, but Norrington was worried for his patron and spoke – not really asking anything in particular, but just wanting to hear his voice. "Well, your lordship?"

"It seems to be as you said it would be, doctor." The light faded, presumably because the man had stood up inside. "It takes a while to get used to the dark in here. It is circular, with a domed roof. I can stand up in the middle, but when you come in be careful not to bang your heads. That doorway appears to be the only opening. I can't see anything else yet."

"Is there enough space for me to come in with you, your lordship?"

"Oh yes, though there isn't a lot of room. Probably best to keep it to two at a time until we work out what there is here, if anything."

Handing two hats back to Bradshaw and pushing his lantern ahead of him, Norrington got down on his hands and knees and crawled into the chamber. Standing up cautiously, he examined the interior briefly, lifting his lantern slowly up the wall, then over his head and down again. Stones such as they had seen outside, obviously selected for size and shape and carefully fitted together to leave no gaps, were piled up skilfully to form a circular domed structure three big strides across. The wall was slightly lower than Norrington's own five and a half feet before it began to curve over to form a roof which was a foot over Thorning's six feet at its apex, where a shaped circular piece acted as a capstone. Then he thought to look down, and realised for the first time that as he had crept from the tunnel to the chamber interior he had passed from an earth floor to a stone one. The floor of the chamber was paved in a manner which resembled the wall, the stones being positioned so as to leave no gaps and meet the foot of the wall exactly, and obviously pressed into the ground with care so as to make an upper surface which was almost perfectly level. Norrington was taken aback: the structure of the wall and roof, though remarkable for its elegance and finish, was not unfamiliar from other such monuments which he had seen, but he could not think of another example of such a paved floor from this early period.

As the two men moved their lanterns from side to side to illuminate the floor, they saw that the interior of the stone chamber was not as featureless as had first appeared. The stones beneath them were arranged in a concentric pattern to match that of the roof above and at the centre, below the capstone, was a large circular stone, which must have been carved to shape; the stones of the ring adjoining it were similarly curved on the inner side so as to fit around it, and those of the outermost ring were curved on the outer side to fit the curving wall. They thought of the countless hours of patient pounding, stone on stone, which had to have gone into the precise fashioning of each piece. However, the most striking feature was the centre stone itself, for even more work had been lavished on it: cut a half an inch deep on its surface, and, being completely protected from weathering, as crisp as the day it was first done, was a perfect spiral pattern, rather bigger than a dinnerplate. Norrington tried to count the number of rounds it did before reaching the farthing-sized cupmark which lay at the very centre of the floor and hence of the mound: about twenty, he thought. He noted that the spiral actually lay within a complete circle enclosing the design: the first departure of the spiralling arm from this was at a point directly opposite the entrance, as was its final turn where it met the central mark. It was fascinating, quite literally, but the feeling of deep unease which had struck the men as soon as the chamber had been opened was even stronger now and both wanted to leave as soon as they could without appearing uninterested in their discovery.

When the two men had crawled out of the chamber to let Bradshaw, Hale and Baines take turns inspecting the interior, they withdrew to the tent to discuss their next move. Neither was very forthcoming. The agreed plan had been to dig down if they discovered nothing in the chamber, to look for the expected interment, but now neither of them felt like espousing the scheme; at the same time, both were unwilling to suggest abandoning it, for lack of a convincing reason. The chamber itself far exceeded their expectations, but they were both feeling deflated at the fact that there was nothing in the nature of a tangible find, a significant artefact, and nothing to indicate the purpose of the mound, for which they had been hoping. They were also depressed by the atmosphere they had encountered in the place, and especially by the thought that they were now bound to return there. At length, Thorning ventured: "I suppose we should dig downwards now, as that was what was agreed."

"Yes."

"There is no reason not to."

"No, I suppose not, your lordship."

The further excavation was to be conducted with at least the same level of care as had been shown so far, and so it was decided that the pavement should not be taken up until the scholars had numbered each stone with chalk and drawn a precise plan, so that it could be laid down again exactly as it had been. However, it was generally agreed that the first priority was to illuminate the chamber as much as possible, not least to try to counter the depressing effect it seemed to have on the whole party. The hooks which had been used to pull the hatch over the entrance open were forced into suitable small crevices between the stones around the higher part of the wall of the chamber so that lanterns could be hung from them. When this had been done, Norrington took chalk and numbered each floor-stone, except for the central one, while Bradshaw crouched in the entrance: no-one felt like being in the chamber alone. The ring of stones immediately around the centre received the numbers one (directly facing the entrance) to six, then seven was the next stone outwards from number one, and so on, until the broken pieces used to fill in the few gaps around the foot of the wall had been chalked. Then the relative positions of the stones were charted on a circular plan. Meanwhile, the odd job man had dismantled the windlass and was taking it back to the castle and Hale and Baines had departed, promising to return later that afternoon to see if anything had been revealed, though actual digging was unlikely to commence until the following day. As he said goodbye to the departing clergyman at the gate in the hedge, Thorning noticed with irritation that Jenkins was watching from the far side of his field.

As the centre stone was larger than the rest and very carefully fitted into its neighbours, starting with its removal would clearly have been the most difficult option, and the most likely to cause damage. It was decided therefore that the taking up of the pavement would start with the prising out of the small fragments at the edges, thus leaving room for the easy levering out of the next line of stones, and so on, working in towards the middle. When the first fragment had been extracted, it became clear that the stones had been laid on a sheet of clay, deliberately spread over the soil and flattened.

Despite his vague misgivings, Norrington took it on himself to start the work, as being essentially his project. He would dig out a stone, and place it in the chamber entrance; Bradshaw would pick it up from there and place it in a gardener's wheelbarrow outside the opening. When a number of stones had been placed in the barrow, it would then be pushed to the end of the tunnel, where the gardener unloaded them and laid them out neatly on the flat patch of scorched earth where the bonfire had been, in their correct pattern, as another device for preserving their original sequence. Thorning tried to make himself useful by checking their progress against the chart, and rechalking any numbers which appeared in danger of being rubbed out. It was slow and, especially for Norrington, painful work, and after a half an hour or so the older scholar had to stop for a rest; Bradshaw took over in the chamber, and Thorning himself took charge of the stones as they came out, while Norrington watched from the camp seat.

It was a little before noon when the pattern of work was interrupted. Thorning was waiting for the next stones to arrive when he became aware of a disturbance down the tunnel. Bradshaw was pushing his way past a workman, who was pressing himself against the earth wall; the young scholar clambered over the wheelbarrow and rushed out into the sunlight, with an extraordinary expression on his face. Thorning fell back and Norrington stood up in alarm: for a moment, both had the unspoken fear that he must have succumbed to the miasma of the chamber and become unhinged. He was indeed overcome, but with excitement: he seized Thorning by the arm and vigorously gestured to his tutor to follow, being unable to find words. He almost dragged Thorning down the tunnel and ducked through the entrance: "Come on, sir!" His lordship stooped as low as he could and shuffled in; even before he could straighten up, he saw by the light of the lanterns what the young man was pointing a jabbing finger at – a bone, stained dark, exposed by the removal of a stone next to the central, inscribed, one. It was not sticking out of the earth, but lying on the surface for a short distance. It looked as though it curved up and back down again at the ends, out of and into the clay, as a bone such as a rib might do.

Drawn in by Thorning's exclamations and Bradshaw's inarticulate jubilation, Norrington again put aside his misgivings about the chamber and scrambled back in; the little room was quite crowded, but each man was all but oblivious of the others, so excited were they by what had been uncovered. The barrow was proved to be a burial place, and the body, or what was left of it, had been discovered – an actual skeleton, older than the Romans, not merely a broken pot which had once contained ashes. Now would follow the excavation of the remains and perhaps of gravegoods, the interpretation of what was found, the deductions and speculations about the people who had built the mound and the life they led. Norrington saw articles in learned journals, lectures, perhaps a book; Bradshaw saw his name in print too, and a brilliant start to his academic career; Thorning saw new social dimensions, his estate visited by distinguished academics and much mentioned in the press. When the initial euphoria had run its course, they quickly settled what had to be done. Thorning at once sent the gardener home and paid off the workmen for the week, though it was only Tuesday, on condition that they said nothing about what had been going on; they were aware that something significant had occurred, but not the detail, and the scholars had determined at once that the discovery should be kept secret until they chose to reveal it to the world. In the meantime, they could manage the excavation themselves. They did not share their secret even with Hale and Baines when they arrived separately later. Baines was quite easily fobbed off with the story that, having found the chamber empty, they were doing no more than looking under the floor to examine the construction more carefully: because the paving was up, it was too risky for anyone to enter the chamber. When Hale came by later, he too did not have the impertinence to challenge his lordship's explanation, but it was clear that he was not fooled: he could see well enough from the scarcely-perceptible furtive glances and the strained formality of voice that they were hiding something. Before he went, he said just enough to let them know that he understood, and to convey just a touch of disappointment that Thorning did not feel that he could confide in him.

"Judging from that," he said, indicating the stones laid out on the ground, "you must be taking the whole floor up, and very carefully too. It must be quite a labour, now that you have, as I see, dismissed the men."

Thorning did feel rather guilty about deceiving the priest, who was practically a personal friend, and rather foolish about being so transparent in his deception. Nevertheless, he was convinced that it was the best way to proceed, and the fairest to his colleagues, who had caused it all to happen.

Resisting the temptation to start liberating the skeleton from the clay in haste, the men finished the task of taking the paving stones out of the chamber themselves, ending with the careful raising and removing of the central slab bearing the symbol of the spiral. They then realised that they were very hungry and thirsty after their exertions, having drunk what they had brought with them and having let the time for lunch slip. However, they did not wish to leave the site unattended at this point, and so determined that Bradshaw should wait a while longer: the two older men would return to the castle, and send a servant back at once with some provisions for him. They would come back later, so that he could have a break until dinner, as he would be keeping watch on the site overnight in the tent in place of the footman George. It was not intended that he should do any work during the periods when he would be on his own. Without a word being said, each of them knew that to be alone in the dark and musty chamber with its ancient resident was impossible, even with someone at the end of the tunnel; to venture in when the nearest person might be Jenkins nearly half a mile away was quite unthinkable.

They returned in the carriage towards the middle of the afternoon and found the young man sitting on the camp seat on the path, just inside the hedge gate, as far away from the tunnel as he could be while still keeping watch over it. He rose and greeted the older men with an unaccustomed reserve, and when Norrington asked gently why he had settled in such an odd place, he replied with noticeable confusion and defensiveness: the hedge provided some shade on such a sunny afternoon, being in the corner would allow him to ambush any unwary intruders, sitting far back permitted him to watch the whole site at once. Too many different glib answers, and none of them really convincing. His colleagues did not press the issue: all of them knew that the place engendered unease, fear even, though to admit openly what they only sensed might invite the charge of being irrational, over-emotional and feeble, as each was unsure what the others felt and wished to avoid embarrassment. Bradshaw was relieved of his post, and asked to return in the carriage around dinnertime, with a hamper of food then being prepared at the castle and whatever he needed for the night; the plan was that they would eat together at the site, and then leave Bradshaw in the tent until morning. In the meantime, before his return, Thorning and Norrington would make a start on taking up the thick sheet of clay which had apparently been spread over the chamber floor to receive the paving stones. This they would simply take up in sections and dump at the edge of the site, as it would not be possible to preserve it and, in any case, it did not, in their eyes, have anything like the same value as the stones. The only care they would take would be to avoid disturbing anything deposited beneath it, especially the skeleton.

When they had relit the lanterns, they began, as with the stones, at the edge of the chamber, where it was easiest to prise up the floor; a mattock was slid between the clay sheet and the wall directly opposite the entrance, as they planned to work backwards towards the hole so as to avoid having to walk on the earth below. A spade was applied with a cutting motion, and a section of clay more than a foot square was levered up and put in the wheelbarrow, inside the tunnel. The clay had been spread to a depth of about three inches and had been pressed down, presumably when laid as well as by the weight of the stones, to form a firm layer. Beneath was soil and small stones, disturbed as though it had been dug before the floor was put on it. After only a couple of pieces had been removed, they came upon another indication of the buried skeleton – a small section of dark bone sticking up to be level with the exposed surface. It was a little over an inch wide and two or three long, but not enough was exposed for it to be identified. They worked on towards the centre, carefully cutting round the supposed rib; several more similar bones jutting into the clay were uncovered nearby, and the men took great care not to disturb them but leave them half-exposed in the soil. Twice, Thorning emptied the wheelbarrow, and Norrington accompanied him down the tunnel to avoid being left in the chamber.

By the time Bradshaw returned, they had stripped almost all of the floor. His sudden appearance in the entrance and his cry of greeting gave them a shock which caused Thorning to drop his spade with an oath and Norrington, who was stooping to peel back the last of the clay sheet, to turn suddenly and lose his footing, so that he fell awkwardly. The others helped him up, and supported him out into the fresh air, while the young man apologised profusely for distressing them. They could not be too cross, for he had had the good idea of bringing a small cask of hot water, carried outside the carriage but still quite warm on arrival, a couple of washing bowls and some fresh clothes, so that they could clean themselves up properly in the tent before eating their picnic together. Norrington sent the carriage back to collect a second camp bed from Thorning's lumber-room and some of his own things, for he had decided, thinking of poor George, that he could not leave his student alone there overnight, and the tent was big enough, at a squeeze, for two. Indeed, contrary to his previous enthusiasm, Bradshaw now seemed content to listen to their account of what the floor was like and of the bones which they had partially uncovered, rather than going in to look for himself.

The sun was beginning to descend behind the top of the tumulus when Thorning, with some reluctance, was pressed by the scholars to take the carriage home at last, leaving them to keep guard till the morning, when the more exacting work of uncovering the skeleton would begin. They gathered some kindling and started a small fire, in a ring of small rocks away from the laid-out pavement. It was more for light than heat, and it gave them some comfort as the shadows began to deepen around the mounds. They sat by it on the camp seats with their pipes, occasionally throwing in a log from the new supply that had been brought down from the castle. As the sun went down, a breeze gradually blew up, and the temperature away from the fire sank rapidly below that of the Summer's day. The tops of the trees started to sway, the rubbing and whistling sounds being audible above the crackling and spitting of the blaze, and the flames on one side of the barrows and the last rays of sunlight on the other caused the shadows of the moving branches to travel back and forth along the ground and around the curved earthworks in a giddying way. The two men tried to shut it all out by discoursing at length on a variety of subjects – fishing and foreign travel, Plato and politics – not even out of interest but simply because the sound of a human voice lent some normality and warmth to that weird and ancient spot, where great shapes from a dark past loomed in a real darkness and the long lost seemed about to return from its resting place.

Norrington had his second heart-stopping moment of the day when a strong voice from out of the gloom cut across a moment of silence: "Be you gentleman all right?" It was Farmer Jenkins, looking over the wall from his field; he lifted a lantern and they could see his features, not as severe as usual but reflecting unaccustomed concern and a great deal of apprehension; his gaze seemed to shift continually between them and where a more profound blackness marked the mouth of the tunnel. They hastily lit a lantern and went over to him: "Yes, thank you. It is very good of you to inquire."

"No matter. I had to see how you was, after what happened to t'other lad. And I saw him go, so I knowed you'd be alone." They assumed he meant George and Thorning in turn. "As you be all right, I'll be off. By the way, young sir, do you have that cross convenient to hand, the one I gived you?"

"Er, yes; it's in the tent. I'll go and get it for you."

"That's all right. Best to keep it by you. It's as well to have the Lord at your side. On such a dark night."

And he was gone: the light of his lantern moved swiftly off to the field edge and then receded as it went away to the far side and eventually disappeared, presumably behind a hedge. They watched it until it had vanished, then shivered in recognition of the chilliness and returned to their fire, though only to take their chairs back to the tent, as Norrington in particular was weary after the day's exertions. There was no need for any discussion: Norrington would retire to his bed at once to sleep, while

Bradshaw would sit by the tent flap, dozing but ready to go outside at once in the event of intruders. He was not solely reliant on hearing their footfalls through the canvas. They had left a thin cord, quite invisible in the dark, stretched across the tunnel mouth a yard from the ground and attached to a delicate but cracked glass bowl lodged in the fork of a nearby sapling; anyone entering the tunnel would pull the bowl from its position to smash on the stones of the pavement spread beneath. Then there was a stout wooden chest, in which the tools had been carried: this had been left in the middle of the tunnel, across its width, to trip the unwary in the dark. Finally, an old wooden door, once part of a potting shed, had been brought from the castle to cover the entrance to the chamber, and small bells and horse-brasses had been hung from the rear side of this to sound if it was moved. At least one of these devices would serve to alert the sentinel, without him having to sit outside all night.

Norrington soon fell asleep, but not quietly. Presently he began to dream, and his dream was the common one of reliving a distortion of the day's events. He was back in the chamber, with Thorning, cutting the clay with a spade while his lordship pulled it up in strips; however, the chamber seemed much bigger, with a huge expanse of floor to dig, and as he looked around he saw monstrous bones sticking out of it. By the dim light of the lanterns, made fainter by the increased width and height of the room, he could make out the bones of an arm bolt upright, ending in the outstretched bones of a clutching hand, staying together in place by dream logic; there was a skull partly-buried, its eyesockets and upper jaw out of the earth far enough to stare and grin at him. He looked back at his work, and was alarmed to find his lordship gone; the lanterns suddenly burnt low, and in panic he threw away his spade and cast around for the entrance; in the dark, he could not find it, though he knew it had to be there. Then he was conscious of another presence in the chamber; the roof was now several yards over his head, and he sensed that the thing at his back towered up with it and was starting to bend over him. He was on his knees, not praying but scrabbling for the exit, and failing that trying to claw his way through the stones of the wall or down through the earth. Then he felt rather than heard a loud voice close to his ear, but what it said he did not hear, for it mingled with the crash and rattle of the old door being violently thrown from the tunnel, together with its attachments, in the waking world. Bradshaw, in the twilight trance between sleep and wakefulness, sprang up with an oath and stumbled forward, almost bringing the tent down before he remembered where he was. He tore the flap open and ran out, carrying the mattock which had been at his knee; Norrington seized his coat and pulled it on as he staggered behind. Their fire was just a small pile of embers, but he could just make out the young man standing on the discarded door at the mouth of the tunnel, resolute but undecided, his hands flexing around the handle of the tool. There was no sign of anyone else.

"Fetch a light!"

Norrington, now fully awake, could see there was no immediate danger, so bobbed back inside and struck his tinderbox; he soon reappeared with a lantern in one hand and a spade in the other, potentially as a weapon. He came up behind Bradshaw, who was swaying as though wanting to enter the passage but reluctant to commit himself to what might become a desperate struggle with ruffians in the dark. There was no-one in the tunnel, but that did not rule out the possibility of someone hiding in the chamber: both men had a vision of a brute waiting inside with an axe or club to fell whoever stooped and stuck his head through the low entrance. "We must see," muttered Bradshaw, and he took a determined step forward. They both gave a small involuntary jump at the sudden crashing noise which came not from ahead of them but from outside, and close at hand. They stared into the blackness to the side of them, without seeing anything. Then they realised what it had been – the glass bowl, dislodged by Bradshaw as he advanced. And at once both men felt a thrill down the spine and a prickling of skin and hair which was nothing to do with the comparative cold of the night, nor with the dark, nor with the fact that they were alone in a remote and mysterious corner: they understood that whatever had cast the door away from the chamber entrance had not passed through the trip-cord – and so had not had to enter the tunnel. Whatever they were dealing with had not intruded into the chamber from their world, but had been in there already, in that abode of darkness and death. Moreover, it was big enough and powerful enough to move a solid wooden door and send it through the air so as to fly over the cord without touching it. They stepped back. A sudden gust of wind breathed brief life into the embers of the fire by them, and their own shadows danced for a moment over the tunnel mouth as the trees nodded and made the field of stars overhead blink and flicker.

Then they were inside the tent, without having consciously run but being dimly aware of having clutched each other's arms as they tripped in their haste over stones, boxes and tools in the way. They stood side by side like soldiers preparing to fight, one with the spade held ready across his chest and the other with the mattock, but they did not dare to open the tent flap to look out. What there could be outside of which to be afraid they did not know and did not want to think; what protection a thin sheet of canvas could be against anything deserving such fear they wanted to think about even less. The mere fact of not being able to see what was outside was a source of comfort, and there was always the desperate hope that not seeing meant not being seen; for this reason, lighting a candle was out of the question. They stood motionless and silent in the dark for perhaps a quarter of an hour. Twice they thought that something large pressed against the tent walls and snorted, but the wind was gusting quite regularly now and it could have been that; twice they thought they heard a low growling sound nearby, but the branches of the trees were rubbing together and it might have been that. At length, Norrington was overcome with fatigue, and cautiously perched on the edge of his bed, still clutching his weapon. A few minutes later, when nothing further had happened, Bradshaw sat down too, but not quite, and straightened up again – there was something hard on the bed. He fumbled for it in the dark, and his hand closed on the wooden cross Jenkins had given him. He resumed his seat, with the mattock across his knees and his hands resting on it, folded, as if in prayer, around the cross. So they remained for some time. Eventually, Norrington nodded off, slumped forward, as Bradshaw could tell from the gentle snoring; at first he continued to keep watch, but the younger man must have succumbed to sleep later because he awoke with a start to find himself lying on his bed with his feet still on the floor and the cross still clasped in front of him. He straightened up and looked about: the walls of the tent were no longer black but grey, indicating that the sun had risen. He looked closely at his watch, but could make nothing of it. After sitting for a while listening carefully, he risked pulling back the tent flap a little way and peering out: the dim half-light allowed him to see that there was nothing untoward outside – just the shapes of the mounds, the dark trees, the detritus of their excavation. He examined the watch again: a little after five o'clock. Shivering from the dawn chill and pulling his head back, he looked across at Norrington, who had long since fallen back onto his bed and dropped the spade. Bradshaw spread a blanket over him, and then lay down on his own bed and covered himself, before falling into a real sleep.

The strange snorting noise again, and the billowing inwards of the tent wall, though now there was no hint of wind. Bradshaw lay perfectly still, scarcely breathing, his eyes fixed intently on the moving grey sheet a couple of feet from his face, tensing himself for sudden action. The canvas sank back, and there was a sound as of something large and heavy shuffling away; Bradshaw relaxed slightly and let out his breath – then sudden it rushed back and tore open the tent flap, and the sunlight burst in. This time the young man really did wake up, and found the Reverend Hale looking in.

"Good morning, Mr. Bradshaw; I hope I did not startle you. You are both long a-bed, despite the excitement of your venture."

"Ah, good morning, Rector. Yes, I am afraid we had rather a disturbed night, with the wind and all, and did not get to sleep until quite late."

"Really? I don't think there was a wind at Stoke Armitage last night – but then, it is some distance away, and in this shelter you are probably more conscious of the weather than those of us indoors."

Norrington was stirring, then quickly got up when he was aware of the visitor; he was flustered: "Rector, ah, yes, indeed."

Bradshaw interposed in case the older man said something embarrassing before he was fully awake: "What brings you here, sir?"

"Literally, your neighbour Jenkins. He arrived at my rectory very early, just after I had risen, and suggested I should come over as soon as possible. Well, he virtually demanded it, in fact. I gather from him that you have been continuing with the excavation, though I had gained the impression that it was to be abandoned – no matter. I had been intending to come over this morning in any case, to see if there had been any developments, so I have made my way over here straight after service."

"Jenkins? What has it to do with Jenkins, that impudent, interfering fellow?" asked Norrington, put out by the farmer's presumption.

"He seemed to think you might have a had a bad night. He was saying something about a young footman from the castle having had a disturbing experience the night before last while on watch here, and seemed to fear the same happening to you. I believe him to be a good man, despite his unfortunate manner, Doctor. Virtue should not be confused with politeness, after all. Here, what is this?" He stooped, and recovered the cross from where it had fallen by Bradshaw's bed. "This is yours? It looks very old – might it be a find from your digging?"

"Actually, Jenkins gave it to me. I am not sure why."

"There you are, you see; he has a heart beneath his gruff exterior. It is certainly old, and a quite exotic wood – olive, I fancy. I would not be surprised if this were to prove to have been a relic from a pilgrimage to the Holy Land."

At that moment, Lord Thorning's carriage arrived and his lordship came up the path, followed by a servant carrying another hamper.

"Good morning, good morning Mr. Hale. I am pleased to see you here, though we were not expecting you."

"Good morning, your lordship. I thought I might call by to see if there any developments in your excavating. I hope I am not intruding." He thought it better not to mention Jenkins' part in the proceedings, or complicate matters for the others.

"Indeed no, you are always welcome at Thorningley." Then he noticed the thrown-down door and the broken glass. "Good heavens! We have had intruders! Gentlemen, what has been going on here? Have you apprehended them?" The two scholars failed even to meet his eye. "It was that rogue Jenkins, I'll be bound! And did you let him get away?"

Bradshaw spoke up: "No, it was not Jenkins; in fact, Jenkins came during the night to check that all was well was us, and has been of assistance." Hale was rather puzzled at this, but said nothing. "The truth is that there has been no intrusion – I broke the glass myself by accident. But there has been some disturbance inside the mound, and that is why the door is out. Or so we think."

"Inside the mound, but no intrusion? What sort of nonsense is this? Do you think this is so?" This directed at Norrington, who could still not raise his head or speak. "Am I surrounded by superstitious fools and milksops afraid of a few shadows? I took you for men of learning and wisdom – "

"Your lordship," Hale risked an intervention, "if I might be permitted to speak, without wishing to gainsay anything you have said, I fear that neither you nor I understand quite what it might be like to be out here at night. I am not talking of fear of the dark, or anything of that sort, but of the power of the imagination. These are indeed men of great learning, and for that very reason their minds team with ideas about such places as this, both facts and stories, and being so involved in the process of uncovering the truth they are bound to be overwrought and unable to sleep, and so prone to fancy. A mere footman with no inkling of what might be here and no sensitivity towards it was, as I understand, overcome by the experience of being here alone, so surely these might be expected to be quite overwhelmed. I take it that you have found something inside the chamber – beneath this floor which has so carefully been raised?"

Thorning was diverted back to the business in hand. "Yes, some bones or other. We are going to work on them today."

"Perhaps you should reassure yourself that no damage has been done by intruders."

The scholars could not undo Hale's efforts by showing reluctance and were anxious to vindicate themselves, so they swiftly prepared lanterns and escorted Thorning as boldly as they could to the chamber door. Hale, having obtained his lordship's permission, followed. Norrington allowed the younger man to lead the way; he entered the chamber, and Thorning followed. After a moment, they reappeared and went swiftly back down the tunnel: "Quite all right. Nothing disturbed," said Thorning briskly, though Hale sensed that he too felt something untoward in the atmosphere of the place and would say nothing further about the behaviour of his guests. Hale bobbed under the lintel and swung his lantern across the floor: he saw the partly-uncovered bones, felt the chill of the place, and retreated to where Norrington awaited him.

Hot water had been brought so that the scholars could refresh themselves and the hamper was opened in the mouth of the tent so that they could sit inside and partake of breakfast. Hale was invited to stay and join them: even Thorning felt that the presence of the clergyman might be of some benefit, in the circumstances, though he could not have explained why. He was in discussion with Norrington as to their next move.

"As I understand it, we slow down now, and uncover the bones as they lie, rather than pulling them up."

"That is the accepted enlightened practice, your lordship, making sketches as we proceed. In that way, we avoid damage to the bones and anything which might be intermingled with them, such as jewellery or weapons, and can ascertain the position in which the body was buried – outstretched, bent, or curled up, as it might be."

"Perhaps we should start with that flat piece at the far side – I rather fancy that it may be the top of the skull. I've seen that before, when poor devils have been left to rot on the battlefield. "

When they were ready, it was decided that Norrington would commence the work with brush and trowel, assisted by his host. Hale was anxious to speak to the scholars about their recent experience – though he was careful to keep the specifics of this from Thorning – so he stayed to talk to Bradshaw. The young man felt able to describe the events of the night to him, and indeed felt relief at being able to do so, in confidence and uncriticised; he also told him what he knew of George's ordeal, and of his encounters with Farmer Jenkins.

Perhaps fifteen minutes had elapsed and Bradshaw had told Hale all he could, when the two men re-appeared at the mouth of the tunnel. Norrington looked even more ashen and crestfallen than when he had been berated by Thorning: he was like a man who had suffered a great disappointment from which his fortunes would never recover, and who saw little point in continuing. Thorning still had some animation about him, but it was of a distracted, or rather distracting, kind: he gave the impression of one who has been assailed from a wholly unexpected source, and who, though quite unaccustomed to being incapable of coping, has no notion of how to deal with this situation. The others saw at once that something was seriously amiss and rose to greet them. When asked by Hale what was the matter, Norrington could once again not speak, but Thorning said: "You had better see it for yourselves, rather than have me try to describe it. In fact, it would be a good thing if you were to see it, Rector; perhaps Providence has brought you here this morning deliberately."

Taking their lanterns, Bradshaw and Hale hastened into the chamber and saw that which caused the rector to send word to Stoke Armitage to apologise for his absence and the whole group to spend the rest of the day wetting and respreading the clay layer over the floor of the chamber and resetting the pavement in place exactly, with the central spiral maze pinning down the point where the middle of the chest of the interred body might have been. Jenkins' old cross was carefully placed in the centre of this stone, as Hale read out some passages, including the eighty-sixth and ninety-first psalms from the King James version of the Bible, and it was deliberately left there when the chamber was resealed. It went on to make them spend the evening hammering the slate slab back into place across the entrance and heaping barrow loads of earth in front of it and pressing the soil in to form a wall from the floor to the roof of the tunnel, with the rector offering prayers at each stage of the work. When they had retired to the castle exhausted, it still made them rise at dawn and, accompanied by the entire conscripted staff of Thorningley, return to complete the filling in of the tunnel and the relaying of the turf. It made his lordship put a padlock on the hedge gate and pay for the estate to replace the old wall and fences around the mounds with more substantial, higher barriers. It prevented Norrington from ever publishing his site, or any of them from ever speaking of what was found, beyond saying that only some stones had been discovered, supporting the middle of the mound.

A shallow scoop of earth, perhaps six inches deep, had been removed around the spot where the bone had been found and then in towards the centre of the room for about two feet. It was indeed a skull which lay in the hole, though the original find had been not its crown but the top of a dog-like snout, with sharply pointed teeth still in place. Behind lay large oval eye sockets and a high dome; but the most remarkable feature was the pair of horns, three or four inches long and curving slightly inwards, which protruded from the sides of the forehead.

"My God!" exclaimed Bradshaw. "What sort of beast is that?"

"No beast," answered Norrington from the entrance where he stooped in the darkness. "Look at the size of that brain pan – it held a brain larger than yours or mine; it was an intelligent being. And examine the neck, and the top of the spine entering it from below and not from behind: this creature walked upright, as we do."

"Was it indeed the devil that we uncovered in that mound?" Thorning asked Hale later when the four were alone.

"Perhaps a devil, if not the devil. I assume it was the enemy, or the god, of the people who raised the mound, unless such creatures built it themselves."

"I am inclined to think that the chamber may have been a place where a ritual were performed to bind it, as it were, probably with the sign of the spiral," added Norrington.

"The one thing we can be sure of," said Bradshaw, "is that there was indeed a burial beneath the barrow, but not of a human being, as we understand the term. We look at the monuments of antiquity and can only think of people like ourselves dominating and directing the world, above the level of mere animals – but who knows what may have inspired, or inhabited, the Sphinx of Egypt and the labyrinth of Crete?"

VANDALISM

It is often surprising, sad, even horrifying, to learn how little regard some people in some periods have had for the art and culture of their own past – and here I am not thinking of mere neglect through idleness or changed priorities, but of outright active vandalism. The blood of anyone with any sense of aesthetics and spirituality must run cold to think of the great monastic churches laid waste for builder's rubble and of Cromwellian soldiers stabling their horses in cathedrals and deliberately smashing statues and glass windows which represented the culmination of centuries of intellectual and artistic endeavour to present mankind with some hint of the indescribable beauty of the world to come. And herein lies the irony: it is not the case that men do such deeds *even* in a religious context, but that they do them *especially* in a religious context, for nothing seems to harden the heart to all that is sacred and inspirational more than excessive religious zeal and the accompanying sense that one can do no wrong. This is as true in our own age of the extremists who desecrate what they see as the profanities of ancient Egypt, Persia and Mesopotamia as it was of the early Byzantine iconoclasts. Tolerance should be central to a true understanding of all the great religions, and along with that tolerance can flourish a love of all the arts that celebrate God and His creation and represent man's attempt to restore something of beauty and order to the world which he has marred.

The church at Dabberley was a minor example of the passive form of vandalism, as it involved great blindness and neglect but no deliberate destruction. Its claim to notoriety, however, lay rather in its being haunted, and no religious reformer or iconoclast has ever succeeded in ridding a place of its ghosts, no matter what they might do to its material structure. Not that the hauntings worried anyone too much: when a house or church has had that reputation for long enough, it is just accepted by the people round about, and they do not care a jot if others believe it or not. It is only new apparitions that cause fear and upset and fierce debate between believers and non-believers. Concrete records of the hauntings at Dabberley did not in fact go back very far, but in the minds of the storyteller and his audience anything beyond the days of, say, our grandparents becomes part of an undefined past which is more a flat tapestry than a tunnel of time. To the untutored mind, history extends back only a limited period of extended time before becoming a two-dimensional world where the Conqueror wins at Hastings but King Harry succeeds in the rematch at Agincourt and the Spanish armada narrowly avoids collision with the last of the Viking longships. And so the local people held that the Dabberley ghost, or ghosts, dated from the long past, though opinion was divided as to exactly which period. Here, stereotypes often take over – a monk condemned for some misdemeanour, say, or a mother grieving for her children – but Dabberley was a little different, for the recurrent ghost was specifically that of a knight in armour, like Hamlet's father on the battlements of Elsinore, rather than the usual Grey Lady, Hooded Monk or Sorrowful Nun.

Now Dabberley is in a cold and damp spot, on a flat place where a slow river winds in leisurely fashion round a broad bend at the bottom of a steep wooded valley, and where frequent mists and fogs and even the occasional will o'the wisp could easily have given rise to tales of indeterminate shrouded and hooded figures, rather than the very precise outline of a knight in armour, complete with helmet and shield. This fact might be seen as giving more credence to the story, for hearers with any credulity at all. The church is a little apart from the small village but on the same level, and when graves have to be dug in the winter it is not many feet down that grey water is encountered. The ground is unstable, and in the days in which our story is set the first thing travellers riding towards the church at Dabberley noticed was a series of six great rough wooden buttresses put up along the north wall of the nave, triangular structures in which the hypotenuse and the base, pushing back against a deeply buried post, held a thick plank flat against the wall; three rows of broad crossbeams between the buttresses, stoutly attached to the planks, completed a structure like one side of a cage, designed to prevent the wall from bowing outwards and so collapsing. If, like the Reverend Hale, the visitor approached at sunset, the impression created was of a church half-opened to the sky, like one of those minsters wrecked at the Reformation, or of the bare ribs of a gigantic decaying beast.

And Dabberley as a whole was in decay – perhaps had been from the start, as it was hard to visualize it as ever having been a thriving and optimistic place. Not only was its population in slow but steady decline, so that there were few young people left and cottages without roofs and windows could be found not only outside the village but even on the main street, but also those who remained there seemed to be fading away, from causes ranging from coughs and colds to consumption. Forty years earlier than our story, the decision had been made not to spend the money needed to rebuild the nave wall; almost the opposite, indeed – the vicarage would be sold to provide a fund for repairs and there would no longer be a resident priest for the dwindling congregation who even at Christmas barely half-filled St. Anne's and whose presence at a weekday service on a cold, dark, misty morning was almost undetectable by the celebrant, as everyone crowded around the boiler at the west end for warmth. This primitive device, and the pipes connected to it under the wooden floor of the nave, had been intended to heat the whole chilly building by means of hot water when put in at some remote period, perhaps a half a century or more earlier, but it had never really worked as intended. Nevertheless, for those who arrived early enough to sit in the back two rows to the south of the main aisle, it was a godsend, though it obliged the verger to enter the church a half an hour before the service to get it lit. Apart from that, a perfunctory cleaning twice a week and the few services themselves, the church was left entirely empty, for, sad to say, anyone shivering to pray for any length of time in its dampness, breathing in its dank atmosphere and smelling its mouldiness, would leave sniffling and feverish rather than uplifted and renewed. Had St. Anne's, Dabberley, been typical of parish churches, one would find some sympathy with the atheist's assertion that there is no-one there when you pray.

Theophilus Hale had been invited to visit this forlorn place by the Reverend Stephen Bennet of Sutton-on-the-Water, in whose care Dabberley now lay. They had conversed at a diocesan function, having been vaguely acquainted before; Bennet had heard something about Hale's involvement with strange phenomena and wished to discuss the haunting with him. "It is something of a paradox, I suppose: I don't believe in ghosts, as they say, and yet I know my church to have one. Can you understand that?"

"Indeed yes – and many of us are in the same situation: it is all a matter of definitions," explained Hale. "The souls of the departed are in the care of Our Lord Jesus Christ and certainly cannot be wandering the earth lost. What are commonly reported as ghosts seem to me to be on the whole mere impressions left by past lives on their habitual abodes; or perhaps some small part of the mortal intelligence, or rather emotion, lingers in a familiar spot when the immortal soul has gone." Hale could actually think of an example or two within his own experience which would at least partly contradict this argument, in favour of there being souls in exile, but he kept them to himself.

Bennet had invited Hale to come and see the haunted spot for himself – "one gets so few visitors at our edge of the diocese" – and Hale had casually agreed; he was reminded of this a month later, when Bennet sent him a pamphlet on the fabric and history of St. Anne's written by his broad-minded predecessor some ten years earlier and including a brief note on the ghost and a sketch 'compiled from witnesses' accounts'. The simple drawing, which could have been copied from a school history textbook or more likely from a funerary effigy, showed a knight of the period of Richard the Lionheart, from the Third Crusade of the late twelfth century: his head was enclosed within a square-topped helmet, and he wore a flowing white robe bearing a cross on its front and gathered in by a belt supporting a sword in a scabbard. Chainmail was evident on his arms, extending to mittens, and through the slits in his robe a coat and stockings of the same material could be glimpsed. He carried a conventionally-shaped shield, which probably would also have borne a cross, slung on his back between his shoulders.

Intrigued, Hale finally took up the offer, and was now at the end of an unhurried day-and-a-half ride across the diocese; he would spend two days here, then return home in time to write his Sunday sermon. Bennet met him, as arranged, not at the church, where it was too uncomfortable to wait, but at the small tavern a half a mile further on. "It is a little late to look inside the church now; as it is not used after dark, there is no provision for lighting. Let us go straight on to Sutton-on-the-Water, where dinner awaits us; tomorrow is the day of the week when my flock there have to forgo their service before work, so that I can be here, though I would have more of a congregation at home even though they have the rest of the week in which to attend." From the Reverend Bennet's tone, he appeared to have little time for his second parish, though Hale could not tell whether this was caused by the nature of the flock there or simply by the dreariness of the surroundings to which he was obliged to travel. After a glass of something warming – apparently not Bennet's first – they rode on a couple of miles to where the valley broadened out and a gentle slope allowed Sutton-on-the-Water to be built above the flood plain. They talked over a meal of steak and ale pie left for them by the vicar's housekeeper, accompanied by more ale and wine and followed by port; Bennet, perhaps ten years older than Hale, sensed that the younger man could not help but note the amount he drank, and excused it on the grounds of health, the need to fortify himself against the cold and fogs of Dabberley and the rigours of his chief pursuit, riding to hounds. As strong drink and hunting were his main topics of interest and Hale stopped at a glass or two and tended rather to favour the fox, they soon found the conversation to be rather forced and floundering and both readily determined on an early night to prepare for the next day.

St. Edward's vicarage was quite small but Bennet obviously spent little on heating it, or on anything domestic. The fires were all but out before they retired and there was no coal in the rooms; it was cold when Hale got up, and there was no sign of anyone laying a fire before they left for Dabberley in the early-morning gloom. Indeed, there was no sign of anyone, and breakfast consisted of tea and bread and cheese; although he was hungry, Hale could manage only a few mouthfuls of this at that hour. Nor was the atmosphere as congenial as it had been at his arrival: Hale guessed that his host was somewhat disappointed in his lack of interest in drink and hunting, and that this visit had been less about research into the supernatural than it had been about Bennet trying to find a like mind amongst the clergy, in the name of friendship. But soon they were on their way back to Dabberley, and as they rode into the narrowing valley it seemed to get darker rather than lighter and it began to drizzle. They tied their horses to the fence of the house nearest the church, next to a watering trough. "The last foothold of the clergy in Dabberley," announced Bennet; "no, seriously; this house used to be the vicarage and a covenant was left on the property to the effect that clergy serving the church are entitled to tether and water their horses here for up to half an hour before the start and half an hour after the end of the service, and that if any clergyman is taken ill or dies here during that period – a not-impossible situation, given the nature of the spot – whether or not he has a horse tethered, he, or his corpse, is entitled to shelter within the house until the ecclesiastical authorities recover him. Quite a sensible provision, if you look round at the place."

The church of St. Anne at Dabberley dated from the earliest days of Gothic, not long after the middle of the twelfth century, and most of the fabric was original; the chancel was put up a generation after the nave, and the tower and porch another half a century after that, when an enlarged window in the Decorated style was put in at the east end. But the bulk of it was in a very hesitant Early English style of twinned lancet windows and pointed arches, in which one could almost feel the mason's lack of confidence, both artistic and technical, in what he was doing, putting up this building in this strange new fashion not seen before in this remote spot and being perhaps his first attempt at it. The builder, perhaps fearful of the consequences of pointed arches, had made it all more massively strong than it needed to be, in the Norman manner, which added to its later problems of subsidence, and he had limited the size of openings, making the interior seem dark and cramped. In the growing daylight, Hale became aware of how bowed the north wall was, and how the very top of it, above the buttresses, leaned out away from the roof. There were cracks in the stonework, some filled in and some not; most marked the separation of blocks and were of limited length, but one or two included actual broken stones and ran almost the height of the wall, these being the places where collapse was most likely. Two of the windows had lost a substantial amount of glass, presumably forced out gradually by the infinitely slow twisting motion. Prudence had made the tower at the west end very squat, barely higher than the pitch of the nave roof; it seemed to be the most stable and best-founded part of the structure, as the rest of the building leaned away from it rather than the other way round, so that the east wall of the chancel seemed to nod respectfully towards the ground in the direction of Jerusalem.

Inside, they found the boiler already warm, and they stood by it to dry their damp coats a little before hanging them up. It was still night inside. As they stood, Hale was conscious of a movement down the nave to his right; yes, there it was again, down at the chancel end; was this the ghost? He caught Bennet's arm, and put his finger to his lips. Bennet gave him an odd look, then the silence was broken by a scratching noise and "Good morning to your Reverends!" A candle burst into flame at the altar, then another, and Hale, feeling more than a little foolish, could see a short, plump figure in dark clothes moving around at the far end of the church.

"Elias, my verger here; in his other life, he keeps a small dairy herd which furnishes much of the village with milk. Good morning, Elias; this is the Reverend Hale, whom I told you about. The boiler seems good and warm already!" Almost aside to Hale again, "Unfortunately, the parish gets all the benefit of it, the poor clergyman none: not even the pipes go as far as the chancel. Elias, by the way, has never seen the ghost despite being here more than anyone," and this *sotto voce*, "though he is very lacking in imagination and decidedly short-sighted."

They passed into the small vestry, where Bennett put on the vestments he had brought in his saddle bags. "They would not last a week stored in the atmosphere here," he explained. They then went back out into the church, empty but for the verger finding the relevant pages for the service and lit only by a handful of candles and the pale light of a cloudy morning at the small windows. Bennet took his seat by the altar and Hale went down into one of the front pews to pray. After a while, he became conscious of people coming in behind him, and eventually Bennet stood to start the service: the bell in the tower was never rung for fear of the damage the reverberation might do. He introduced the visiting clergyman; Hale looked round briefly and bowed towards fewer than a dozen people huddled on the back pews, who made no sign in return. Their responses in the liturgy were similarly muted, but that is not to say that the church was quiet. The wind and rain had strengthened, and throughout the service the prayers were accompanied by a bizarre collection of sounds – the gurgling of hot water passing round under the floor, the banging of heating metal from the pipes and boiler, the wind playing and fluting round the loose edges of the swaying and creaking roof, sounds of dripping water, the coughing and sneezing of the congregation. Bennet rattled through the service as quickly as Hale had ever heard, with the shortest sermon; this was preceded by the excuse, "On account of the rain, I shall not detain you long this morning", and Hale imagined that this was a version of a formula which played a regular part in the weekly ritual – "on account of the snow, on account of the harvest, on account of the ice, on account of the flooding," even perhaps occasionally, "on account of the heat". There was no accompanied music: there had once been a small organ, but the diocese had taken it away when there was no longer anyone to play it.

When this extraordinary service was over, Bennet made his way swiftly to the door, as the congregation got up and began to leave immediately. Hale followed him, noting that they were almost silent, whereas in every other parish he had ever seen there would be some talk between neighbours, or at least hearty greetings and solicitous enquiries as they left the church; here, each seemed wrapped up in his or her own stern purposes and presented a grim face to the outside world which forbade any friendly approach. They at least shook hands with their priest as they went out; he had a word for each, though they were almost all on the same theme: "Pity about the rain; sorry that you have got so wet coming out; dreadful weather again, isn't it?" The responses they gave were at least of two distinct varieties, though the subject matter was the same: there was, "The heating seemed a little better this morning," or there was, "The heating seemed very poor this morning". Perhaps a warm and water-tight building is after all a pre-requisite for spiritual thoughts, mused Hale.

At the end of the queue was an old lady, who could have been approaching eighty, obviously hanging back; a middle-aged man who had not been to the service, presumably son or nephew, was apparently waiting for her impatiently in the porch, stamping up and down to keep the cold out. She addressed Hale rather than Bennet, and did not acknowledge the latter's introduction: "Miss Alton, who has lived in the parish nearly all of her life and was our school mistress for about thirty years, until there were not enough children, is that not right?"

"Have you come to see the ghost?"

Hale was rather taken aback and could only think to say, "If there is a ghost, I may see it."

"Oh, there is a ghost. But be very careful. I have seen it several times, and each time something bad has happened. I saw it just before my niece Betty died, giving birth to her twins, and I saw it the night my brother Alfred died. I was in here praying for him – it was more like a proper church then – but when I got back it was almost all over and he just had time to see me before he went. Consumption, it was. That must have been nearly forty years ago. We had a priest here then, not one coming in just for the odd service. I was sitting just there. Mark my words, if you see the ghost something bad will happen, very soon."

At that point the man waiting could contain himself no more and took the terrible step of entering the church itself – then stopped and looked embarrassed. The old lady broke off, smiled at the two clergymen, and tottered past him and out; he followed. While Elias tidied up and Bennet retired to disrobe, Hale began to examine the interior fabric of the church. Much was entirely predictable, and familiar from the pamphlet, but there were two intriguing features: firstly, the wooden floor of the nave, now subject to rot, particularly where it met the leaking north wall. He knew about the pipes under it but was puzzled by the fact that the floor of the chancel was stone-flagged, so that, as Bennet had pointed out, the heating pipes did not reach there. Also, the chancel was approached by a tiny step up, not four inches. He knew of buildings where the chancel and the nave shared a floor and of buildings where the chancel was elevated above the rest of the church by steps, but of none where they were divided by a feature serving merely to threaten the undignified tripping up of the unwary. Then he understood: there had once been more than one step up, but the wooden floor had been put in later and at the eastern end the planks had been rested on the top step below the level of the chancel floor, reducing its height by their depth. It was not the case that the heating pipes had been put in below the floor: they had been laid on the original stone floor and then a wooden one had been put in over them. He checked at the entrance from the porch: there were indeed five steps up from the floor of the porch as one entered the nave, of a slightly different colour and texture from the rest of the fabric there and certainly not marked by centuries of being trodden. The doorway had presumably been recut at the top, but it was hard to tell, as the original arch had clearly been reused; however, the topmost yard of the stone jamb on either side looked newer than the rest of the surround.

The second oddity was a kind of recess in the middle of the fragile north wall of the nave, cutting most of the way into the thickness of the masonry at floor-height. It was two yards long and a yard high, with a kind of tracery of stone hanging down for a foot or so from the top edge: this was basically a trellis of stonework with small shield-shapes and stylized flowerheads set where the lines crossed. Nothing else in the building was as delicate and as sophisticated as this work, but its purpose was obscure; but for its position, it might have been the canopy of a tomb, but there was no inscription to indicate who might have been buried there. The wall was badly cracked at this point and the floor was particularly water-logged, blackly-stained and rotten.

When Bennet rejoined him, he drew his attention rather to the top of the building, where the worst problems were: they looked up to the join where north wall and roof were supposed to meet. The line of the top of the wall was wavy rather than straight, dipping out and down in between the buttresses; there were rotting planks covering gaps, patches of cement filling gaps, remaining gaps through which the sky could be glimpsed. Similar amateurish repairs were evident where the western ends of the nave walls were pulling away from the eastern side of the tower. As tends to happen, those parts of the interior which were prone to suffer from the weather looked, by contrast, more battered than the exterior; stains from rainwater, splashes from repeated droppings from nesting birds and crumbling from the effects of frost were evident. At least it had stopped raining for the moment.

Hale had studied the historical pamphlet carefully, and knew that the church had been founded in the late twelfth century by Sir Ranulph d'Abberley, whose seat was at Sutton-on-the-Water, to serve his outlying lands. A list of the incumbents, painted in gold on a wooden board, hung at the back of the church: it was hard to read much of it, as the names up to the middle of the sixteenth century, when presumably the list had first been drawn up, were in a flowery antique hand and all were peeling badly. Hale tried his best: Stephen the Clerk, 1185-1207 – Stephen Bennet did not seem to appreciate Hale's joke about a homecoming; Thomas d'Abberley, 1207-1233 – could that be the younger son joining the Church while his brother took the estate? James of, possibly, Sarum, 1234-1267; Nicholas Wellman, 1267-1269 – not so well then; simply Peter, 1269-1286; Ralph of Durham – a long way from home, 1287-1314; Andrew Cornish, 1315-1348; and then the terrible period of the Black Death: Henry Parsons, 1348-1351; Friar John, stepping into the breach almost literally, 1351; Richard Tharp, or Thorp, 1353-1377; and so down to the last incumbent, William Cutler, MA (Cantab.), who, according to the pamphlet, was virtually killed by the place. Having retired rather early from a busy urban parish, he found the physical rigours of Dabberley and the fear of its walls coming down very depressing and succumbed to a chill caught at a funeral within two years of arriving. It was at that point that the parish was merged with Sutton-on-the-Water (the list concluding with the names of Stephen's two predecessors at St. Edward's, as serving priests; Hale recognized the last as the author of the pamphlet) and the building was left to cope with a limited repair fund.

"It is my belief that the building will become unusable in ten years' time and fall down in twenty; but I hope that it will not be while I am here. It is sad that such an ancient place of worship should come to such an undignified end, though it was the height of folly to build the house of God almost literally on sand." For a moment, Stephen Bennet seemed to soften a little and a touch of the romantic showed itself.

When they had toured the church, which did not take very long, and the Reverend Bennet had said all that he had to say about the ghost, which was not much, as he had not seen it himself, an awkward silence fell between them again, as it had done the night before. They had so little in common that they had nothing to say to each other once the one thing which had brought them together had been exhausted. Hale made an effort to rescue the situation: "I would really like to talk to some of those who claim to have seen the ghost. Miss Alton, for example, seemed to me to have more to say on the subject."

Thereupon Bennet, quite obviously relieved to be rid of him for a few hours, commended the idea warmly and offered to conduct him to the houses of some who had stories to tell. First they went to Tom Gardner's house, only to find the old man being attended by the doctor; then to that of Margaret Hawes, who entertained Hale with tea and the story of her uneventful life for nearly an hour before saying that she did once see the knightly figure exactly as shown in the pamphlet – but that at the time she had been napping during a sermon shortly after reading the newly-published monograph. Shortly afterwards, Bennet returned and saved him from more autobiography –"yes, she does like to talk" – having been home but also having made sure that Miss Alton would see him in the afternoon. By now, Hale was starving, and, remembering that Bennet's ideal of a meal did not include a great deal of food, offered to pay for them to go and eat – anywhere. Bennet laughed this off: he had booked the private room for them at the tavern and their late dinner would be ready within the hour.

The pork in cider continued a mealtime motif of meat cooked in alcohol, but Hale could have done without the cider. As he watched Bennet consume another tankard of porter, he came up with his plan for the evening – a convincing one, and one which might have occurred to him in any case, but which here served more than one purpose. "If you are willing, I should like to spend the night in St. Anne's. It will give me the best chance of detecting whatever might be there. Unfortunately, it will mean forgoing your company for the evening."

"If you are quite sure – though the church is not a very comfortable place, as you have seen." That was all the protest Bennet made, and he did not volunteer to accompany him. The plan was that, after instructing Elias to put the church boiler on at dusk and leave a supply of fuel in the porch and then going back to the vicarage to make preparations, the two clergymen would later return to Dabberley. Hale would be left in the church, with blankets and food, and Bennet would bring the horses back to Sutton-on-the-Water, to return early in the morning, though Elias was expected to call on Hale first. Hale would probably need to rest on Thursday after a largely sleepless night, though he was welcome to join a ride Bennet had planned for that day from the castle, with a few of the local minor gentry, presumably supposing, before meeting him, that his guest would appreciate it.

In the meantime, they called on Elias at home, to make the necessary arrangements and so that Hale would know where to go if he needed help in the night. They then moved on to the small cottage where Miss Alton lived, and Hale was left alone with her for half an hour. It was clear that her world had stopped some three decades before, and that on her own ground she was freer and less focused than she had been in the church. She knew Hale as the "young" clergyman she had seen that morning, but chose to see him as someone who had called on her for a social visit – that is, to give her an opportunity to talk to someone new – rather than someone who had come with specific questions. Although from time to time Hale tried to steer her back to discussion of the ghost or at least of the church, she focused only intermittently on what she saw as the decline in the building and the services; the bulk of what he got was an account of several highlights of the first half of her life, some of them more than once. It is true that the ghost featured briefly in a couple of those stories, but he did not really learn much more than he knew already.   .

"Oh yes, I saw the ghost. My sister Molly, she was the oldest: first Molly, then me, then Kate. Anyway, Molly married Tom Jackson up at Sutton Cross, and had a daughter, Betty. Then Betty was having twins, and she was in a terrible fever so that the midwife didn't know if she or the babies could be saved. They had the doctor in from Sutton, old Doctor Marsh. We were all in such a state, but Doctor Marsh, he thought he could save them. In the evening, I went to St. Anne's before it got proper dark to pray, because you could go in and pray then; it wasn't enough to freeze you the way it is now and there wasn't rain coming in through the roof. And I was kneeling with my eyes closed, asking the Lord to save Betty and her babies, and I felt that there was someone else in the church, so I looked up and there it was, drifting rather than walking through the pews just in front of me. I jumped up and I think I screamed and I ran out of the church and it was years before I would go there again on my own or in the dark. Father said I had been dreaming, but I hadn't. I didn't sleep all that night but had a candle by me."

"Could you describe the ghost?"

"White-like, with a flat hat on and a long flowing coat, like the crusader. It had a shield, but on its back instead of by its side. It wasn't very big, and it just floated. Anyway, the next morning word comes before we set out that Betty had died, and her babies with her, for all that Doctor Marsh could do, and that is why I say, death and destruction always follow seeing the ghost."

And again:

"We didn't always have the ghost; I don't remember it when I was a child, and children usually know most about such things because they pass stories on. The ones I used to teach always passed stories on; the most awful things, I can tell you. No, I don't remember being frightened of the ghost when I was small. But church was different then; it didn't freeze you to death and rain in on you, and we had a proper vicar, not one who just calls in when he can be bothered and then goes away again as soon as he can, and we had the crusader in those days."

"The crusader? What crusader would that be?"

"Everything was different then. That's when I started at the school....."

And again:

"You saw the ghost again when your brother died?"

"That's right. It was a mistake of course, but you can't blame me; it's natural to go to church and pray when you need help, isn't it? You know about that, being a vicar and all, but when I saw the ghost I knew it was wrong, that death always follows seeing the ghost. I had hardly been inside the church on my own since Betty died while I was praying there, but I felt I had to go for dear Alfred's sake, and then I saw the ghost and I knew it was all over."

"Did the ghost look the same then?"

"Oh yes. I didn't scream this time but I left the church quick and ran home, and he was at his end...."

When he had finally escaped from Miss Alton, Hale discovered that his horse was not at the tavern where he had left it but was waiting outside for him, tended by a boy on a pony. Before he could speak, the lad addressed him: "If your honour be Mister Hale, I be sent by Mister Bennet to take you to the old castle, if that be what you want." At least Bennet's attempts to minimise the time they had to spend together were ones calculated to interest his guest. As they rode back towards Sutton-on-the-Water together, Hale learnt that this was not just a waif Bennet had found idling but the son of the farmer on whose land the castle stood, and he had been invited to tea with the family; the vicar, as far as he could make out, was entertaining some friends to make arrangements for tomorrow's ride. They passed St. Edward's church and the vicarage and made their way down the main street and out of the other side of the village to where a low wooded hill dominated the river. A path led through the trees, where a few pigs were rooting, and then Hale could see the castle clearly: "not a proper castle like in the pictures in the books," the boy had apologised. It was a perfectly formed Norman motte standing on the existing high ground, an earth mound with a flat top which would once have been enclosed by a wooden fence. Through the thick grass could be discerned a track which led to the top by making almost a complete circuit at a steady incline. This they followed on foot; on the top, there were a few stones which hinted at a small round tower put there at a later date, perhaps by Sir Ranulph himself, since this had clearly been his headquarters. From this high point, Hale could see traces of earthworks in a ring around the mound which would have enclosed other buildings, but the site had never developed into a major stone fortress, since from the end of the thirteenth century interest had shifted to Sutton Hall, first as an adjunct to the castle and then as its replacement.

In the farmhouse, set amongst fields of cabbages and potatoes on the other side of the hill, Hale was shown some objects which had been found, or turned up by the pigs, around the castle, especially around the foot of the mound and on the outside of the earthworks where rubbish might have been tipped in a ditch now overgrown and scarcely discernible. There had never been ploughing or digging by antiquarians at the site, but nevertheless

Farmer Roberts had several interesting items to show his guest, some being clearly connected with the castle, such as a simple spur with a single cruel prick, which Hale tried on his own boot but found to be considerably too small. Other pieces could have been from any age, such as a number of large nails and a worn spoon with a broken handle, and Hale had not the heart to tell the farmer that the two old clay pipes were definitely from a much later period. Finally, the three great treasures were produced: a silver penny which a friend of the squire had declared to be of Henry the Third, a pewter goblet which Hale privately thought might be considerably younger, and the hilt of a broken sword with a frail six inches of the blade remaining, very much abraded by time and weather. The hilt itself was in quite a good condition, and its very square cruciform design, with large bead-shaped terminals at the ends of the guard and of the grip, led Hale to express his belief that this could have been of the period of Sir Ranulph himself. Roberts explained how they had searched a long time to find the rest of the blade, wherever it had flown "when snapped off in the middle of a ferocious battle", and again Hale refrained from the inglorious suggestion that it might just have been damaged and discarded. After a hearty tea of Mrs. Roberts' fresh bread, jam and cake, Hale took his leave with profuse thanks and a coin for the lad Tom.

Hale was glad of this foundation of crusty bread when the evening meal turned out to be a chicken stewed in wine with little else to accompany it except drink. Again, a pot had been left simmering, and Hale never did see any domestic help: presumably someone came in during the day but did not tarry. At about eight o'clock, Hale began to get ready for his vigil, putting on his warmest clothes and packing two thick blankets, a pillow, some bread and cheese and a small flask – Bennet had several such things, for the field – filled with brandy. A notebook and pencil, his watch, a tinderbox, some candles and a lantern completed his equipment. He rode to Dabberley with Bennet, who was to return with the horses when he was settled. Fortunately, the night was not too cold and it was dry, though the almost complete lack of stars and the watery appearance of the moon suggested that this would not last. A strong wind was beginning to get up and the waving and rustling of the trees along the valley was eerie because of its great scale.

In the church, Elias had indeed lit the boiler, which was warm, and there was a supply of wood and charcoal in the porch. Several candles had been left out in strategic places, and a few large ones were lit so that the newcomers could at least make their way in in safety; Hale decided to leave these on for the time being. He wanted to stay as warm and dry as possible: that meant staying on the south side. He decided not to sit right at the back, in case the warmth of the heater made him drowsy, so settled down in his blanket three rows down the aisle. These two apparently trivial decisions turned out to be extremely important ones. Bennet left him, at around half past nine. It was darker inside the church than out, as the walls and tiny windows largely shut out what twinklings of stars and reflections there might have been, and at first the candles were mere spots of light which illuminated nothing. As his eyes grew more accustomed to the conditions, he found he could make out the distant east window, which was slightly lit by moonlight, and was aware of some corners and arches in the structure. Nevertheless, had he not seen it in daylight, he could not have judged whether he was in a chapel five yards by ten or in the greatest of cathedrals. He prayed silently, until he closed his eyes at about ten o'clock; opening them, he found that an hour had passed and the candles had burnt down noticeably. It had also started raining a little, and the wind was now quite strong, bringing new sounds to the building, and not pleasant ones. He shivered and pulled his blankets around him: then he recalled that the boiler would need refuelling. It was not an easy choice, to get up from his warm nest and walk several yards in the dark to get two logs, but he resolved and did it, despite stumbling twice on the steps in the porch and burning his hand slightly on the door of the boiler. He settled down again, and resumed his prayers.

He opened his eyes as the sound died down: there had been a loud noise – he could not tell what; or had he dreamt it? – and it had shaken him from his slumber; the candles had burnt down to nearly half of their length and it was very cold. He fumbled with his tinderbox and lit a small candle; by its light he looked at his watch. One o'clock. Holding the ineffectual candle in front of him, he shuffled out of his pew – his joints and muscles were all stiff – and, feeling his way gingerly, over to the boiler. He opened the door with a handkerchief wrapped round his hand: the fire was out, and he had no means of getting it started again so as to be able to burn logs. The metal was still quite warm and presumably the water would be for some time, but he had to be resigned to it getting progressively colder now as dawn came on. The wind was stronger, and the candle flames were dancing around in the draughts; they had burnt down more quickly than they should have done because of this, as they flared out in one direction and then in another. A couple had actually been put out, and Hale shuffled down the church to relight them with his. It was while he was walking with the uncertain steps of a newly blind man down the central aisle that he encountered the ghost.

It was just as undramatic as that: so swift was it and so sleepy was he that he scarcely registered it until it was over. From his right side, the south side of the church, a figure basically in white swept in front of him at a fast walking pace and disappeared into the darkness of the north wall. He registered the top of a flat helmet on a level with his own chest, the flowing surcoat, the scabbarded sword sticking out behind, but did not catch the face; stunned, he stopped and gazed after it, at the shield bearing a cross slung over its back, and in particular he looked down. The drawing in the pamphlet had been very precise in most details, and in particular in one respect, in that it had stopped at the knees and shown no feet. The ghost was so short because it floated not above the wooden floor but, as Hale thought it might, above an original floor below the existing one. It was silent, it was all white and grey, and it was gone in a moment. Putting aside the instinctive fear of the unknown and inexplicable and the dread of mortality which are what cause ghosts to be frightening, he followed it to the wall, and found himself standing by the curiously decorated niche. For a moment, he felt a drop in temperature so extreme that he thought that the ghost must have touched him – but no, it was a splash of rainwater on his hand, then another on his head, and he backed away from the leaks.

He made his way back to his blankets, already grown cold, and wrapped them round him again as he shivered and chattered. He had seen the ghost – there had been no doubt, he had been awake, and even moving. But there was no escape for a few hours yet. It had started raining strongly, and even if he didn't mind getting drenched and muddy he could hardly wake up Elias' family at this hour. A swift bolt of light shot diagonally across the east window – not another phantom, but lightning outside; there was a crash, and a squall of wind roared through the open edge of the roof and around the enclosed space, putting out the candles. This time, Hale did not feel like getting up, but pulled himself deeper into his nest. Rain lashed against the windows and roof intermittently, driven by the wind instead of falling steadily, and sometimes a bucketful would actually fall inside the church, producing a gentler but far more bizarre sound. Hale found himself praying for deliverance; what was it Miss Alton had said about the appearances of the ghost? "Always death and destruction follow"? Hale had not thought much about this warning until now. Candlesticks fell over, the board listing former incumbents rattled on its nail.

There was a sudden flash, which lit up the whole interior of the church, accompanied by a heat which Hale felt on the back of his head and a burning smell, acrid and sulphurous as a whiff of hell might be. It could not have lasted any time at all, but the brightness seemed to hang in the air like a mist for several seconds, allowing Hale time to look around. His eyes went instinctively to the top of the north wall, where there seemed to be movement beyond the illusion caused by the sudden creating, shifting and passing of shadows. Yes: the waves in the wall which had been physical and static before, being caused by the sagging of the stones, were now pulses of energy, making the structure sway, and for a mad moment part of the watery disc of the moon flashed in and out of sight where once the wall had met the roof. As the light faded, Hale could hear stones crashing to the ground or bouncing off the body of the wall and landing outside or inside the church: one smashed into a pew two rows in front of him. As soon as it was properly dark again, the sounds which had had preceded it were wrapped up and doubled in a huge tearing, followed by a confused noise of gargantuan proportions, including roaring, breaking, shattering, falling. Something bodiless was already pressing Hale from behind, and he suddenly found himself no longer sitting but bending over the pew in front and then being pushed over it to fall onto the seat and then slip down onto the kneeler. He was aware that he had banged his head badly and there was a pain in the wrist of his left hand, which he had used to stop his fall, but in a strange way he seemed to be too stunned to worry about such injuries and he regarded them as a remote observer rather than as an immediate sufferer.

Some instinct made him stay safely where he was, and even to push himself further under the next seat, rather than to get up and try to run away. The wall was collapsing basically within the narrow confines of its original line and the framework of the buttresses, rather than falling over, but even so its debris was spreading a long way: loose stones were bouncing on or smashing through the wooden floor, breaking and dislodging the water pipes; broken glass from the shattering windows was sprayed across the nave. By wonderful chance, or divine providence, the roof stayed in place, though swaying dangerously, and did not fall to complete the process which would have brought the rest of the nave down, at least. And so Hale was preserved, and within the hour was taken out of the rubble and dust of the south nave by the verger and some helpers, to recover in the former vicarage, in accordance with the terms of the old covenant. Bennet arrived soon afterwards, but it was decided that the visitor should stay where he was till morning.

In the daylight, it was easy to see what had happened. Lightning had struck the west tower, on its northeast corner, where the north wall of the nave adjoined it, albeit tenuously; the shock had shaken that wall so badly that it had finally come apart and fallen down, the buttress-structure making it collapse straight down rather than falling outwards in the direction in which it was leaning. This had perhaps been helpful in reducing the dragging on the roof, which miraculously had not followed it down, on top of the Reverend Hale; the rest of the building still stood, more battered than before, but lacking only one side of the nave.

Nevertheless, the whole structure was so dangerous, the falling of the roof being seen as merely delayed, that entry into it was forbidden at once, and within a matter of weeks the roof and the south wall of the nave had been carefully taken down, with the west tower following them. A temporary wooden wall put up at the west end of the chancel to keep the weather out was at the same time replaced by a short extension of the chancel and a porch on the west end, using some of the fallen stone and paying for the labour by the sale of the rest. The repair fund was largely spent on the proper restoration of the east wall, and the resultant chapel was sufficiently large to accommodate the few church-goers of Dabberley, in a somewhat more intimate setting than before. However, one thing of great interest was recovered from the ruins of the nave and found a home in the porch of the restored part of the building. As Hale had surmised, it was discovered, when the wooden floor was taken up, that it had been laid on top of pipes which rested on the original stone floor, or at least on supports standing on the flagstones. However, that was not all that had been covered over: lying under the wooden boards beneath the mysterious niche in the north wall was a crusader – an almost life-sized effigy of a man in armour of the type already described, with hints of chainmail showing through a plain surcoat, lying on a plinth about six inches high. His hands were held in the attitude of prayer on his breast and his legs were crossed, in the manner of crusaders, revealing mail leggings. His feet rested on a strange little dog which turned its head to look at him and his head lay on a stone pillow. He wore a flat-topped helmet showing his face and a short beard and moustache; a sword hanging from a belt was carved down the outside of his left leg and his right leg was covered by the left hand half of a shield. Apart from wear on the hands and the nose, which looked more like the result of touching for luck than the deliberate mutilation one finds elsewhere, the figure was perfect, just escaping the discoloration and crumbling from repeated soaking which affected the wall surrounding it. This, evidently, was the 'crusader' to which Miss Alton had made unexplained references. Originally, the effigy had been at the bottom of a niche nearly two yards high and serving as a canopy to his tomb, before it had been ringed in with gurgling pipes and covered over with timber in an act of cultural blindness of the kind considered as this tale started.

The figure was taken up and preserved in the wide porch of the restored chancel, which was henceforth all that remained of St. Anne's church; it was found to be possible to prise up the stone plinth on which it rested, using wooden wedges of progressive sizes until slings could be put around it so that it could be hauled up using a frame as a crane. The plinth turned out to be the lid of the tomb: an open stone box just over two feet wide and two feet deep and six feet long contained the remains of two ancient skeletons, much corroded by damp, which were later buried with due ceremony in exactly the same spot, in what was by then part of the churchyard; the ghost never walked again. Examination of the bones by the local physician found one to be female, aged fifty to sixty, and one to be male, perhaps ten years younger, with evidence of a healed broken arm. It appeared that the male had been buried first, then moved to one side in a skeletal condition to accommodate the woman. Etched on the outward-facing edge of the plinth was the inscription "Hic iacet Ranulphus Abberliensis. Requiescat in pace." There was no record of the name of the lady who awaited his return from the crusade and then in widowhood awaited their reunion.

DREAMS

The Reverend Hale had no clear idea as to what sleep and dreams might be, apart from a definite, professional insistence as to what dreams are not, namely portents of the future or guides to personality and fortune – though it had to be admitted that they often contained fragments of what had been. Like most people, even most intelligent and educated people without specialist training or knowledge, he gave them little thought: they just happened, and with a regularity and universality which rendered them too commonplace for speculation. If pressed, he would have pointed to the body's need for recovery from its exertions, by means of enforced immobility, and perhaps have spoken of dreams as a process of ordering the experiences of the day or organising the memory. With prompting, he might even have described the nightmare in terms of the manifestation of deep fears and anxieties, but the notion of the unconscious mind, yet to be identified in his era, would not have featured in his account. His own sleep was generally sound and his dreams never recalled, except for the occasional nightmare drawn from life, the image of which lingered in the mind for days or years, and the occasional vivid narrative dream the impact of which was such as to be recalled clearly for the first few seconds after waking, dimly remembered after a few minutes and then the subject of frustrating attempts at recapture for the rest of the morning. He was aware that people varied enormously in this respect, just as they differed in the amount and quality of sleep they enjoyed: some claimed never to dream at all (though Hale suspected this was actually a failure of memory), while others were able to recount their dreams at length the next day, and some, such as his friend Joseph Stannard, deliberately sought, by device or practice, to develop their skills in this.

The Reverend Joseph Stannard, vicar of All Angels, Chelmsley

Magna, had been a contemporary of Hale at St. Michael's College and, despite being a theology student, was well known for his obsession with sleep and dreams, though he was saved from outright condemnation by his stout denial of the possibility of any kind of fortune-telling involving them.

He would often stay awake the whole night himself in order to observe, with permission, the manner of other people's sleep; it was not unusual for him to appear at morning lectures drowsy and bedraggled – or not appear at all – as a result of such a session. Initially bizarre, Stannard's request to watch one sleeping soon became an Oxford joke, then a commonplace, and a surprising number of students agreed – though on at least two occasions he forgot himself so far as to address his request to young ladies of his acquaintance, who had responded with more than verbal violence. They need not have worried: his obsession extended only to the recording, minute by minute during the night, of movements, utterances, breathing, and above all of the eye movements which he believed were linked to dreaming and what he called "sightless vision". Hale had been his subject on a couple of occasions, and he recalled being woken up periodically in a very sharp manner and questioned rapidly and brutally as to the detail of what he had been dreaming, before it faded. Despite a close run-in with the college authorities and his bishop over a pamphlet in which he expounded the view that the Book of Revelation was in fact an account of a particularly vivid dream of St. John, Stannard had just scraped through his degree and eventually acquired his small living through the good offices of a titled uncle by marriage. Since that time, the two clergymen had exchanged occasional brief letters of a factual nature, with lengthy intervals between them, and it had been years rather than months since Hale had last heard from him when his unusually familiar letter arrived one morning.

Expressing a desire to renew their friendship – it had never been very close, in fact – and to combine it with healthy exercise which would, he said, benefit them at their time of life, Stannard proposed a brief walking tour along a section of the south coast famed for its heathland and sand dunes and rich in reptiles, rare flowers and butterflies; he clearly remembered Hale's interest in natural history, and played on it. He had even gone so far as to secure invitations for himself and a companion to two comfortable coastal vicarages whose incumbents he knew, less than twenty miles apart, as the road wandered. So as to avoid difficulties over Sunday services, he proposed riding down to one on a Monday and staying overnight, sending their horses on ahead, then spending four days exploring the country before staying on Friday night at the second house and returning on Saturday. Should the weather prove inclement, they could simply divide their time between their two hosts.

Hale was somewhat taken aback by the presumption of the letter, but its tone, despite the directness of the summarized contents, was more pleading than hectoring, and he could see how Stannard had tried to make it into an expedition which he would indeed enjoy, even if simply meeting for a dinner and a talk over a bottle would have been a more conventional way of renewing an acquaintance. Eventually, Hale decided the charitable thing was to accept, and, being able to call on a locum at short notice, he agreed to a date of some three weeks ahead.

They met at a crossroads, one coming from the east and one from the west, and after a few moments of greeting (for despite the exchange of letters during the preceding three weeks, mainly of a practical nature, they had not met again until now) they continued a slow ride southwards side by side. Hale noted that Stannard looked older than he would have expected, though he would have recognized him from his gaunt features and eyes which tended to stare unblinkingly and then roam restlessly with a distant focus. As they inched nearer to the coast, their talk took many turns aside from the prosaic matter of parochial duties to embrace art, natural history, books they had discovered or rediscovered lately and other subjects they rarely had a chance to air in the solitude of the vicarage and the rectory. Stannard talked of his interest in rereading Herodotus and the Greek view of the Persians, while Hale discoursed on the differences between the main groups of butterflies and the characteristics of the ones they were most likely to see. Engaged in this process of entertainment and enlightenment, without revealing much of their thoughts and feelings, they caught their first glimpse of a streaked-silver sea as the sun was going down over a small harbour at the west end of a bay ringed by low cliffs, and they broke into a trot. St. Edwin's, their first place of lodging, stood boldly on a promontory, with a cluster of cottages inland of it and a ruined priory next to it. The vicar and his family made them welcome, and after dinner, conversation and some music from the vicar's wife and daughter, the two visitors withdrew, the Reverend Hale to the guestroom and the Reverend Stannard to a disused servant's room in the roof, an arrangement the latter, acting very much as the leader of the group, insisted on, to ensure that his colleague slept well: "For I," he said, "can fall asleep at once anywhere, and similarly awaken again." The others laughed at this absurdity, but Hale wondered if it were in fact literally true.

Hale passed a reasonably comfortable night for one never easy the first night in a strange bed, and awoke feeling no more than a slight ache in the limbs, as though he had been riding hard for part of the previous day rather than merely ambling most of the way. That morning, Stannard was very concerned to question him as to his state, and Hale was reminded of the interrogations about dreams; but he soon subsided into his breakfast in the bosom of the Reverend Trimmon's family. Two men were hired to tend their horses for three days and then take them to Over

Sandleigh at the other end of their journey, and the two holidaying clergymen, having thanked their hosts immoderately, set off with their knapsacks into a blessedly sunny day. Initially they took the greensward at the top of the cliff, but soon they were obliged to fall down to the beach beneath and so arrived at an old harbour, where they inspected the sailors' chapel and a ruined tower which Stannard claimed was a Tudor gun emplacement, and took refreshment at the local hostelry. That afternoon, they entered gentler green country, where pasture gave way to sea-washed meadow around a broad estuary. Here they passed some time, Hale increasing his tally of butterflies by at least three – two species netted, one observed and one possibly seen – while Stannard took a nap in the shade of a tree. As the afternoon wore away, they went a little way inland to cross a bridge and made for the highway and the remote inn of which Stannard had heard. Starting with its over-explicit signboard, The Queen's Head was a somewhat less comfortable place than they had envisaged, being mainly a place of gathering and drinking for the men of the area, and providing accommodation more often for visiting family members or incapacitated customers than for true travellers, but the people were reasonably hospitable and the hot food they got together was adequate; in fact, though Hale and Stannard did not realise it, they were on their best behaviour and made a special effort, being somewhat in awe of two obviously learned men of the cloth together in their humble establishment. Over supper, the clergymen swapped memories of student days, and then retired early, as the day had tired them.

On waking, Hale rose immediately, and paused only briefly in front of the mirror, in the sconce before which a candle had burnt out; he straightened his short fur-lined and -collared jacket and adjusted his hat to show the jewels to the best effect, walked from his curtain-hung bed and clambered into the waiting carriage. For a few moments he was swayed and bumped over cobbles through crowded streets filled with garish market stalls; through the small windows he caught sight of jugglers and acrobats, pedlars and hucksters, soldiers carrying crossbows, a masked executioner standing on a scaffold with his crossed hands resting on the shaft of his upturned axe. Invisible grooms opened the door as the carriage stopped, and he sprang out with the vigour of youth. He hastened down an avenue lined by huge heraldic statues bearing carved shields, passing by men strumming lutes, waving quill pens in the composition of sonnets, declaiming in English and Latin, all to the accompaniment of the calls of peacocks. Passing through a flattened arch, he turned into a wooden panelled room with an enormous stone fireplace, in front of which the familiar figure of Bluff King Hal, as painted by Holbein but with the even more familiar disproportionately thin facial features of the Reverend Stannard, was warming himself.

"Come in, my friend! And sit yourself down."

A huge wooden armchair upholstered with leather and tapestry appeared and Hale sat in it. Stannard thrust a deep silver goblet of red wine into his hand.

"Unfortunately, you are most unlikely to remember anything of this in the morning, beyond perhaps a general sense of having been somewhere exotic. One of the reasons I chose you for this experiment, you see: I knew from observing you at Oxford that you have a vivid and rich dream life but take nothing of the experience away with you and hardly ever recall anything at all. I would not be surprised to hear you deny that you ever been to Persia."

"I have never been to Persia."

"But you were there, only last night – both of us were. You proved to be surprisingly good at polo and horseback archery, considering it was the first time you had tried them. But as was saying, it was ideal for my purposes to have a subject who could participate fully in the dream without calling me to account for it later."

"What do you mean by 'subject'? And what manner of experiment is this in which I seem to have a part?" Hale was shaken, for a snatch of a hazy memory involving riding at speed and wielding what looked like a croquet mallet had passed through his mind.

"I am sorry, my friend – I did not mean any disrespect by my choice of words; I was merely following the modern tendency in discussing matters of natural science."

"Natural science? Surely we are both asleep and I am dreaming this."

"In a sense – though it would be more accurate to say that we are dreaming it, and that you have entered my dream and I have entered yours. Look, you are plainly confused, so let me go back a little; as you will recall nothing of this, it really does not matter what I reveal to you, and I have long wanted to explain my work to someone who might just begin to appreciate its significance and ingenuity. I have long been, as you know, a student of sleep and dreams, and have devoted much of my life to their understanding, and to developing them in myself. In particular, with much patient practice, I have learnt how to be sufficiently conscious in sleep to observe and shape my dreams, making them learning tools and places of retreat. I can go where I will in my dreams, be who I want, and achieve whatever I desire – within the dream. The sense of liberation, and simple power – unmoderated power indeed but also power the exercise of which can hurt no-one – is indescribably exhilarating. As king, I have just sent a Tudor duke to be executed – and he will be, though no-one will die. What does the waking world offer to match that? Perhaps in every generation a mere handful of dictators will have

107

such power, though not even they will have the lack of accountability which I enjoy, nor be able to exercise it in every known place and era."

Hale saw a hint of madness in his friend's eyes, and brought him back to the idea of an experiment.

"Ah yes. The ultimate extension of the power of the active dreamer, as I term myself, would be to control other dreamers, to have others enter and leave one's dreams, as their own dreaming selves and not as simulacra in one's own dream. And so here you are. The technique I have developed has several elements, the simplest being the planting of suggestions during the day. You may recall that I described that ruined fort we passed today as being built to house King Henry's cannons; whether it was or not I know not, but it put King Henry into your mind. Then there was the choice of this inn, possibly of the same date, with Anne Boleyn on the sign for The Queen's Head. I pointed out some resemblance between the wood on the walls in the dining room downstairs and the Tudor panelling of the dining hall at St. Michael's. Although you did not notice it at the time, you were being primed throughout the day to have Tudor motifs feature in your dreams."

Stannard was interrupted by a blaring of trumpets outside, and there was a heavy knock at the door; he called out, and in walked the masked executioner Hale had seen earlier, except that now he had no axe but what looked like a bloody bath towel. He opened it up, and inside was a pale head with a coronet still around his brows, Stannard took a small packet out of the purse at his belt and threw it to the silent man, who caught it and flourished it as he backed out of the room with the horrid trophy in his other huge hand.

"You saw him earlier partly because of the account of the killing of Anne which I insisted on giving when we arrived here, though you substituted the axe for her sword through force of association, if you understand me."

"But what if you are simply a figure in my dream? You may be lying in your bed dreaming of All Angels, for all I know, and I may have built up all this story from recalling your interest in dreams at Oxford. And even if we are in the same dream, who is to say who is in charge, whose dream it really is? I may have brought you here, after all."

Stannard thought a moment. "I assume if I can answer your second point then I have also by implication answered the first." He carried on before Hale could protest. "I say that an animal will walk through this door when I open it. I defy you to make it otherwise. I shall also tell you what kind of animal it will be – a camel; if you wish to test my claims, then make it into a different beast. You do not need to tell what you would make it, if you would prefer to avoid the embarrassment; you will know yourself if you succeed or not."

Stannard pulled the door open, and, ducking its head to avoid the lintel and then having to stoop to squeeze its hump through the entrance, a dromedary slowly made its way into the room, chewing from side to side and swaying slightly. Just below its sagging hump, above its neck, a screeching monkey wearing a miniature turban and Turkish costume was perched precariously on a small saddle. Stannard turned and smiled at his silent victory as the camel faded into the wall, but behind Hale's impassive expression were not defeat and resignation – for the monkey had been his addition.

"If I may continue? Having planted the Tudor idea in your mind, I then had to dream myself into that period and then summon you from your own petty dream – it was something about netting a

109

yellow butterfly, by the way – and into mine, which action your dream interpreted as a waking up. The Tudor details came largely from your own knowledge or half-knowledge – the crossbows were a little out of place, I think, and I think you might have located the execution somewhere a little more discreet than the marketplace – aided by a dash of Hampton Court palace. On reflection, you may recall that the dream process typically eliminates some unnecessary links and details in the story: you got out of bed fully clothed, for example."

Despite his unwillingness to accept what he was being told, Hale was nevertheless moved to ask questions.

"But what if I had had no existing knowledge, even faulty knowledge, about the time and place from which to furnish the dream?"

"Normally, of course, you would not dream of such a place at all: your visit to ancient Persia last night was entirely prompted by me. When the sleeper has limited accurate knowledge of the setting of the dream, then the background and details will be approximations – for example, making ancient Egypt look like classical Greece – or simply omitted; in dreams, buildings can lack features as basic as walls and backdrops are often cloudy. The Persia you were in lacked any specific details beyond well-watered gardens and high towers of vague exotic design, unless I was able to put them into your dream, and focused almost entirely on human characters – with high headgear and curly beards. It rather depends on the intelligence and imagination of the person involved: if the sleeper is limited in these respects, he may simply substitute his own contemporary details for those most blatantly missing."

"I am still unclear whose dream I am in, yours or mine. You talk of summoning me into your dream and then of how I furnish my dream: as it is the same dream, I think you are being inconsistent. I think this also raises the question of where the dream is – in my mind or in yours."

"Yes, a good point. To be honest, my ideas on this are still not fixed, as I have had only limited experience so far of bringing people into my dreams in this way. I believe it is a mixture of the two: the main direction of the dream is mine, some of the details are contributed by you. But I fear that I tire, and we must now end this stage of the experiment." Stannard began to yawn mightily, and he fell into the armchair which Hale vacated. Hale moved swiftly backwards out of the room without looking round, and found himself literally flying past heraldic animals, an executioner with a block, jugglers and men at arms, faster and faster until he was through his own door and into his own bed, without even changing his clothes. He was at once asleep within sleep, dreaming of dreaming of pursuing yellow butterflies with a net.

The next morning – it was Wednesday – Hale awoke with a confused notion in his head of watching William Shakespeare leaping around the stage of the Globe Theatre with a butterfly net while reciting some lines from *Hamlet* about 'stranger things than are dreamt of in your philosophy'. This image had faded by the time his eyes were fully open and was forgotten in the time it took him to yawn once. He had retired early and slept through the night, after their day of walking in the sun, but he did not feel as refreshed as he should have been, as though his slumber had been disturbed. Nevertheless, he said nothing of this in response to Stannard's inquiries, when he went down and found him already breakfasting. He felt his friend was watching him oddly as they ate, as though expecting him to say something; he asked if anything untoward had happened overnight, which he had missed, but in reply he only asked what he might mean by that and changed the subject to their itinerary for the day, which they were able to follow without any hindrance, the weather continuing

111

warm and sunny.

They returned to the coast from The Queen's Head, and then their walk took them around a bay into which the several mouths of a river meandered across sea-meadows and mudflats; the stream was not a large one, but having descended from the hills inland with some force it slowed down and spread out when it hit the plain and was divided between patches of boggy ground and a number of minor channels which carried at least a faint memory of the river to the sea. The tide being out, the travellers ventured out across the dark sand marked by ridges left by waves, solid enough to hold them despite wobbling like a pudding and filling their footprints with pressed-out water. They hopped across the narrow channels carrying fresh water to mix with the brine, skirted the shallow pools and hastened on whenever they felt greater suction tugging on their boots. In the distance, gulls circled and waders pecked their way along the water's edge, effects of the shimmering light and heat sometimes making them look close at hand and sometimes far out to sea; just above the horizon, Hale could see clumps of what looked like trees where he knew there could be none.

He called Stannard's attention to the phenomenon, and for a while they discussed the mirage, which led Stannard to speculate on what life in the desert might be like. For a moment, as he spoke of the Bedouin tribesmen, a curious image of a monkey on a camel entered Hale's head, but it passed as soon as it had come. He was more immediately puzzled by the man's tendency to switch from saying little – which had always been his habit, not being given to small talk – to discoursing suddenly at some length on factual topics little related to the moment. It occurred to him that Stannard might over the years have deliberately schooled himself to do this, in order to overcome his reticence, though it actually served rather to draw attention to his lack of social ease, so forced did his little lectures sound. They certainly did little to promote conversation, for at the end of these expositions Hale was left unsure how to respond and generally a tense and awkward silence ensued. At the far side of the bay, they called in at a small village which had no tavern but a shop where they were able to buy some basic supplies for a picnic, which they ate once they had passed on away from the blank gaze of the fisherfolk.

That afternoon was largely spent in a narrow wooded valley between sea-cliffs on the one hand and steep downland on the other; its sheltered clime was home to butterflies and wildflowers, and they progressed slowly along the path with frequent stops so that Hale could inspect another notable specimen. It was during one of these pauses that Hale, turning quickly to his companion to make an observation, caught sight of a momentary expression which changed at once to a forced smile; what he saw troubled him, although he was careful not to show it, and made him wonder. In that brief moment when he had caught Stannard off-guard, he had realized that the man was barely tolerating him: it was not merely impatience with the frequent halts, for the look directed at his back had been one of disdain and dislike. It was clear that Stannard's apparent interest in what Hale pointed out was entirely false, that his bonhomie was faked. Was it just that he had failed to understand what such a trip might entail and was finding it hard to feign enjoyment, or that he was disappointed to find that Hale was not as he remembered him and was anxious to be away from him? Or was there something else involved in this walking tour, some hidden purpose, of which Hale was unaware? Whatever the reason for Stannard's attitude, they would be together at least until they reached Over Sandleigh, another two days' meandering walk according to their plan and at least one even if they chose to hurry, and so Hale determined to do what he could to ease any friction there might be between them – initially, by not indulging in the inspection stops which seemed to

113

be vexing Stannard so much.

He followed this up by insisting that Stannard should again chose their resting place for the night. There were two options, according to his information: The Ship at Paget's Folly, apparently converted from the farmhouse when Paget gave up trying to cultivate the cliff top, and The Bull at Carbrook, which was a homely inn on the edge of a picturesque village two miles further on. Hale liked the sound of the latter, next door to an interesting Early English church with a Norman tower, but, despite it being more expensive, Stannard preferred to walk back to The Ship for its view out to sea from their rooms on the top floor, and especially for the fine old four-posters they contained. In truth, Hale did find the bed comfortable, but he would have slept well on flagstones after another day in the fresh air and a good dinner with claret and port; not even his troubling speculations about why Stannard should dislike him and why he was persisting with his show of friendship could keep him awake for long. Perhaps he was reading far too much into one expression – perhaps Stannard had been yawning or had discovered a blister; the man had been pleasant enough all day and had been an affable companion at supper, despite bringing up again, in a rambling way, the topic of Arab nomads and the geography of deserts.

Hale was on a fine horse, looking out over a landscape of sand dunes, featureless except for a distant clump of trees, hovering above the horizon in the haze; he was conscious of a short beard and loose, eastern clothes, and of being, again, considerably younger than he was in the waking world – the Hale who persisted in his head rather than the one who confronted him in the mirror. "We have been here before, have we not?"

"Yes," said Stannard, "though then it was ancient Persia and now we are rather in Arabia, I think. That was two nights ago. This is

114

very interesting: you clearly remember nothing of the dreams when awake, but are able to remember something from dream to dream, as people remember from one waking period to another. It supports a belief I have long had, that the dreaming self has a capacity for memory of its own; it explains how the same dream can recur on different nights and why dreamers often report feelings of recognition or familiarity."

"I recall how to use this." Hale took the short recurved bow from its holster on his saddle and reached up to draw an arrow from the quiver over his shoulder.

"Let us see," said Stannard.

A pair of pale antelopes with long straight horns galloped in front of them and Hale urged his horse forward. With Stannard in close pursuit, he chased them thunderously towards the clump of trees, the dunes marvellously flattening and the sand hardening before them. He drew alongside the lagging one just as they passed the oasis, and, twisting sideways in the saddle and using only his feet and thighs to steer and encourage the horse, took aim. He was conscious of Stannard immediately behind him on the other side, watching him intently and urging him on. He released the shot – at a large fruit, rather like a melon, hanging from a palm tree, which smashed to pieces as the arrow passed through it. The riders slowed as the antelopes disappeared.

"That was deliberate!" said Stannard. "A great disappointment: I had been hoping to observe what consequences there might be to a killing in a dream. I have had people killed off-stage, as it were, like that poor fellow that was executed last night, but never actually done it or seen it done."

"Why do you not try it for yourself?"

Stannard looked at him curiously. "An interesting idea, but I would rather not take the risk, in case there are consequences. I would rather let someone else do it."

"Someone like me?" The dreaming Hale was beginning to dislike Stannard at least as much as the waking Stannard seemed to dislike him. Stannard merely smiled, irritatingly smugly. "But," Hale countered, "if you wanted me to kill, why did you not just make me do it?"

The smile froze; Stannard merely said, "Enough," and trees, dunes and horses vanished.

On Thursday morning, two miles along the coast from the Ship, they came to the foot of a long slope which took them up across the brow of a great cliff which stood like a mountain half of which had fallen into the sea. As they walked along the edge, Hale pausing occasionally to examine a wild flower, they looked down over collapsed terraces of rock on which still stood the shrubs and stunted trees which had grown on top of the hill before the encroaching and undermining of the sea had caused their footings to slip down the cliff-face. Far below, at the foot of the cliff, the sea broke in white plumes on broken stumps of rock, while on the landward side, there was a slope down to woods which flourished in the quiet shelter so provided. Hale sat down on the cliff edge, enforcing a short break; he had not slept very well, and felt vaguely disquieted, though he could not have said why.

"When you were in Italy," asked Stannard, "did you visit Sicily?"

"Unfortunately, no," said Hale, "though I should dearly love to do so."

"Indeed, I also have not, but this scene reminds me of the passages in Lucretius in which the poet describes the sea raging around the island of Sicily and rushing into caves to cause the eruptions of the mountain Etna: *quam fluitans circum magnis anfractibus aequor / Ionium glaucis aspergit virus ab undis.* Does it not strike you so?"

"Perhaps." Hale failed to see any obvious similarity with this English seascape, but did not wish to contradict his friend. Stannard persisted with his line.

"Have you seen a volcano?"

"No, but when in Italy I saw paintings of Vesuvius and the bay of Naples. It must be an impressive sight."

"Of course, Lucretius talks about Empedocles, the Sicilian philosopher, whom some say threw himself into the crater of Etna. I wonder if it really was an elaborate suicide, or just the tragic ending of a scientific investigation, misunderstood. If it happened at all."

Stannard's train of thought, which continued in this way for some minutes, struck Hale as somewhat bizarre, and he did not encourage it.

Their stay that night – the penultimate of their trip – was at an inn run by a man of Scots descent and called nostalgically The Edinburgh Castle; the board outside featured a very convincing painting of the ancient fortress atop of its rock, clearly done from an accurate sketch or print if not from life. "Of course," said Stannard, "men of science say that the crag on which the castle sits was once a volcano, in the infancy of the world."

"Indeed."

"Yes; have you visited Edinburgh?"

"No. I believe it is considered a very fine town."

"It is; I went there some years ago, in the course of my study of sleep – do you remember that? I consulted an eminent physician at the university there on the subject."

Hale had grown so used to Stannard's rambling style that he actually heard very little of what followed; if he had listened to it, he would perhaps have noted how much of it was devoted to descriptions of the rocks on which the castles of Edinburgh and Stirling stood, and of other Scottish hills, and strained comparisons between them and the volcanoes of the Mediterranean. At supper, they were tempted to try a little of a curious dish of oatmeal and offal which the Scotsman called haggis, and to drink a shot of the whisky of his homeland, which gave Hale a burning sensation at the back of his mouth and nose and made him cough – as though they had swallowed a volcano, said Stannard. They retired to bed soon after the meal.

Hale was standing on the edge of a crater on the top of a high mountain, with a clear blue sky above and the deeper blue of the sea around it. It was an almost circular depression some forty or fifty yards across with a rim only a yard or so wide around it, and it sloped steeply down fissured barren rock perhaps two hundred feet; there was a great pool of steaming brown mud at the bottom, through which bubbles burst in white steam to reveal glowing red and yellow underneath, like liquid embers. The great heat and the sulphurous stench which the pool gave off made him feel dizzy immediately and he had to make an effort to keep his footing. He was aware of laughter tinged with madness at his side, and there was Stannard.

"I am sorry, my friend, but your notion of a volcano is that of a schoolboy – a perfectly regular crater on the summit of an otherwise ordinary, pristine mountain peak. Etna is actually a mound of ash and cinders hundreds of feet deep and covering many acres, with smoke and fire breaking out of vents all over it.

And I think you may be confusing it with a geyser. But it is your dream, so we must allow you it."

"I assume the idea of the volcano was yours, however; you planted this idea so that I would dream it, is that not so?"

"Exactly so. I mentioned volcanos several times during the day; I needed to labour it somewhat, as I soon grasped that they featured little in your view of the world, unlike the desert, old Persia and the time of the Tudors."

"I understand."

For a short time they stared into the seething caldron that in some way they had both brought into being — not that it really existed.

It was Hale's father, the old rector, sitting on a garden chair and nodding over an open book on his lap. Behind him was the garden of Hale's childhood, and beyond its trees and shrubs the back of the rectory itself, so that Hale could pick out the window of his own bedroom. His father gave a kind of snore and snort and there was a slight jerking of his head and limbs as he opened his eyes; he leaned forward and pushed back a little the straw hat which was shading his eyes. He looked as Hale remembered him last, as an old man in his latter days, but he spoke as Hale recalled him speaking to him many years before, when he was a small boy: "I shall help you as much as I can, Theo, but there is a limit to what I or any man can do: for any more, you must rely on yourself and the Lord."

Hale turned towards Stannard, who clearly saw the old man too, which puzzled Hale: surely his father was part of only his memories, not Stannard's; as far as he could recall, Stannard had never met his father. Stannard was clearly angry at the intrusion: "Whoever that old fool is, he is not supposed to be here! I did not suggest him to you! Get out of here! You will spoil everything!" His rage was tinged with fear, when the old rector merely grinned at him from beneath the straw hat and began to chuckle.

At that moment, some sleeping but still functioning part of Hale's brain suddenly saw the reason for the inconsistencies and aberrations in the dream world which Stannard forced him to share with him, and hence the basic flaw in his method which perhaps he had not grasped himself. He did not have the vocabulary which a later psychologist would have for describing what was happening, but at an intuitive level he understood well enough: in controlling another's dreams, Stannard had to enter them to some extent, had to project himself into the fringes of his subject's subconscious mind and so expose himself to whatever might be lurking there. In short, whatever threatened or frightened his subject in dreams might arise to threaten or frighten him too when they shared a dreamworld; whatever fears and memories plagued his subject could plague him too – might even, perhaps, become in time as rooted in his mind as his own fears and memories.

Hale began to run, as in the guise of a young man he could. He forced himself to concentrate on the idea of escape, sensing, or at least hoping, that the slight exercise of will with which he had experimented in conjuring up his father might serve him in his extremity. At all costs, he had to avoid plunging into the crater, which appeared to be Stannard's intention for him. As he ran, he felt that moving downwards might aid him more than moving upwards and making himself an easier target, so he willed the road to slope downwards; Stannard did not interfere with this, perhaps because he could thus chase him more quickly, and he soon found himself going downhill quite steeply. He was heading away from the picture-book volcano into a valley, not one of sunny summer meadows between grassy downs but one of grey scree tumbling down bare fellsides under a cloudy sky. He stumbled, tripped and staggered as the path narrowed and became increasingly rocky and uneven, and the gathering gloom and the shadows of the mountains made it darker the lower he went. This was no good: this forbidding landscape was of Stannard's making, to dishearten him and might soon produce monsters from his own dark unconscious. He stopped; did not look back; closed his eyes; concentrated hard.

The late bishop was standing in front of the high altar of the cathedral, crosier in hand, with Theophilus, newly ordained, kneeling on the steps before him. The bishop signed the blessing over him, and he stood up. The old rector, now in conventional clerical dress and smiling radiantly, came forward and took him by the hand to congratulate him, and, yes, he was now kneeling by his bed, flanked by his parents. He remembered their nightly prayer from his childhood, the ninety-first psalm: 'Thou shalt not be afraid for the terror by night; nor for the arrow that flieth by day; nor for the pestilence that walketh in darkness; nor for the destruction that wasteth at noonday'. He opened his eyes; then opened them again; and he was in his bed at The Edinburgh Castle.

Stannard was restless at breakfast, and seemed troubled about something; all he would say was that he had been called back to his parish suddenly, on urgent business, though how such a message had reached him was unclear. Recalling the glimpse he had caught, two days before, of what he imagined his alleged friend really felt about him, Hale chose not to question him further: for whatever reason, Stannard wanted to terminate their trip prematurely, and Hale felt quite relieved about it. A lad had already been sent to Over Sandleigh to fetch their horses, with an apology to their prospective host there, and it only remained for them to await his return before travelling back to their parishes. By tacit accord, they filled in the time apart: Hale announced his intention of going for another walk along the cliffs, and Stannard briefly wished him well without offering to accompany him. By the time Hale returned to the inn, he had already gone, having borrowed the innkeeper's horse so that he could meet the returning ostler half way. In due course, the lad came back with the borrowed horse and Hale's; Stannard had apparently taken an inland route home instead of coming by the inn.

What had caused this impolite behaviour Hale never knew, for he never heard from the Reverend Stannard again - which suited him admirably.

OBSERVATION

You may, dear reader, be starting to doubt the veracity of my accounts of the experiences of the Reverend Theophilus Hale, Rector of St. Mark's, Stoke Armitage; you may be questioning whether a scholarly man living a quiet life in a remote rural community is likely to have been involved in so many events which we might term bizarre. My immediate response would be along two lines: firstly, that it would perhaps be exactly such a person – spiritual, contemplative, unhurried, well-read, enquiring, sympathetic and empathetic – who would be most open to such experiences and to whom others might bring theirs, and secondly that it is perhaps a mistake to emphasise active ideas of happenings and involvement. Rather, we should perhaps be thinking in terms of how individuals observe their surroundings: how detailed a view they take, how rich and varied is the interpretation they are prepared to make of it, how imaginatively they engage with it. An event which might seem mundane and uninteresting to one person, and perhaps even fail to be noted at all by a second, may be a rich and illuminating milestone in life for a third. Let us consider an example or two. I know those who, when excitedly told there is a rainbow outside, will perhaps grin in a placatory fashion and continue with the sewing or the newspaper, but also those who will rush out of doors despite the shower to view the marvel of a phantom multicoloured arch overhead and spanning the horizons on a scale immensely beyond human design. I have pointed out a heron flapping heavily down a river, craning its neck back as if to face the sun, only to be greeted by an indifferent grunt, while my heart has taken wing with the impossible large and paradoxically graceful bird as it makes its way to its secret haunts far from the homes of men. Just so could another man have trod Hale's path without ever seeing a ghost, sensing an unseen presence or stepping into a legend, even though he saw and heard essentially the same things.

I put to you another case. Are you one of the many who open a door and think no more of it, or one of the few who push it open and just fail to catch proper sight of whatever it is that immediately disappears in a blur round the back of the foot of the door? You either know what I mean or you do not: if of the latter group, you will perhaps recognize my description of the brownish haze which is just on the point of leaving your sight as you look down at the floor. No, there is nothing behind the door, nothing stuck to the wood of the door itself and fluttering out when in motion, nothing like a cobweb over your eye. And yet you saw something moving along with the door but not of the door, something which seemed to want to avoid your gaze, something faster than your reactions and even perhaps knowing of your actions slightly in advance. Or probably more familiar is its much taller brother, the shadow at the corner of your eye which flickers and moves away even as you notice it and turn slightly to face it. Was it just a shadow, inside this dim room, with no obvious object to cast it and no obvious source of light behind? It seemed that there was something there, but such a thing as could exist only at the periphery of our senses, of our world, and was bound to vanish as soon as focus was brought to bear on it. Was something there, or was it not? Was it merely a mote in the mind's eye? Perhaps we attach too much weight to the simple and tyrannical dichotomy we inherited from the Greek logicians, the all-inclusive, mutually exclusive categories of being and not-being; perhaps these are just two of several possible states, or the extreme points of a spectrum, and there are many things which exist independently, to some degree, without the kind of reality, power of manifestation or appeal to the senses which we would normally expect of something which 'is'.

Now the Reverend Simon Bryant was both acutely observant and also one of the least fantastically-inclined or superstitious men ever to take religion seriously. Indeed, he had been the last student at St. Sidwell's Hall to receive the Tranter Prize for an undergraduate essay on the theme of "The Spiritual Life" from the hands of old Professor Tranter himself – Tranter, who had famously declared that not one penny of his bequest should ever benefit one who demonstrated any willingness even to entertain the idea that there could be any afterlife or supernatural domain other than that which is, in its blessed portion, occupied by Jesus Christ and his saints. (It is, I am sure, pure malice which identifies Tranter with the ghost of a troubled old man, sadly shaking his head, said to have been encountered by students working late on moonless winter nights on the Theology gallery of St. Sidwell's library.) And yet the Reverend Bryant was convinced that the shadowy images which he encountered more often than most at the corner of his eye were, in some sense, real things, and indeed even beings, since capable of movement and response.

It may be that he actually saw more out of the corner of his eye than most of us, as his peripheral vision was exceptional. He had quite a thin face and his eyes might have seemed quite far apart, but there was nothing abnormal in his appearance to suggest that he would be so capable of seeing sideways without moving his head. He had discovered the ability at an early age, when it gave him an advantage in certain childish games, for no-one could creep up on him undetected and he did not need to make a warning turn in order to identify the one behind him who was moving. As children will cultivate their own special talent, he practised and developed this art, and in later life would often cause astonishment with the trick of greeting those who considered themselves to be standing virtually behind him. It was somewhere in between these periods, as a senior schoolboy, that he began to pay attention to the shadowy ones.

As he was conscious from a very early age that his range of visual perception was exceptional, so he soon realised that his awareness of and interest in the shadowy things tantalisingly glimpsed at the corner of the eye or in the briefest intervals of movement were outside the experience of other people, and he was careful to keep them secret in order to avoid the labels of 'different' and 'strange' which children fear so much having attached to them. He persisted in this into adulthood, the only evidence for his peculiarity visible to others being the occasional sideways flick of the head which they ascribed to a nervous tic but which in reality marked a moment when he forgot himself and tried to outrun with his eyes a shadow which fled from them. Even Mrs. Bryant knew nothing of it, although very rarely she did notice him behaving oddly. For example, on one occasion, a year after their marriage, she chanced to see him, unaware that he was being watched, opening and closing his study door repeatedly, sometimes quite slowly and sometimes very quickly, while apparently staring at the ground. He was, of course, trying to get a clear view of whatever it is that seems to follow the edge of the door and then disappears round it, in the twinkling of an eye. Asked what he was doing, he found a convincing answer in a convincingly brief moment of thought, and said he was looking at the amount of dust on the floors, particularly behind the doors. Unfortunately, this resulted in unfortunate exchanges later between Mrs. Bryant and the maid, and hence the departure of the latter, much to the inconvenience of the house; the Reverend Bryant had to pray a great deal about this development and for forgiveness in the following week.

However, he did not desist from his strange habit, but merely became more circumspect in his practice of it. He would take the opportunity of being alone to stand quietly – standing giving freer and further movement when turning rapidly sideways than sitting – and soon, very soon, the hint of something just out of focus would flicker at the corner of an eye. He would wait a while to lull it into confidence, then blink deeply and rapidly a few times to dispel the need to wink, and finally flick his head round quickly, trying to keep his focus. Sometimes he did this so many times and so violently that he gave himself a pain in the back of the head or the neck.

Nevertheless, by his fortieth year, he had grown accustomed to the idea that his little eccentricity was an unwinnable game, that he would never catch up with the swift glimmer at the edge of sight, and that perhaps it was in the very nature of things that this should be so. And then it happened: whether this shadow was a particularly slow or complacent one or whether his own speed of reaction had sharpened more than he had realized he knew not, but the fact was that he turned in time to face it full on. "Stop!" he shouted, and pointed straight at it so that there could be no doubt that he truly had caught it at last, and that it should know it. Then he hesitated, for in all the years he had pursued this aim he had never actually given any thought to what he would do if this came to pass, or even to what the purpose of the quest was. The shadow also seemed uncertain how to react: there was nothing in his command or gesture to compel its obedience, but it did stop and wait, as though guilty and found out. In truth, there was no precedent on which either of them could act, for such a thing had never happened in the history of the world. During the millennia, in the Reverend Bryant's view, in which men had glimpsed the movement at the periphery of vision, or during all the millions of years, in reality, in which man and his ancestors had sensed it, it had never before been shown that the shadow had a real existence outside the workings of the human eye and brain.

Nevertheless, what kind of existence this might be was unclear as there was scarcely anything to indicate the shadow's presence. Most of what had been perceptible as it moved was the motion itself, the partial interruption of the background scene, a sequence of interference; when it came to rest, it was as insubstantial as it was almost totally transparent, and its outline could not be traced. Less tangible than pipe smoke two minutes old and more like a thin sheet of plain glass propped against the wall, it would have been scarcely recognized as an entity in its own right, distinct from the tints and shadows around it, unless one knew it was there. This was passing through Bryant's mind when a monstrous possibility sprang forth in response: if it could not be seen at rest, or against the swift movement of wind or in the smothering effects of rain, it might be the case that there were many of them unobserved in the world, not just the odd specimen at the corners of individual eyes. Trembling, he looked around the room: yes, there by the window, a kind of washed-out stain overlapping curtain and wall; a faint wavering of the air at the side of a chair; a slight distortion of the glass in the front of a china cabinet. The thought of how densely they might throng the world outside filled him with professional horror and sent him in haste to the window itself: there was one by the gate, one under the appletree, one just visible against the dark laurel... he thought of the city streets, where hundreds hurried day and night while thousands of the unmarked shadows looked on. And what were these shadows? Angels? Spirits? Ghosts? And what did their lingering presence on earth suggest? He stood, bewildered and terrified by the vision which had suddenly befallen him, while the detained shadow tiptoed quietly out of his perception. Just as he had never planned what to do if he saw one clearly, so he had never really thought about what the shadows were; now that he had seen one properly and had finally proved to himself that they existed independently of his mind, he was forced to account for them at once, and tried to do so within the boundaries of the cosmos as he understood it. The only explanations for them which presented themselves to him filled him with fear and more than dispelled the initial elation he had felt at the capture, for they undermined the faith which had controlled his whole life and career, and thus left him comfortless.

Mrs. Bryant, returned from visiting, found him still standing there half an hour later, gazing vacantly at the wall and muttering partly audible, partly coherent things: "It cannot be, not souls, trapped here, for what would anything then mean?" and so on. Failing to engage his attention fully, she led him to bed and sent for the doctor, who diagnosed fatigue and prescribed bed rest. Then the fears started: it was not that he woke up screaming, but that he screamed when he awoke, as though seeing something terrifying when he opened his eyes. He would suddenly roll over and bury his face in the pillows or against the wall, even in the middle of a conversation. What was happening was that he was regularly catching glimpses of the shadows in his room in a way he had not experienced before, and was reacting to them with what was now fear, though he could not explain this to anyone. Why he should be so frightened after living with them at the edge of his entire life is not easy to explain, but it can be understood best as a fear not so much of them, as they were creatures of little or no worldly power, as of what their presence might reveal: even a universe of lost souls with no eternal rest or reward. He remained thus for a week, and then seemed to revive a little with a spell of sunny weather which banished all shadows - so much so that he ventured down to his church to take morning prayers, only to be so aghast at what he saw inside the ancient building, in addition to forty-odd pious men and women, that he had a kind of fit and positively swooned away. He was carried back to his bed and the bishop was informed.

Mr. Osborne, the curate sent to officiate at Penningtree during the vicar's indisposition, was not an unreasonable man, but the vicarage was not large and he had to be accommodated in it, despite his obvious unwillingness to be under the same roof as someone whom he imagined to be little better than a madman; the sooner he could return to Oxford to finish his commentary on the non-Pauline epistles the happier he would be. Furthermore,

Mrs. Bryant was obliged to have her own bedroom, on account of the nature of the vicar's condition, and that was the house virtually full. Everyone was therefore full of hope that the bishop's men would be successful in restoring Mr. Bryant to health, the bishop's men being Doctor Pownell, his personal physician, who took up temporary residence at the Green Dragon, and the Reverend Hale of Stoke Armitage, who was due to travel over to Penningtree on Tuesday mornings and stay at the inn, returning to his parish on Wednesday afternoons, for as long as was necessary. The Reverend Hale had been requested by the bishop to complement the doctor's work by spiritual direction and counselling, as the bishop had heard something of the nature of the patient's ramblings and held Hale in high regard as a comforter of the spiritually distressed (and unofficially knew something of his experiences as a helper of those even more afflicted).

When Reverend Hale first saw Bryant, Doctor Pownell had already been attending him for several days, and he reported to him what he had so far learnt; fortunately, in their case there was no tendency towards distrust or disdain between laity and clergy or between science and religion, as they had known and respected each other in their different fields for some years. In any case, the great rift between religion and science was still then some years in the future. Pownell was unable to tell him much about the nature of his affliction, partly because the patient had, since his initial frantic collapse, refused to say anything definite about what was troubling him. Most of what the doctor could tell him was negative: it was not brain fever; it was not dementia; it was not a general hallucination or the result of poisoning. Bryant had no apparent disease or deformity and there was nothing in his medical history or that of his family to suggest a tendency towards these symptoms. All that Pownell could say with any conviction was that Bryant appeared to be suffering from a particular, localised illusion which was frightening him not because it seemed to pose a physical threat (indeed, the word 'shadow' had been used in an unguarded moment) but because in some way its presence challenged his religious faith. Although Bryant let little slip, the sudden and unexpected fit appeared to be accompanied by a sudden and even less expected religious crisis, and from time to time he would cry out things which suggested a spiritual desertion: "Eloi, Eloi, lama sabachthani?" Though the doctor had been able to do a little to control his angriest outbursts and soothe his most tortured periods, he felt, alluding to the Scottish play, that his patient had more need of the divine than the physician and readily made way for the priest at the bedside.

The Reverend Bryant, whom Hale thought of as a confident, inquisitive, intelligent man, was lying at the edge of the bed, facing the wall, his face barely six inches from the plaster; he had drawn all the bedclothes tightly about him, though it was not cold, and had made a kind of hood of them around his head. He was lying still, in a twisted kind of pose, with his eyes closed, though he was not asleep; fortunately, he was clearly in the quiet phase of his illness. The curtains were drawn though it was barely afternoon and enough of the sunlight penetrated to make the room dim rather than dark. As Hale entered the room, he turned inward even more, burying his face in the pillow.

"It is only I, Simon; you have nothing to fear." Hale pulled up a small chair, but still had to address the man's back across a yard of sheeted mattress.

"Who is it?" asked a muffled voice.

"Theophilus Hale."

Bryant had so far been made to encounter no-one but his wife, servants and medical men in his condition, all of whose feelings he could assume or ignore; an old acquaintance was another matter, and a long pause ensued in which Hale sensed embarrassment struggling with his fears. Eventually, he seemed to reach a compromise between etiquette and his own needs and he turned from the wall to his visitor and sat up against the pillows, though covering his face with the improvised hood.

"Please excuse me. My condition is such that I am able to see things which I would rather not see and so I cover my face lest I should glimpse them accidentally. I do not need to be in bed, but I have such perturbation of spirit that I am frequently sleepy; furthermore, it is easier to protect myself from what I might see by lying in a darkened room and covering my face." His voice was shaky, his words at times hesitant, but he was far from the incoherence and raving which Hale had been led to expect.

"And what is it that you can see which you must avoid so urgently?"

There was a long pause. Hale fancied the sheeted form in front of him trembled and could see the hands being rubbed against each other and twisted round in the action usually described as 'wringing'. He repeated the question.

"That which no man should see. That which no man was ever intended to see. It is my own foolish inquisitiveness which led me to see them. And now I must look on them for the rest of my pitiful life." The voice was rising hysterically and the hands were working faster. Hale's next question was obvious, but he held back for fear of maddening the man.

"Be easy, Stephen. There is no-one here now except us."

There was a kind of laugh from the sheets. "That is all that you know! The earth is full of them. They are in this room now. There is probably one at your shoulder, another in this bed." His own thought seemed to frighten him, and he ceased talking with a great shudder. Hale knew that, whatever 'they' were, Bryant was talking nonsense, but nevertheless the passion and urgency with which the man spoke made him feel a little nervous, and he glanced briefly over his right shoulder.

"Whatever troubles you, man, think on Our Lord Jesus Christ, who has freed us from all fears, even the fear of death, and whose strength and protection never desert those who believe in Him."

There was another long pause, without any hint of the 'Amen' or other response which Hale hoped to hear. Eventually, he asked, "Would you like us to pray together?"

"No." It was clear, flat, definite, and, given its source, shocking.

Hale was silent for a moment. "Perhaps you misunderstand. I was asking if you would like us to pray together, 'for where two or three are gathered together in my name, there am I in the midst of them'."

There was a shorter pause, then a brief speech which had clearly been thought out in the long hours during which Bryant had lain alone in his misery but which had never been voiced before. It was as though he had held his peace until he had an audience who might understand him, and now was letting all his thoughts flood out.

"Suppose your Jesus Christ has been replaced as a prophet, just as he replaced the prophets of the Old Testament. Suppose the New Testament is due to be replaced by a Final Testament. Suppose that, with the passage of time, we have entered the last of three ages of understanding, and that man has now reached the stage where he can accept the harsh truth of the world untrammelled by myth and vain hopes. We have reached the stage of enlightenment about the scientific reality of the world, and through mathematics we can understand the mechanics of the universe; and shall our religious faith remain that of desert tribesmen or Gothic peasants? No: we are ready for a new, mature understanding of the world not based on superstition and blind faith but on what we can see and what we can reason out."

Hale had thought of Mahomet when Bryant spoke of new prophets, but now he seemed to be preaching a kind of humanistic atheism and Hale waited to see how far this would go, controlling his pressing urge to contradict him.

"And now I must tax your patience further, my friend, for I believe that I may be the new prophet, the first of those who see clearly how things are and reject the old falsehoods. For I see that which has not been seen before and I understand what it means."

"And what is that?"

Whether he feared ridicule or rejection by Hale or whether he was simply overwhelmed by the enormity of his own message, Bryant seemed to find another great obstacle to overcome in being this specific, and lost his composure. The shuddering and hand-wringing started again, violently. A great cry went up from the sheets, as of a soul so vexed that it had to relieve itself by means of such a physical venting, devoid of thought or meaning, and the bundle rolled over into the wall again. Doctor Pownell entered the room, but there was nothing to be done except leave the patient to calm down; the two men withdrew.

A few hours later, after a long and harrowing interview with Mrs. Bryant, Hale returned to the patient when, judging from the cessation of sounds of snoring, he had awoken from a troubled sleep. This time Bryant was less forthcoming, almost as though he regretted having said so much the first time; Hale got little more than grunts from the sheets, and withdrew in order to try again later, as he understood that he was generally in a better state after dark, presumably when he could not see whatever it was that troubled him. It was then that he would sit up and eat and drink, though keeping his eyes cast down and not stirring from the shelter of his bed. Indeed, when Hale returned after supper, Bryant had changed again, and was even more willing to speak than at their first meeting; this time, his manner was almost conspiratorial. It crossed Hale's mind that madmen often impart their crazed distortions of reality in just the same confiding, conspiratorial way.

"I have seen things which I should not have seen, and now I know things which I should not know. I did not want to know them, but now it is too late; too late! Far too late. But I have to pass on what I know, while I still can. It is my destiny! I must tell you and then you must tell others. It is the new truth, the new New Testament, the Newest Testament, and I must be its prophet. Yes, me! Who would have guessed it? Do you know what the life hereafter is like?"

Hale was determined to remain straightforward and steady. "For those who have served the Lord God and done His bidding, there is a place prepared for them in paradise. The fact but not the details, which we could not comprehend, have been vouchsafed to us by Our Lord Jesus Christ. There is quite another place prepared for those who have lived a life of sin and defied God's commandments. Of course," and here Hale lapsed into teaching mode to complete his account, "the Papists would insert other stages in between, as though the soul could continue its progress to salvation even after judgement."

Bryant, who was sitting up in bed, though, as far as Hale could tell in the near-dark, with a sheet wrapped round his head and most of his face, began to giggle – yes, giggle like a maid. Hale was unsure how to react to this unseemly response, but suddenly the man shuddered and the giggling stopped. He jerked upright, throwing back the sheet and clutching at his temples. Hale almost fell backwards from his seat, uncertain whether he was having a fit or about to attack his visitor. But Bryant merely wailed out, "No, no, nothing could be further from the truth! There is no heaven, no hell but here on earth! All else is a fable!"

Bryant was now crouching on the bed, and Hale could make out a hand stretching out as if to seize his arm. He swiftly jumped up and backed away.

"No, no, I mean you no ill! Come back!" He slumped back against the pillows and put his arms by his sides. "I must tell you, but it frightens and maddens me even as I think it."

Cautiously, Hale resumed his seat, and called out that it was all right, as he could hear someone approaching the door.

"Listen. The souls of the dead, ghosts, spirits, call them what you will, are all around us. By some mischance, I can see them. I suppose others may have seen odd specimens of them – that is the origin of the ghost story – though I am the first to see them clearly and understand their true natures. They are legion – several in a room – I cannot guess how many millions in the wide world. They are so many that all the dead must be among them. There is no heaven, no hell, no reward, no punishment, merely the life of a shadow when the body has died. That is the truth of the world."

"And what are they like, these ghosts?"

"Scarcely anything at all. The Greeks were close to the truth when they described the souls in the underworld as flitting, insubstantial things, though in fact they have no resemblance to the people they once were. They hardly exist at all, though they must have some kind of awareness and responsiveness, as they attempt to avoid detection. Except of course with me. They know that I know them and they have given up trying to elude me. Perhaps from now on everyone will come to see them, now that it is known to be possible, just as anyone can now see through a telescope what once only Galileo saw in the sky."

"Is there one of these ghosts here now?"

"Oh yes, there will be more than one here in the room. They are fearfully crowded, the poor things, even more than we!" He began to giggle again in the darkness of the room, which Hale found even more disconcerting than his words.

"Show me."

"Ah, they are hard enough to see in the daylight, and are quite invisible in the dark – though in fact they are best seen in slightly subdued light. Not even I can see their flimsy forms now – which is my one blessing. Come back in the morning and you shall be the second to look on them and understand."

And so Hale returned an hour or so after dawn, two hours after Bryant had had his second frugal meal of the night.

"Are you ready to show me your phantoms now, Simon?"

Bryant, who was lying on his bed with his eyes tightly shut, nodded. Hale pulled back the curtains to their fullest extent so that a pale light filled the room, and stood at the foot of the bed. Bryant sat upright and, with an effort, forced his eyes open. After a moment of adjustment, he spoke in a strained, tight-lipped way, as though not wanting anyone to observe his speech.

"There is one just behind you, immediately to your right, next to the fireplace." He turned his head to the left and stopped; "There is another over by the dressing table". And to the right; "A third stands by the casement".

Hale turned to stare at the wall next to the fireplace, but could see only a watercolour of a spray of flowers against the pale stripe of the wallpaper.

"Where exactly?"

"You are looking straight at it, man! Concentrate!"

Hale stepped forward. "I cannot see it, but I shall attempt to touch it." Hale half-hoped to break Bryant's delusion in this way, but he found his host's tone of voice so convincing that he was less than fully confident. He tensed himself and prepared with the sign of the cross for whatever might be the consequence of, perhaps, sharing a space with a ghost, the sudden great drop in temperature being only one of the sensations which might befall him, as he knew. He stepped cautiously into the place the vicar had indicated, and nothing happened. He shuffled forward again, to be almost up against the wall.

"Am I near it?"

"You are right behind it – or even inside it; I can see it in front of you, making you a little less clear, insubstantial as it is. You are touching a ghost!"

Now the Reverend Hale had as much right as anyone to say that he had seen a ghost, or that he had seen whatever it is which people see when they claim to see a ghost, for he was loathe to define the word; and this was nothing like seeing a ghost. Not only could he see nothing, but he could feel nothing – no breath on his cheek, no localized coldness in the air, no prickle in his skin, no inward sense that he was in the presence of a Something. There was only the vicar's tiled fireplace. He turned and stood looking at Bryant with a quizzical expression. The vicar closed his eyes and fell back on his pillows. "Only me, then. The rest of the world is not ready. 'A prophet hath no honour in his own country', or in his own time." He sounded infinitely weary.

As soon as he had heard of the details of the case, Doctor Pownell had contacted his old colleague Preston, one of the best eye doctors in the country, in the hope that the problem was indeed to do with sight and not with mind. The bishop was willing to meet London fees, and Preston was anxious to assist both his friend and the hierarchy, so word soon came to Penningtree that if Bryant could be got to his surgery everything that modern medicine could do would be done for him at once. The first part of the journey was easy enough, in a closed coach all the way to the capital, stopping only after dark, but the actual arrival at the doctor's premises in a busy street was fraught: though he was marched swiftly from the vehicle across the pavement and inside, Pownell on one arm and Mrs. Bryant on the other, Bryant was filled with the old despair at seeing so many ghosts unheeded amongst the thronging crowds so that he cried out like a madman and tried to break free of his companions. Once they had him indoors and calm again, he was subjected to a very thorough examination and a series of tests which extended over two days, with his wife and the bishop's doctor on hand to provide stability and support when it became hard for him. Several times he asked for Hale, who had returned to his duties in Stoke Armitage. At the end of the period, he was returned home in the same way, and Pownell sent Hale a copy of the report which Preston had given him for the bishop.

In Preston's opinion, the unusual degree of peripheral vision which Reverend Bryant enjoyed was largely caused by a distortion of his eyes, a kind of horizontal stretching, the retina in particular being pulled sideways and covering a rather larger area than is normal but without containing any more of the structures we now call rods and cones which gather light and begin the mental process of interpreting what is perceived. The long-term practising of extreme vision, exercising the muscles which control the shape of the eye for the purpose of focussing, had pulled them apart even further. The result, in crude terms, was that minute vertical gaps had opened in the retina, leading to the experiencing of areas of vision in which definition was lost and blurring occurred. This accounted for the vertical patches which he seemed to see; these could well have appeared quite suddenly, as the structures in the eye pulled away and suddenly tore apart. There was no remedy for the damage done, but further deterioration might be prevented by desisting from the habitual straining to see sideways. Otherwise, it was not impossible that small actual gaps in his field of vision might develop, though at its present stage the mind could manage to fill in from the surroundings most of what should be in the damaged area, minimising the loss and distortion of vision.

Unfortunately, as the doctor explained in his accompanying letter, whereas, despite the irreparable damage done, everyone else had taken it as good news that Bryant's problem was a simple physical and not a mental one, the patient had rejected the diagnosis utterly, becoming angry and abusive towards Preston when it was explained to him and reducing Mrs. Bryant to tears. He had suffered incalculable harm from the loss of his faith in coming to terms with his own version of events, but now he clung to that new belief even more doggedly, raging heatedly against a superstitious humanity who dreamt of immortality and put their faith in scientific quacks. They had returned to Penningtree in a closed coach with Bryant under opiate sedation.

Hale resolved to go to Penningtree as soon as he could, in case he could be of any help, but when he finally arrived he found the Bryants already gone and the Reverend Osborne in place as the new incumbent; the new vicar, recognizing the part Hale had played in the matter, gave him accommodation for the night and explained what had happened. The bishop had been convinced from the accounts he had received of Bryant's behaviour after diagnosis that, even if the cause of his problem had not been a disturbed mind, such a disturbance was its result. It was not possible for him to undertake any parochial duties or represent the Church in any way until he had recovered, shaken off the heresies he was proclaiming and resumed a more normal and stable manner. Almost as soon as they had arrived in Penningtree, word came from the bishop's palace that they were to pack in order to move into an almshouse in a row not far from the cathedral, until Bryant should be well again. The Reverend Osborne was confirmed as vicar, to avoid further disruption to the spiritual life of the parish.

A few months later, Hale was in Bristol on diocesan business and chanced to have a few hours of leisure; he resolved to visit the Bryants, though unannounced. He knew the ancient row in which they were housed, and after inquiry soon found himself at their door. Mrs. Bryant made an effort and looked quite pleased to see him, but the overwhelming impression she gave was of utter weariness and joylessness. The house was very small, and filled to overflowing with their possessions, though everywhere the excess was simply of quantity, as the mark of neglect and decline touched everything from Mrs. Bryant's wan cheek to the faded wallpaper and the darned fabrics. Hale understood that they had virtually no income beyond charity and Mrs. Bryant was obliged to do all the housework and even take in mending and sewing. But worse was to come: she briefly showed him her husband, sitting up in bed in earnest nonsensical dialogue with a space of vacuity which he addressed as 'Mister Locke'. He did not seem to know Hale, but introduced him to the ghost of the philosopher John Locke, who had, apparently, some interesting things to say about perception and understanding. Hale was deeply moved by the sight of the man's complete collapse, and stayed behind briefly to pray with Mrs. Bryant that her husband might be restored to her as she knew him.

But, of course, that which whips behind the door as it opens and that which flees from sight at the corner of the eye wanted the existing state to continue, and to be as it always has, and were relieved that their secret remained just that.

IN BED

The bed has many symbolic meanings and connotations in our culture, amongst which is a curious connection to ideas both of security and of insecurity, which can perhaps be summed up by reference to the old image of one pulling the bedclothes over one's head to hide from something or shut something out. Perhaps this is because we retain even today a deep-rooted fear of the dark, lingering from the early days of the species when there was no source of artificial light, the return of the life-giving sun was not guaranteed and nocturnal predators with far better night vision accounted for many fatalities. Furthermore, the enforced inactivity of the night has always led to speculation, the free working of the imagination on all the shadows and strange noises which suddenly achieve prominence when the busyness of the day has subsided. Sleep is the easy way to overcome these anxieties, if it can be achieved, but it leads to its own perplexities and worries, not only in its kinship to death and the bizarre activities of sleep-walkers and sleep-talkers but more especially because of the regular phenomenon of dreams, which many early cultures seem to have barely distinguished from waking experience; strange images and narratives from somewhere unknown and unseen visit the sleeper while the normal activities and rules which apply in the hours of daylight are suspended. It was a short step to seeing the night as a time when other realities came into play, other worlds coincided with our conscious one and the mysterious force and realm called death, and even the dead themselves, might touch the living. For the dead, though gone from us physically, being interred or devoured or drowned, evidently remained with us in less tangible ways, in memories and as actors in dreams; they survived in a different form, and might be glimpsed when night brought anarchy to normality. Knowledge and enlightenment might result from such contact, but the survival response to what is alien, unpredictable and uncontrollable is to avoid it, and the best way to ensure avoidance is to implant fear, which inhibits getting into a position where there is even a slight risk of an unwanted encounter. Hence, even the ghosts of our own kin, though viewed as insubstantial spectres incapable of physical action and presumably kindly disposed to us, become objects of terror.

In this context, the bed is not just a couch on which to sleep comfortably off the cold and hard ground: it is an island of safety in the great sea of the dark, a tangible reminder of the day precisely located in a familiar domestic space, the physicality and ordinariness of which can be set against the uncertainties of a darkness in which our senses are distorted or do not function and the few feet of space to the bedroom wall become extended to a possibly infinite void. The elaborate beds of the past, the box-bed and the four-poster, may well have been designed primarily to keep out the draughts when windows might have imprecisely-fitting shutters rather than glass, and to secure some privacy when rooms were few and large and did not have specific purposes; but also, the sliding doors and curtains served to shut out the night, to define a square of normality and safety for the occupant, and to hide him or her from whatever might pass by in the hours of darkness. In the absence of these fittings, pulling the bedclothes over one's head serves a similar purpose.

For the reasons already set out, the setting of the sun brings night-fears, and the worst terrors of all are those which invade the apparent security of the bed. Many accounts of hauntings and poltergeist activity include such details as the moving of occupied beds, the snatching off of sheets and scratching sounds around headboards, and many storytellers have exploited the idea, with descending canopies, ghostly impressions on the eiderdown and thin voices from within the curtains – those very bedcurtains the tearing down of which symbolises Scrooge's lonely death in

Dickens' best-known Christmas tale. The bedclothes themselves can be involved, the image of the corpse in its shroud giving rise to the conceit of a ghost, or its imitator, draped in a white sheet – a Halloween, cartoon and comic book convention which goes back at least to Shakespeare's 'sheeted dead'. The most disturbing of all M. R. James' stories plays on these fears, making an apparently innocent empty bed and its coverings the habitation and temporary embodiment of a sinister and vengeful supernatural entity.

Though he did not hunt as many clergy of his time did, travelling around his parish and beyond and working in his garden gave the Reverend Theophilus Hale more exercise than most of his colleagues took, and as a result he usually slept soundly. Although he had more experience than most people of phenomena scientifically inexplicable or attributable to unworldly causes, he was not particularly afraid of the dark, nor superstitious or nervous, and anxiety rarely troubled him enough to keep him awake. On this particular day, he had taken far more exercise than he was accustomed to and was certainly ready to take to his bed as soon as was decently possible.

Following a taxing mission for the diocese, he had been granted a fortnight's leave from his parochial duties; as he had recently been in correspondence with an old college friend who was now vicar of the parish of Torcastle, on the western edge of Devon, he had decided to take up an invitation to visit him. When the locum from the bishop was safely installed at Stoke Armitage, Hale took horse for the west; after spending Friday night at an inn in Exeter, having passed some time exploring the cathedral, he set off again early, intending to cross the moors – not taking the main road which skirted them – and arrive at his destination perhaps an hour or two before nightfall. He soon found that he had considerably underestimated the roughness of this unfamiliar terrain, and was pushing his horse a little more than usual.

145

Disaster struck less than fifteen miles out from the city, as he headed away from Moretonhampstead, where arable fields had long since given way to rough grazing: his horse stumbled, cast a shoe and proved to be slightly lame in that leg. There was a cottage in sight, half a mile away, and he gently led the creature there, where he inquired as to the possibility of hiring another mount, getting a farrier to attend to his horse or finding lodging for the night, or any combination of these. The cottager was not unkindly but blunt: the nearest village was another couple of miles further into the moor, off the main road, and there was neither horse nor room for him in this small house, even though he was a man of the cloth. Hale considered his limited options: he was sure to find assistance in Moretonhampstead, but it was much further away than the village, which was relevant, since the horse could walk slowly but could not be ridden. He made his mind up when the cottager assured him that there was a decent inn and a smithy in the village, and so he began to lead his horse westwards again, towards Morston. The climb was very gradual, but served to slow horse and man down further, and the country through which they passed became bleaker and emptier. Trees thinned and eventually disappeared altogether, apart from lone, bent and stunted specimens in dips or behind features which gave some shelter from the prevailing wind; the dominant colour of the landscape turned from grass- and leaf-green to the browner shades of gorse-heath and bog; the path itself, once he had turned off the road at the ancient fingerpost marked "Morston", was narrower and less well-tended and soon was no longer a badly paved highway but a mere causeway of stones intended to stabilise the mud which hooves and wheels churned up. The slow walk which the horse forced him to adopt made the journey even more tiring than it would have been if he could have strode out at a comfortable pace; as it was, he was conscious of every step and could not let his mind wander free of the immediate moment. The sun was two hours past its midpoint when he reached the top of a rise and spied a cluster of buildings perhaps a mile ahead. Another half an hour – the cottager had considerably underestimated the distance and the journey had taken fully two hours from his door – and he was outside the Moorland Inn at Morston. He already knew that he had made a mistake, and that he would have been better advised to have returned to the town, which he could have reached in much the same time, but he had to make the best of the situation in which he found himself.

The village was merely a short line of low buildings on either side of the road, between a clapper bridge and the stone walls of a farm; from it, rough lanes and paths could be seen stretching up the surrounding fells to isolated cottages and crofts for which it was a centre, of sorts. Hale spotted the sign of a bakery; next to the inn there was a small shop with a jumble of agricultural and household equipment in the window and signs advertising animal feed and medicines. There was no-one about to take charge of his horse – indeed, there was no-one in the street at all – so he took it to a stone trough of stagnant and rather green water, swaying from thirst and weariness himself as he watched it drink deeply, and then knotted its reins in a ring in the wall. He entered the inn, which was no more than a house larger than the surrounding cottages, with its parlour turned over to public use and presumably one or two of its bedrooms let out to the occasional traveller. He had evidently been observed arriving, as the landlord was waiting for him. He was not a particularly welcoming or expansive fellow for mine host, though he was quietly polite and his seriousness could be taken for concern; as Hale was to discover, his manner was friendly and forthcoming compared to that of the grim characters amongst whom he lived, as he had much more to do with outsiders than they did and his trade required him to be civil – though, as it turned out, he had more to be aggrieved about than most.

Hale sat himself on an armchair by the cold fireplace – there was no-one else in the room – and bluntly asked for a drink, without any preamble, so thirsty was he; the landlord was not concerned to ask about his journey or comment on the weather, but swiftly brought a tankard of weak ale and withdrew. Hale thought his behaviour unusual, but it suited him well enough at this moment. After he had taken a couple of deep draughts, the rector called him back and made enquiry about the smithy and the possibility of hiring a horse or other transport to get across the moor. The first question was soon answered: the smithy was at the far end of the street. The second the man took a little time to consider: few people around had a horse, and those that did would be unwilling or unable to part with it, especially on a Saturday, since it would be needed to get them to the nearest chapel on the morrow – "for we be chapel-folk hereabouts, if you pardon me, sir, and not of your persuasion at all". Hale thanked him and paid for his ale, and led his horse down the street – which was still deserted – to a dark and cramped cottage to which was attached a small forge, though there was no sign up. There was no activity in the workshop, and he had to bang on the door to gain the smith's attention. A tall, broad-shouldered man with a face fiery with prominent veins and marked by engrained soot threw the door open and curtly asked what he wanted: Hale began a brief account of how his horse came to be lame, but the smith cut him off short:

"I be finished for the day and it will soon be Sabbath-eve, so I don't see as how I can help thee until Monday."

"Monday! But I need to be across the moor today!"

"The fire be out, and you wouldn't want me to be sinning by working on the Sabbath, would you, vicar? In any event, that horse o'thine needs rest for a day or two to fix his leg."

There was the hint of a sneer in the word "vicar", and so Hale did not press him further. The smith unbent to the extent of agreeing to shoe the horse first thing on Monday morning, and in the meantime he took a look at the leg: he was a good deal more sympathetic to the animal than he was to the man, and applied a poultice to take away the lameness. He instructed Hale to let the horse rest for the next day in the inn stables – he took it for granted that Hale would be staying there as there was nowhere else – and dismissed him by waving aside as absurd his suggestion that there might be other transport to be had in the village at short notice. Hale trudged back to the Moorland disappointed: he was going to have to spend two nights in this miserable place, while his friend was expecting him today or tomorrow at the latest, and there was no way he could get word to him that he had been delayed. He returned to the landlord, whose name was Whitton, and enquired about lodging; the man was not surprised, having seen the condition of his mount and knowing what response he would get from the smith, and by way of answer he called a boy from the back of the house to take the horse round to the stable and bring the saddlebags in under Hale's direction. The stable was a wooden lean-to behind the inn, with three straw-filled pens in it, pungent with animal smells though they were empty; when the horse had been settled in one, Hale and the boy re-entered the building and Whitton led them up a narrow staircase to a landing with several doors leading off it.

"This be your room, sir, if you like."

There was a bed with a dark wooden frame of some age, somewhere between a double and a single size; a press and a chest of drawers of similarly dark wood; an armchair with threadbare upholstery; a folding table on which stood a basin and jug of common blue and white earthenware. The furniture was of simple but solid construction, undecorated, probably locally made and almost certainly as old as the house itself. The walls were rough and whitewashed, apart from around the small hearth, which was surrounded by a line of natural stone and had no mantelpiece. On one side of this was the single small window with plain hessian curtains; the foot of the bed was under this, with the press and cupboard along the other wall. It was a small and ugly room, but the worst thing about it, which Hale noticed at once, was the dreadful smell – not a fusty or damp odour, but something very unpleasant underneath and partly masked by the smell of soot from an unswept chimney. Hale remarked on it at once and immediately crossed the room to open the window; this did not, however, clear the air – in fact, the smell was magnified several times over, undisguised by the sootiness. He guessed what it was. Pushing the window wide and pinching his nose with the other hand, he leaned out and looked down: just below him – and, given the lowness of the rooms, not far below him – was a great midden; the stable lean-to was immediately next to it, indicating the source of most of its contents. Hale slammed the window shut and turned on his host: "This is intolerable!"

The weariness of several hours of plodding along on uneven stones in riding boots, the frustration of being late for his visit and having to spend two days in this remote hamlet, the resentment at the rudeness which he had encountered, all finally took control, and at this final outrage he lost his usual composure and for once in his life he was actually angry – though, in truth, at that time many people, especially in rural areas, would not have regarded the situation as out of the ordinary; Hale was perhaps somewhat refined for his age in this regard, as well as being at this point less than wholly rational. Whitton, who had never thought of his domestic arrangements as being unacceptable and who was scarcely conscious of the smell, appeared somewhat overawed, rather than presenting his usual taciturn front, which Hale might have ascribed to a natural desire to please his guests but which actually derived from the fact that he had rarely heard anyone speak for such a length of time before.

"I am expected today by the vicar of Torcastle, but the smith of Morston will not entertain me until Monday; and now I am expected to sleep in the meantime on top of a dung heap!"

At the end of his diatribe against Morston in general and the Moorland Inn in particular, Hale had spent his rage and began to realise that he was overreacting and taking out his feelings about his own predicament on the unfortunate landlord. However, he resisted an urge to apologise and pressed on. He demanded another room which did not have this offending feature – one at the front of the house. Whitton muttered something inaudible and made a gesture with his hands.

"You do have other rooms? This is an inn?"

"Well, we have one other room, sir. We have few people stay here, it being out of the road, like."

"And this other room, it is not taken then?"

"Well, no, not taken as such."

"And it is at the front of the house and not overlooking a midden?"

"Aye."

"In that case I shall take it."

"We don't normally use it, you see, sir."

"Well, you now have a paying guest who needs it."

"But it is not – not ready; not aired. We weren't expecting… and it is not comfortable, sir. Not as comfortable as this room. Not at all comfortable."

"I am quite prepared to put up with a little dampness and mustiness in place of that abominable stench. And as for comfort, it could hardly be worse than this room, unless you have the rack in place of a bed. Now please show it to me."

Hale was pleased with his witticism and did not notice the expression on the landlord's face, and particularly the boy's. All he noted was that Whitton shrugged and gave in and the three of them crossed the landing to another door, which the landlord unlocked. Inside was a room similar to but at least half as big again as the other, with a full-sized bed, as yet unmade, a tiled fireplace and a small writing desk in addition to the usual furniture. It had two windows, with a view over the hardware shop and towards the fells beyond. The only drawback was that this room was much colder than the first, perhaps because it faced north and had not been used for some time, as the landlord had implied. Hale was inwardly relieved, but was relentless:

"So you thought to give me the second-best room? Perhaps my calling offends you, as a chapel-goer."

The landlord apologised in a general way, assured Hale that the agreed rate would still apply, and went away to get bedclothes; Hale, determined not to appear pleased, called after him that he would need a fire as the room felt cold. The boy, who had not entered the room, stood at the door and held out the bags for Hale to take from him, and then ran off down the stairs. The rector was feeling ridiculously pleased with his petty triumph, while at the same time realising that it was quite out of character for him; he put it down to tiredness and being thwarted in his plans. While Whitton made up the bed and set the fire, he went down to the stables to check on his horse's leg and organise provender for him. Returning to his room, he set out his things and then sat down for a moment to study his surroundings a little more carefully. The longer sides of the room ran with the front of the house: on the exterior wall were the two windows, flanking a dressing table and a large mirror, somewhat crazed and clouded with age. In one corner there was a press and in the other a bookcase on which were some pots but no books. The bed occupied the wall opposite, against the interior wall, with a washing table at its head and a chest at its foot, and beyond that the door; the mattress, Hale had been relieved to note before it was covered, was quite clean. The short exterior wall contained the fireplace, with an old armchair at each side of it; the interior wall had a chest of drawers and two stand chairs pushed against it, and the small round table to go with the chairs stood in the centre of the room. Apart from a general feeling of dust and disuse and an unseasonable chilliness, the room was perfectly acceptable, and Hale felt rather less vexed as he settled in one of the armchairs to read a little of a book he had brought with him, before his dinner.

For Hale's supper, Whitton produced a mutton pie – or rather, he served a pie which appeared to have been made by a woman glimpsed or heard occasionally in the background, presumably his wife. She seemed vexed, and Hale was aware of hard words being exchanged in the kitchen, though voices were kept low and he could not make them out. He assumed that she was put out at having to accommodate him at short notice, and at having the trouble of making the spare room ready. He was eating alone at a small table in the corner of the parlour, or at least he might as well have been alone, for the two men in shepherd's attire who had come in only to drink Master Whitton's small beer by the cheerless hearth ignored him completely, even though he had greeted them civilly enough when he had come in. The effect of this lack of politeness was lessened, however, by the fact that they all but ignored each other as well, and also their host, who came in to refill their tankards when they were almost empty, as though silently summoned. On Whitton's last appearance, when

Hale was almost done with his food, they both drew out some coins, handed them over with a curious grunt, and left. The host paused briefly in front of his remaining guest, with the tankards in his hands, and made a vague inquiry as to the pie; Hale made an equally non-committal reply – in truth, the mutton had been tough, the crust burnt and the gravy congealed, but he had been so hungry that he had made a fist of eating most of it. To cover his lack of enthusiasm about the meal, Hale added a half-jocular comment about the lack of conversation to be had in Morston. In truth, he regretted his earlier angry outburst in front of the man and hoped to atone for it a little by being more friendly in his manner. Whitton hesitated in his movement to the door, swayed as if in indecision, then stopped:

"It's true, sir, them hereabouts aren't given much to talking. It's as if being alone so much, out on the moors, with no Christian soul to speak to, they lose the habit, or never get it. It don't mean as though they're stupid nor nothing like that, sir: just that they keep their thoughts inside them. Sometimes we have gentlemen like yourself passing through and I have to remind myself to talk civil-like, and then when they've gone I have to remind myself to keep my peace and not upset my reg'lars with chattering." An unaccustomed smile spread over the man's face, and Hale grinned back.

"You can't have many passing through and staying here – it's off the main road and not on the way to anywhere, as far as I can see."

"Some travellers making their way north-south across the moor pass through this way, though most folks go east-west and miss us. A merchant comes to sell goods to the store across the way a couple of times a year, sometimes a lawyer or doctor or visiting preacher comes out from Exeter and has to spend the night somewhere. No, the trade don't amount to much; just enough to make us keep a room prepared."

"Which is why it is not worth keeping the second room ready, I suppose."

Whitton was silent; Hale would have gone on to take the opportunity to apologise for putting him to the trouble of preparing his room, but at that moment two more surly characters came in and took the seats by the fireplace. They exchanged nods with the landlord, and he hurried off, with, "It's my reg'lars as is my real trade, you see," only to return swiftly with the two tankards refilled, and some cheese for Hale. "Pie," said one of the men, in a manner which made it at once an inquiry and an order, and the other grunted with a rising tone. The landlord nodded again, and returned to the kitchen. By the time Hale had eaten as much of the hard local cheese as he thought prudent before retiring and the men had downed their draughts, he had returned with two more dishes; the men fell on them ravenously, distaining the niceties of cutlery, and Hale decided it was time for him to leave. As he crossed the passage to the foot of the stairs, he called out a cheery goodnight to Whitton, who bobbed out of a door to wish him a peaceful night; Mrs. Whitton was just visible in the shadows, peering round the edge of the doorframe at him. Hale repeated his goodnight as though to her, but got no response. He ascended the stairs, but it was quite dark at the top and he groped for his door; he heard someone follow him, sensed a light behind him, and turned to find Whitton with a double candle.

"Sorry, sir, I was forgetting how dark it has got. You will need a light." He turned the handle and stepped into the front bedroom, which was dark except for the pool of ruddy light now given off by a low fire. Crossing to the fireplace, he proceeded to light the five-candle holder on the mantelpiece, and a fat nightlight on the table next to the jug and basin. "I would leave the little light on if I was you, sir, in case you wake up and find yourself in a strange place. It'll burn through the night and no harm will come of it. You have a tinderbox in case you need to relight the candles, sir? Good. There are logs in the box if you want to keep the fire going – it still isn't very warm in here, I know. I hope you have a peaceful night, sir," he repeated, "and if you need anything we are just down the passage on this side of the house. If you need anything at all."

The Reverend Hale was, as I said near the beginning of my account, very tired after the day's events, and, since there was clearly no call on him to be sociable downstairs and there was nothing else to do in this place, he proceeded to take off his day clothes and prepare himself for sleep. When he had prayed a while, kneeling by the bed, asking especially for forgiveness for his hard thoughts and words that afternoon, he found his mind wandering from the matter in hand; he had a vague notion that if he went to bed early he might wake early and have time to get himself to a church in time for the service, though he had failed to ask Whitton where the nearest outpost of the Established Church might be and he feared he would have to walk back to St. Andrew's at Moretonhampstead in order to observe the Sabbath. This prospect – perhaps five or six miles each way – daunted him: that, and the thoughts that began churning in his mind concerning the mechanics of perhaps hiring another mount back in town with which to complete his journey and reclaiming his own horse from the farrier's later, prevented his mind from shutting down even after he had extinguished the candles and closed his eyes. For some time he tried to lie still and blank out his thoughts, but then some noise from below, more likely the banging of a door than the sound of voices, would disturb him again. He rose and, noting the lack of a moon, closed the windows in case that improved matters, but there were no sounds from without to vex him and it only served to make the room airless. Nevertheless, he still felt cold, and after another few minutes he rose to put another log on the embers and add his coat to the bedclothes. He turned to the wall, so that the renewed glow from the fire should not disturb him, and made a determined effort to launch himself into slumber.

The log, not being of the best sort, cracked with what sounded in the confined space and the silence of the night like a loud explosion, in his scarcely-started dream. "This is intolerable!" he muttered for the second time that day, and sat up. After gathering himself, he swung himself out of the bed and attacked the fire with a poker, so that it flared and guttered; he staggered back and lay down again, his eyes on the ceiling. At length, the fire died down, and the room was almost completely black, apart from the faint squares of the windows, struck by starlight. There were no longer any noises from below; to complete the effect of darkness and peace, he leaned over to blow out the nightlight and lay back.

At first, he assumed it was a dream; but then it occurred to him that if it were in a dream, he would surely not be able to dismiss it as dream. No, it had to be a dream – this was not his bed, not his room; but then he remembered where he was, and soon afterwards what had brought him here. He became fully conscious of his position: he was lying on his side, facing into the room, with the windows in front of him and the fireplace beyond his feet. He knew the fireplace was there, because he could see a merry blaze in the grate, though he knew it had been extinguished; he also knew there was no-one else in the room, but in the glow he could see him sitting in the chair and looking into the fire. Not distinctly, of course, as the back of the chair was towards him, but he could make out the top of a head, an arm on the rest, legs stretched out towards the hearth. Despite the fire, it was colder than ever, though that was not the only reason for the shuddering which Hale felt, the chill which seized especially his back, despite it being the most snuggly wrapped part of him. It was the ancient terror of supernatural forces, the instinctive avoidance of the unknown which is as deep-seated as the fear induced by snakes. Hale could not control the ancestral emotional response, though his reason told him there was nothing to fear.

"Has it occurred to you how – trite this story seems? Perhaps being in it you haven't noticed, but you have been acting out the lead in one of the oldest ghost stories of all: a traveller is stranded in a remote spot at dusk, seeks shelter in a strange old house, has a – bizarre encounter during the night. By rights, you should be found strangled or at least deranged and white-haired in the morning. Oh sorry, how thoughtless of me – nothing of that sort is likely to happen, not in your case. If you had been one of the charming fellows mine host entertains below, you might well be jumping out of the window or breaking your neck on the stairs by now – if I had been able to wake you out of their snoring, drunken stupor. But you are clearly a different matter altogether, and I fancy what – sport I have with you will be of a wholly different order too."

The voice, though low and thin, was cultured, urbane, old-fashioned even, with accents of the city and even of the universities. Surely it was a dream: no-one in Morston could sound like that. And yet it was odd: there were frequent pauses, usually before more sophisticated words, sometimes momentary, as though judiciously weighing the most apt expression, but sometimes longer, as though searching for a forgotten word in a long-unused language.

"I must apologise again – after so long without needing to exercise them, one begins to lose one's manners – I have not introduced myself. My name is, or was, Charles Danvers, sometime scholar of St. Stephen's College in the University of Oxford, late resident of Torcastle, in the county of Devon."

Hale started up, then at once instinctively drew the bedclothes up around his neck, as though shielding himself. His pulse was racing, the hairs on his neck had risen, he felt a prickly sensation on his skin, though he knew that what was before him had no material substance with which to cause him harm. Indeed, it seemed almost friendly in tone.

"Yes, I know you are going there – I heard you tell Whitton. That was partly why I have appeared to you; that, and the fact that you are clearly an educated and intelligent man. I saw you were reading Herodotus earlier – one of my favourites: interesting stories, and not too long; the rest of them do tend to go on so. Thucydides! How tedious!"

"Am I right in thinking," Hale was encouraged by the stranger's words and even more by his tone, "that you are – no longer wholly with us; for you speak of yourself in the past tense." He hoped that the ghost, if that was indeed what it was, would not notice the strangely hoarse and cracked quality of his voice.

"Yes, I am what is commonly called a ghost. Do not avoid the word on my account: I am quite accustomed to what my – situation is. I lurk in the shadows during daylight, and can only be – discerned clearly in the dark, if that is not self-contradictory. I haunt this room." There was a pause. "I assume you would like to ask some questions? I know people have an endless fascination with the condition of which I partake – I will not say "which I enjoy", because there is little delight in it. For the first few years, causing panic and being immortal are quite jolly, but then it becomes repetitive and dreary, and being stuck in the same place with no hope of change is, after all, very much what hell is all about – or so I have heard; fear not, I am not an evil spirit, though I have encountered one or two, briefly. You would definitely not like to meet one of *them*."

Hale took up the offer.

"You say you lived at Torcastle? You must know the vicarage and the Reverend Bryce-Turner?"

The half-seen ghost chuckled. "You have not quite grasped my position. I know the vicarage because it was home for my twenty years of life; the Reverend Bryce-Turner I do not know because – let us see, how old is the Reverend Bryce-Turner? How long has he been at Torcastle?"

"He will be my age, coming up to forty, and has been the incumbent for about ten years."

"In which case, there will have been at least one and possibly two or even more vicars at Torcastle between my father's death in that office and your Mr. Bryce-Turner's arrival. You see, I died, as near as I can tell, some fifty years ago."

"You died fifty years ago, at the age of twenty?"

"As near as I can tell; time ceases to have any meaning when mortality ends and one becomes – stuck and unchanging. And if you know your ghost-lore, you will realise that I must have died close to where I haunt – in this room in fact; and that I stay here because of the violent nature of my end, as I was murdered."

"Murdered in this room?"

"Just so. In that very bed. Do not be alarmed: they changed the mattress afterwards."

"But why?"

"Because there was blood on it. No, I know what you mean; forgive my little joke. I was staying here overnight – forced to stay, as I understand you to have been, by the lameness of my horse, and become the first protagonist of the trite old story, as I was travelling home for the Long Vacation. I was murdered by another guest, sleeping in the little room opposite, a farmer who had been – declared bankrupt and had lost his land. He killed me with a knife in the heart and a pillow over the face as I slept, for the sake of a few coins in my purse, imagining me to be a richer man; he then stole my horse from the stable and tried to escape across the moors on it, not realising it to be lame. He was caught within a few hours, taken to Exeter, as I heard men say, and swiftly tried and hanged."

"And you – some part of you – has been here ever since?"

"You may say the best part of me, the – consciousness, the intelligence, the wit, such as it is; but I am not so sure – what value have such qualities if there is no use to which they can be put? Only the actions of that mass of living clay which perished here that night gave real meaning to my existence, and half a century effectively serves to take the edge off the intellect as well as being damnably dull. Oh, as I say, at first there was some fun to be had, frightening guests and so forth with rappings and disembodied laughter; after a short time, one makes the effort to appear to them rather in the hope that they might stay and converse, but by then the damage is done: one is the notorious and feared ghost, to be fled from and cursed."

"For fifty years you have been entirely alone, and, what is more, aware of it, with human feelings of loneliness; how dreadful! Such qualities are not usually ascribed to ghosts; if they were, people might be more sympathetic to your kind."

"Indeed. The last clergyman we had staying in this room – it must be thirty years ago or more; they are rare in these parts, as you may have gathered – tried to exorcise me when I appeared and tried to address him, but he got into such a panic that he muddled everything and only succeeded in summoning Tom in, which scared him into a dead faint!"

"Tom? Do you mean Mr. Whitton, or perhaps his predecessor?"

"Oh no, I am sorry. When I said I was alone here, I was discounting other spirits in the immediate neighbourhood, because I have scarcely more in common with them than I do with the living. Tom haunts the shop next door; he was the dealer in feed and seed before the current owner – no, there have been two since Tom, I think. None of them seem to have made much of a living at it, but Tom did very badly and hanged himself in his kitchen. He has to stay there as a sort of – penance, for his suicide, and it has added further resentment and bitterness to the despair and melancholy with which he died, so that he barely recognises anything outside his own misery and never speaks a word. Shrivelled and graceless as he is, though, he is – conviviality itself compared to the thing which lives in the cellar."

Hale felt another chill along his spine. "And what is that?" The ghost made a sound analogous to a physical shrug.

"It is hard to say. It has been there so long that its shape has become quite blurred and it has lost the power of speech through disuse. It must have been there for centuries; I suspect it was buried down there secretly – probably in the cellar of a previous building. I glimpsed it just a few times, in the early days, when I could still stretch myself that far, but I haven't seen it since and no-one seems to speak of it. I doubt it can appear as much beyond a vague glow and a coldness. That is the fate of all of us ghosts, I suspect."

"Excuse me for being inquisitive, but what did you mean when you said you could stretch yourself?"

"Again, I have only my own experience on which to draw, but it seems to me that as time passes one becomes increasingly tied to one's location. At first, I could, with some effort, drift through the walls and visit the rooms and cellar downstairs and the attic above, but now I seem to be unable to leave this room, unless it is to descend the staircase and enter the parlour, as if retracing my last journey to that fatal bed. The old mole in the cellarage is by now, I suspect, limited to hovering over his grave. And before you ask, what the next stage after that might be, I have no more idea than you – though the question does frequently occur to me. Do you wish to ask any more questions of your own?"

"One thing does trouble me a little. You said at first that you intended some, I think your word was "sport", with me. What exactly might you have in mind?"

There was another thin laugh. "Do not fear – I do not intend anything sinister; merely that we might have some pleasant conversation, which I lack so badly. In truth, I can do nothing sinister – no ghost can, as far as I am aware. Whatever misfortune may follow from our appearances, in the form of heart failures, falls from balconies, or what have you, is purely the result of the feebleness and fright on the part of those who encounter us. You, may I say, are something of an exception in being apparently quite unperturbed by my appearance."

"I am not without previous experience of beings such as yourself."

"Ah, indeed! As I was saying, we can do nothing in the physical world except impart some faint impression of ourselves on human senses – through sounds heard, through faint images seen, through a touch reduced to the mere sensation of coldness or breath. Even to lift a piece of paper is usually beyond our powers. For decades I have longed to read a book again – any book, it matters not its subject or style; even to cast my eyes along lines of print in an unknown tongue would go some way to appease my – craving. But I cannot open a volume; if by chance a guest leaves a newspaper on a table or book open – it would have to be a traveller; people around here do not trouble themselves with such things – I read avidly what is on view, then pine to see the next page. The last guest in this room – a smart young man, I think he may have been travelling to his own wedding, or at least a romantic meeting – left a letter from his sweetheart on that table in the middle of the room and went down to supper. I must have read that page twenty times before he returned, yearning to see what followed. When he came back and pocketed it, I appeared rather too precipitantly in order to beg him to show me the rest. He screamed and yelled and almost threw himself down the stairs, and they have not used this room since. It must have been six months ago, no, a year ago, or perhaps two. The years do run together so, being all much the same."

The ghost's thin voice had begun to sound even more melancholy, perhaps nostalgic. There was a pause. Then he seemed to brighten a little.

"Which is why I so enjoyed the Herodotus earlier, standing behind your chair and reading over your shoulder – I hope you do not think that rude of me, in the circumstances. But I must say you do read very quickly – I was barely into the facing page before you were turning over! I got quite vexed at times. But I suppose my Greek is very rusty, after so long a period of disuse. We must read some more of it together later."

The Reverend Hale felt distinctly uneasy, imagining the ghost looking over his shoulder, unseen, just as Scrooge would find it disagreeable to learn that the ghost of Jacob Marley had often been by his side, and the prospect of entering into a reading party with a spirit seemed quite bizarre. He changed the subject.

"There may be some reason for it which I do not know – in which case, please forgive me – but so far you have not really appeared to me, not face to face. It does seem rather strange: people speak of seeing ghosts, but not of conversing with them through chair backs. Would you mind if I were to see you properly?"

Again there was a pause, and the ghost spoke more slowly and even more quietly. "I thought it best if you did not, immediately. As I have said, the responses I have inevitably encountered on manifesting myself have been fear, loathing, panic, flight, in other words the stock responses to phantoms, monsters, the unknown. I could not be sure that you would not react in the same way, and I feared losing the opportunity of conversing a little with someone who might, if not forced to confront an apparition from beyond the grave, be prepared to be more – sociable. But as you will."

The ghost stirred. So far, Hale had only seen what might have been the top of a head above the chair back, an arm on the armrest, the shape of legs stretched out in front, all pale and indistinct in the glow of a fire in an otherwise totally dark room. Now he saw more of the ghost, from the back, as it rose; but it did not stand up as a living man would, pushing up from the seat and straightening its legs to gain its full height. Instead, it floated straight up, still in its bent posture, and forward a little, so that it could straighten its body and let its legs hang down. Clearly, it had not been sitting on the chair as we would sit on it, so that it bore our weight, but had merely flexed itself to fit into the angled shape in imitation of physical sitting. A pale human shape, in parts transparent but in others more translucent, hung a foot or more off the floor, facing the fireplace, its arms and legs very slightly spread; then it slowly turned to face Hale, without apparent effort, like something suspended and blown round by the wind – or, thought Hale, a hanged man turning on the end of a rope. It looked in Hale's general direction, without precisely focussing on him – but that would have been hard to discern, as

165

the eyes were not distinct. Indeed, the features in the gaunt-looking face were all somewhat blurred: the nose was flatter than it would probably have been in life, the lips were crooked and down-turned, the chin was merging into the throat.

"As I feared, you look a little shocked, though you try to hide it. No, do not deny it. I know that I have started to – dissolve, and that I now have the face of an old man rather than of a youth of barely twenty. As I told you, ghosts age too, if more slowly than humans, in that the longer they are out of human company, the more they lose of their human features, intellect and emotions, I believe, until, judging by my friend in the cellar, they become merely – localised energies. Perhaps I have fifty years more of a human face, a hundred more of language, two hundred more of coherent thought, before I too become just a dip in the thermometer and a will o'the wisp."

The ghost fell silent and hung limply. Hale could see the fire clearly though the shape of his legs, but the mantelpiece was harder to make out through his chest. He was dressed, if that was the right word, in the fashion of half a century before, a wig of tight white curls, stockings and pumps below tight, short breeches, a frock coat over a waistcoat, frills at neck and wrists. The ghostly clothes seemed somehow to be of a piece with his head and hands, as though they were his body rather than merely covering it. Hale had often wondered at ghosts appearing clad, as though their garments had spiritual survivals as well as their beings: now he saw that they manifested themselves much as they would look when living, not now wearing clothes but making themselves into the appearance of clothes, where they would have been in life. The appearance of costume was in fact an integral part of the ghostly entity, in place of the appearance of skin. Hale had now become quite used to the idea of conversing with a spirit: the hairs on his neck were settling, his heart rate was returning to normal, his voice was strengthening. He risked another question.

"You said before that you are the best part of Charles Danvers. Are you in fact what we call his soul?"

A kind of expression passed across the face of the ghost; it was not easy to say what it represented – frustration or regret, perhaps? The spectre seemed to shiver a little in the air, and after a short while, during which Hale wondered if he should change the subject, it spoke again.

"It was easy enough to talk about souls and angels and heaven and all that at home with my father the vicar or at college with the tutors, but when one is actually living the life of a spirit, I do not say a spiritual life, it is harder to be objective about it, and, strangely, equally hard to be sure of one's facts. I do not actually have a simple answer for you. I have no clear understanding of what a soul is or knowledge of whether I am one, though it is a question which has troubled me greatly over the years. The religion in which I was brought up tells me that my soul, after death, should be in heaven, or perhaps the other place, but I am clearly in neither. Whether there is some other part of me which has passed on to such a place, I know not; all I can say is that I feel a continuity with the person who was Charles Danvers when alive – I believe that I have his memories, his feelings and his convictions, though all of them were much more distinct when I first passed into this state and I fear that in time they will fade like my form. Sometimes I fancy that I may have slipped into one of those places that are neither heaven nor hell, which the Papists invent to solve their theological problems – a purgatory for the cleansing of souls or a limbo for the sheltering of the unbaptised innocents. I have not seen the face of God, nor been aware of judgement passed upon me, nor been conducted by angels, nor experienced any of the things we are led to expect at death. But some, or all, of Danvers I definitely am, and am not just a nameless spirit adopting his identity."

"Perhaps you will not be able to answer this either, as it is an idea connected to my last question. Do you know why is that you, an innocent victim, have become a ghost, when others who have died have not?"

The ghost's sepulchral voice became even more melancholy, and its utterances briefer.

"No. Perhaps it was because I was murdered. I was not ready for death and so could not wholly die. I do not know. Perhaps I am only in your dreams, and not a spirit at all. If I were only a dream, a message sent from − somewhere, then your concerns about souls and spirits would perhaps be answered."

There was a pause, during which Hale hoped the ghost might continue, but it did not: it merely hung in front of him, its head hanging even more limply than the rest. Hale was about to break the silence which was becoming embarrassing when it suddenly spoke again, quivering and undulating in the air as it did so, in what appeared to be the equivalent of strong agitation, so that Hale feared that it was about to assail him in some way, and crossed himself.

"I lie! And perhaps it is because I lie to you as I have lied to myself all these years that I am condemned to this death worse than death. I did not die as an innocent victim. When − I forget the name I heard mentioned at the time − killed me he did so because he had heard the chink of coins in my heavy saddlebags and knew that I carried a sizeable sum." Another pause. "My chief reason for appearing to you like this, if I could but admit it, is to confess an ancient wrong. You see, I did tell you that mine was an old, oft-told story. If I am merely a dream, and you are actually asleep in the bed while dreaming of me, then I am not an apparition but an echo of some ancient deed heard now for a

168

specific purpose." And another. "I ask you, as a clergyman, to hear my confession and pray with me. Do not worry: I do not expect you to say that you forgive my sins, like a Popish priest, but it would relieve me, wherever I might be if not here in this room, of some of the burden which I have carried so long, and might earn me some respite from what I have come to believe is my punishment. It may be mere chance that you, a clergyman, have come here in this manner, but perhaps it was ordained that you should be here for my aid."

Hale agreed readily, and slipped out of bed, onto his knees. The ghost sank down too, its lower legs passing through the floor, though it could not actually kneel. When Hale had crossed himself and called on God, the spirit of Charles Danvers, now penitent in tone rather than urbane, told briefly, though with many hesitations and self-corrections, the tale of how he had called at the offices of the college bursar one day when that official had chanced to be out for a moment, and had idly tried the lid of an ornately carved box on the desk, only to find it unlocked and containing several bags of what were obviously coins; how he, being always short of money, had given way to temptation and put two bags into each of the capacious pockets of his coat before slipping out again unobserved; how he had at once taken horse out of Oxford, fearful of having been seen and wishing to distance himself from the ensuing investigation; how he had, in his confusion, headed for home, not knowing what else to do, but had stopped at this place on his way and had almost convinced himself that he should go back and either confess or else try to return the money anonymously, when his potentially good intentions were thwarted by his death.

"And do you repent of your theft, and are you sure that you would, given the chance, return the money and face the consequences of your actions?"

169

"Indeed yes, most assuredly. It was a moment's weakness, soon regretted."

Hale closed his eyes and began to pray, and he could hear the ghost hesitantly and rustily reciting the creed and the paternoster in a quiet, stumbling echo behind him. Then, more strongly, he heard the voice with an unaccustomed note of eagerness in it: "I fear we shall not get to read Herodotus together again!" He opened his eyes, and he was alone in a room pitch-dark except for the very dim pale squares of the windows. Trembling again, he pushed himself up on the edge of the bed and fumbled for his tinderbox on the table; he got the nightlight going and then crossed to light the candles on the mantelpiece. He sat on the armchair – no; he checked himself, turned, and looked at it for a moment before sitting down, and for some minutes tried to get his thoughts in order. At length, he closed his eyes and began to pray again, for Charles Danvers, for himself, for all troubled spirits – the thought of the suicide next door and whatever it was that inhabited the cellar forced his eyes open and chilled his spine again briefly – and in due course he threw himself on the bed and fell asleep, to awake the following morning with the candles burnt down and brightness forcing its way around the edges of the curtains.

"Did you sleep well, sir?" asked Whitton, clearly nervous and rather surprised to see his guest apparently in good spirits as he took his place at the small corner table to break his fast.

"Yes, indeed, thank you, landlord. My long walk here yesterday made me very tired." He reserved the unsettling proviso until Whitton showed relief and was off-guard. "Though I was awakened for part of the night." The landlord froze midway through wiping the table and continued to stare downwards, though Hale leaned slightly towards him and emphasised his words. "Yes, I know why the second bedroom is kept locked and unused."

The two men occupied the chairs by the fireplace while talking the matter through. Hale was encouraged by the landlord's apparent honesty, now that the truth was out, and Whitton for his part was grateful that his guest was not outraged at what had happened and was reacting in a sympathetic and objective way.

"I have allus known the story, from being a lad, so I don't worry too much about it. I knows it can't really do no harm, you see, just being like a cloud, I suppose. Well, I suppose I'm a bit frightened of it and don't like to see it, but it tends to stay where it is and I haven't seen it too often. My Molly, she's never got used to it, and it upsets her sometimes, and the lad too, though they don't seem to meet it on the stairs in the dark anymore. But I do need to be careful about letting people in there – I've never used the room excepting when someone really needs it, and even then only if I think they're up to it. It's been a long time now – the last two or three made a devil of a row about it, if you'll pardon my language, so it's stayed shut up, until yesterday.

"It were before my time, sir, in my father's time here; well, when my father was still working for his father, in fact. A young man was murdered in that very room by a man called Fitch, a local man he were, fallen on hard times. They say he was not always a bad sort, but had been made desperate by ill luck and poverty. He had lost his place and was staying in the other room upstairs before moving on; they say he had thoughts of taking ship to the new colonies in the Americas, as they was then. But he must have seen that the young man, his name was Danvers as I recall the story goes, had money – he was from the university, you see, and the son of a clergyman like yourself – and he killed him for it as he slept. Put a knife in him. They soon caught Fitch, and he was tried and hanged at Exeter. His body hung on a gibbet by the road across the moors for a long while; you used to be able to see the old gibbet, but it rotted and fell down a couple years back. Ever since then, the room has been haunted, as they say. Though it does no harm, folks are frightened when they sees it, I suppose it's because they don't understand it, like. It doesn't worry my reg'lars, though – it'ud take more than an old ghost to keep them from their ale!"

Hale felt a powerful but imprecise emotion at having his experience of the previous night validated, by hearing the ghost's story confirmed in this way, and was emboldened by it. "So you would not be distressed to learn that the house is no longer haunted?"

"No indeed – Molly would be mighty relieved, and I would have another room to let!"

Whitton looked at Hale oddly, as if expecting some explanation for the question, which came swiftly.

"In that case, I think I can assure you that the ghost, the ghost of Danvers," he was suddenly more precise when he remembered the phantoms next door and in the cellar, "will trouble you no more. You see, I did more than merely see him last night, and I believe that he has finally found peace." The landlord stared at him in astonishment. "If you need some evidence that I am not merely raving, then if you check the story you will find that his name was Charles, that his father was vicar at Torcastle and that he was twenty years of age and a student at Oxford."

"Oh, I am not doubting your worship, not at all. I am just, begging your pardon, amazed by your words. That you should have laid the ghost in a night, with no fuss nor nothing – after all these many years."

"Ah," said Hale, smiling broadly, leaning forward and laying a hand on his arm, "you see, not all the ministers of the Established

Church are merely hunting gentry – some of us have our uses!"

Another matter concerned Hale now, for he did not feel that the story of Charles Danvers had yet concluded satisfactorily: he wished that he could convey to those who might think of the young man merely as a thief that he had, at the end, decided to put matters right and had even finally repented, if in death. However, he did not know if the disappearance of the money in Oxford had ever even been linked to him. He asked Whitton in a casual way if he knew anything about the money which Fitch stole; he thought that it had been recovered from the murderer, but whether it had been sent on to the victim's family he had no idea. He had nothing to say on the question of why Danvers was carrying so much cash, and did not even know what sort of sum was involved, and there Hale had to leave it.

Having abandoned the idea of trying to get to a church, having risen later he intended and his mind being over-exercised by his recent experience, he fretted in inaction for the rest of the day, though waited on assiduously by the Whittons and treated to the best – limited though it was – that the house could offer, as being in some measure their saviour. Towards nightfall, he was slightly worried that a reappearance of Danvers might belie his assurances, but he slept through undisturbed. When he rose on Monday morning, he found that the landlord had already taken his horse to the forge and had evidently spoken to the smith and settled his fee, for the animal was returned soon after he had breakfasted, shod and with a new poultice and bandage applied. The verdict was that it could be walked or trotted gently on a soft surface, but not pushed any harder for the following three or four days. Hale left almost at once, having forced the reluctant landlord to take at least part of the agreed sum for his lodging and having been kissed on the cheek by the ecstatic Molly, and made his way back to the main road, leaving Morston behind forever. Keeping his horse on the grass at the side of the highway but not stopping more than he had to, for fear of being benighted in a lonely spot which footpads might frequent, he made Torcastle at dusk, and presented himself at the vicarage with profuse apologies for his lateness. The evident condition of his horse earned him forgiveness, but he decided it would be prudent to omit mention of the ghost from his account to the Reverend Bryce-Turner of what had delayed him.

Nevertheless, the next morning in conversation with his friend he mentioned having heard on the moor the story of the ancient murder with the Torcastle connection. He had been longing for an opportunity to bring the matter up as though casually, and it came when they were inspecting the parish church together and paused in front of a wooden board on the wall by the door, on which were listed all the vicars of Torcastle back to Walter of Totnes, died 1227. The last name on the board was James Andrews, MA, who had been there for almost forty years, and before him was Dr. Edward Danvers, with a much shorter residency. With a good appearance of surprise, he remarked that he had just come across that name in Morston, as belonging to a young man murdered in the inn where he was staying, during the time when Dr. Danvers was the incumbent. Hale pushed it a little further, adding that, by a coincidence, it was thought that the victim was the son of a clergyman. That was enough: yes, Bryce-Turner had heard something of the story, that Edward Danvers, a widower, had been all but broken by the tragedy and had been forced to retire through ill-health a short time after; he had gone to Bath, where he had family, and was the only one of the last six vicars not to be buried in the churchyard. He knew no more about the story, not why or how the son had been murdered – the precise location of Morston was new to him – and no, as far as he was aware there were no descendants of the family in Torcastle. And that was that.

It seemed as though there was no tradition of villainy attaching to the faint memory of Charles Danvers, but in the coming weeks Hale was troubled from time to time by thoughts of what might have happened in Oxford all those years before: had the bursar been in trouble over the missing funds? Had Danvers been implicated? Had there been a pursuit of the fugitive, ended only by the report of his death? What had become of the stolen money? He would never know the whole story, but his mind was put somewhat at ease when, about a year later, he chanced to be in Oxford and to be introduced to the librarian of St. Stephens' College, an elderly and kindly scholar by the name of Dr. Ward, who had apparently scarcely been further afield than Magdalene Bridge for forty years. Hale, remembering the story and sensing a unique opportunity, expressed a keen interest in the history of the college, throwing in one or two obscure facts about St. Stephen's which he happened to know. As he had hoped, Dr. Ward needed no encouragement to talk about this, his pet subject, and Hale arranged to meet him the next day in his library to view the ancient records of the college.

After politely inspecting several charters, a box containing various medieval lists and bills and an enormous volume of minutes from seventy years of meetings of the college fellows, Hale risked mentioning the name of Danvers, saying only that he had once heard the story of the murder of a St. Stephen's student, while on the moors in Devon. Dr. Ward hesitated for only a moment, then went over to a bookcase and slowly put a low set of steps in place and mounted them; reaching up with some difficulty, he drew out a folio volume, and Hale hurried over to relieve him of it before the weight of it pulled him over. When Ward had climbed down, they moved over to a table and opened the book, which turned out to be a bound collection of a local Oxford journal, for a year half a century back. "At the start of the Long Vacation, I think, this year or the one after it, perhaps." Ward was turning pages and peering at them. "No, it is here – see." There was a brief but emotional paragraph on the tragedy of the murdered scholar, including the apprehension of Fitch, but no mention of the money. Hale asked if he might read further, and Ward agreed, as he needed to speak to the Master at that hour and would be away for perhaps twenty minutes.

Hale turned pages, looking for anything which seemed relevant to the case. In an edition a couple of weeks later, there was a brief mention of Fitch's trial, and later again his execution, but still no mention of his motive. There was something on the grief of Edward Danvers, but nowhere could Hale see anything suggesting that the student had been suspected of theft. Finally, he turned back and looked at the edition before the one describing the murder: yes, there it was, a very brief mention of an outrageous theft from the college bursary in the middle of the day, the bursar being shocked and unwilling to think that a member of the community could have committed such an act. That was all there was: if guilt had been apportioned, the journal would surely have reported it, so presumably no innocent person was charged and no serious blame attached to the bursar himself – Charles Danvers was not held responsible for the theft, and he was not responsible for anyone else being accused of it. Providence had, in advance, taken heed of his change of heart and had allowed him to die all but guiltless; Hale called that Divine Justice, and he slept in his bed all the more soundly because of it.

COVENANT

Murdo McCann fitted a common, paradoxical southron stereotype of the Scot in both the thriftiness of his daily life and the wildly romantic nature of his imagination: for forty years he lived alone in disciplined frugality in order to save for the eventual fulfilment of his grand ambition. His one enthusiasm in an otherwise humdrum and passionless existence was the past of his own country as presented in popular histories and the novels of Sir Walter Scott, borrowed from the free library – a story as colourful as his own life was drab – and his dream was to recreate some part of it with himself as the hero. In place of the workaday city, he would have the sweep of mountains as his backdrop; in place of his terraced house, a fortified mansion as his residence. He pictured himself as the kilted laird striding manfully across the heather, unaware that, all questions of anachronism and poetic licence aside, his true soul was that of the humble and methodical bookkeeper whose role he had filled all his working life. In the interests of one day securing his dream, his one expense (apart from the indulgence of an Arrol-Johnston motor car – the only car in the street, or indeed in many streets around – to enable him to visit historical sites not easily reached by public transport) was the bare maintenance of himself and the house in the suburbs of Edinburgh in which he had invested; every other penny which could be saved went into a deposit account at a bank other than the one in which he worked, so that by the time retirement came, he had far more capital than anyone would have imagined the quiet and unassuming clerk to have at his disposal. When that day came, not long after the ending of the Great War from which his age had spared him, he slipped away from the bank almost unnoticed, with the gold watch which was the sole token of his employer's gratitude; being in charge of such arrangements himself, he had managed to delay the engraving of it so that it might fetch a better price at the jeweller's shop he visited on the way home. The house was already sold, along with its meagre furniture, and within a very few days – for he had hardly anyone to whom he had to bid farewell and there were no other complications or commitments in his life – he had moved himself and his sparse possessions into the spare room of the post office at the village of Inveravond, until his new home should be ready.

But I move ahead too quickly. For a complete understanding of what was happening, and perhaps a fuller picture of Murdo McCann's character, we must look back some two years to the time when he first began, without a word to anyone, to make substantive plans for his future new life. His aim was to be the lord of a castle – a small one, to be sure, but a castle nevertheless, with battlements, turrets and (unlike himself) a history, dominating some valley of the Borders, or a Highland pass, or a Hebridean islet. (There were always mountains in his visions: he associated the Lowlands with the flatness of his working life, to be left behind – though in reality that was all he knew.) He was realistic in his grand aim to the extent that he was quite prepared to undertake extensive restoration work to bring this about, either through his own labour or through the spending of what he had saved. He envisaged himself dining heartily at an oaken table on a dais in a tapestry-hung hall, in front of a great roaring fire, or gazing from his four-poster through a Gothic window down to a mist-veiled loch ringed with hills touched by the dawn light. The pictures in his mind were, admittedly, populated by no-one but himself, but this was not a bleak prospect in his view: he had been practically without family since the death of his parents some thirty years before, the few friends he had had in his youth had soon lost interest in him, and he had been used to fending for himself and making his own entertainment, as cheaply as possible, for most of his life.

However, he soon came to realize that not only were castles for sale a rare commodity but also they invariably fell into one of two classes – those that were comfortably habitable and hence astronomically expensive, and those that were inexpensive but completely ruinous. The result was the same in either case: the sums involved, either as purchase price or as rebuilding cost, were well beyond what he would have after selling his modest house. In the case of the ruins (for in those days such monuments were still invariably in private hands), the length of time before the building would be in a state fit for occupation was an additional problem. And so, on returning from a pointless and difficult three-day journey in his car to a remote spot north of Inverness to see what amounted to little more than a jumble of stones, he had resolved to concentrate on disused churches as a more feasible alternative: they had the necessary archaic features and scale, even if they were less than a century old, and they were more likely to be in a reasonable state of repair, being but recently abandoned. At that time, places of worship were rarely left without congregations, and there was a strong feeling that converting them into private residences was disrespectful, even blasphemous; it was not until much later, and a further decline in faith, that such ideas waned and the practice became commonplace, and in the meantime Murdo McCann benefited from the comparative lack of competition for the few properties that came onto the market. It must be understood that he was not what is called a religious man, nor a superstitious one, despite his literary and antiquarian interests. For him, ancient churches and abbeys were simply picturesque settings, and what went on in them were just some of the colourful rituals of the Middle Ages; the spiritual played no part in his severely material view of life. Similarly, ghosts and witches were part of the richness of folklore and tradition, but the supernatural had no currency in the bank or in his mundane Edinburgh suburb.

Unlike ruined castles, redundant churches generally featured roofs, floors, windows and doors; there might even be running water and some rudimentary form of heating. However, Murdo soon learnt that they were never quite as appealing as they initially seemed: apart from the usual rot (wet and dry), leaks, insect infestations and cracks in masonry, all of which fell within his expectations of repair and maintenance, there was always some proviso, covenant or exception to the sale. If a splendid rose window was the one redeeming feature of a drab brick box in the high street of a depressed little town, then in the small print there would be a reservation of title to it, so that it could be removed bodily by the vendor; if the subsidence which had opened up a split in the north wall could be overlooked for the sake of the lustrous paneling and carved screens, then the terms would include the removal of all woodwork and fittings prior to sale. The commonest kind of provision, he soon learnt, was that concerning access, rights of way or boundaries. One church was on a narrow but busy street with nowhere convenient where he might safely park the car for which he had cared for a decade and which he hoped would serve him for as long as he might need it; another had a small lawn around it which was the common of the village; yet another had had its land sold off to the extent that the only access was over a stile and across a field by courtesy of the farmer. The most usual case concerned access by visitors to the attached burial ground, which might even still be in use; a clause of this kind was attached to the former Episcopal church of St. Andrew in Inveravond, but that did not make Murdo hesitate for a second, so perfect was the building for his purpose.

Built in the early years of the nineteenth century in an eclectic Gothic style to replace an older church, it stood near the point where the River Avond flowed into Loch Avond, to the southeast of Fort William, where it had served the community of Inveravond until the tenth year of Victoria's reign. Then Sir James Anderson, the owner of the estate and the occupier of Inveravond Castle on the far side of the loch, had decided to improve his view by moving the untidy settlement a couple of miles back down the valley, out of his sight – a practice not unknown in those days. The old buildings were torn down and the site landscaped, leaving only the rough, narrow road which came down the valley and around the loch to provide access to the castle, and the church, deemed sufficiently picturesque to be allowed to remain in the scene. It continued to be used as a private chapel for several decades. Every Sunday, after the service in the new church in the new village, the Episcopal priest would ride to St. Andrew's; the Andersons would be rowed across the water, leaving the boat at a small jetty now rotted away, and the castle retainers would dutifully walk around the loch and trudge back again afterwards. This arrangement lapsed, to the relief of most of those concerned, when Sir Colin Anderson's horse fell and rolled on him, leaving him partially paralysed and partially agonized by much movement; confined to his bed as the nineteenth century passed into the twentieth, he eventually ended his misery with the aid of a service revolver on receiving news of the death of his only child, a lieutenant of infantry, in the Boer War. His widow returned to her native Perthshire, simply abandoning, in her grief and confusion, what little remained of the estate to the care of a few unsupervised and irregularly paid servants, who soon forced open the wine cellar to relieve the tedium and take their remuneration in kind. It was not long before a fire broke out in the castle; with no-one capable of dealing with it, it raged for a day and two nights, watched disinterestedly from across the loch by groups of villagers who did nothing to spoil the spectacle. The burnt-out ruin was left to the mercy of the weather; the widow died; the estate passed in shares to several distant relatives of the family, and now they had, after much wrangling by proxy, agreed to realise one of the few remaining assets of value by selling off the isolated church – and so it came

181

to Murdo McCann.

He was taken with Inveravond from his first arrival, on a day in the middle of Spring. The place had actually benefited from Sir James' cavalier action in moving it onto the main road past the valley, and, though still a village, it boasted a small distillery, a weaving business and several shops serving the surrounding area. There were two good hotels, catering for the more adventurous tourists from the south, and even, Murdo was pleased to see, a small garage, Robertson's, to service their cars. He made his way to the high street office of Alexander McRae, the notary who was handling the sale for the estate, and from there the lawyer drove him the short distance down the valley, relating to him what you now already know about the recent history of the place. He also took the opportunity to assure him that his clerk could conveniently deal with the purchase on his behalf, without any conflict of interest, if he should choose to save the extortionate fee of his Edinburgh solicitor and make use of local knowledge. Murdo's habitual caution evaporated as the car rounded the bend which brought it to the side of the loch. It was very nearly the pool ringed by hills of his daydream, caught on a perfect day, with the ruins of the castle clearly visible on the headland opposite and the church on its knoll facing it over shining water.

The building was as promising as the setting: a traditional construction in the local stone, with a two-storey battlemented tower at the west end and a porch protecting the entrance in the middle of the south side. There was a chest-high stone wall marking off the plot from the rough road and the surrounding moor, pierced by a small gate opposite the porch and a larger farm-style gate by the tower which, Murdo noted, would allow the entry of his motor car; there was more space to the west of the building than elsewhere, where the vehicle could be parked comfortably, off the road. A gravel path from these gates ran around the church, flanked by a yard or so of lawn or shrubs on either side, dotted with odd weathered stumps of memorial stones. The wall extended down either side of the building, which was positioned lengthways along the loch, but it ended at the bank, so that the northern edge of the site was bounded only by a couple of yards of shingle and stones sloping down to the water. There was a third gate in the middle of this side wall, by the tower, and walking over Murdo saw that there was another enclosure beyond it, larger than the kirkyard itself, full of slabs and crosses, set out in rough lines amidst long grass and nettles. McRae quickly pointed out that this burial ground was no longer in use – a new one had been established beside the new church – but was not included in the sale; he apologized for its condition, and explained that occasionally someone came from the village to clear the weeds and cut the grass for the benefit of those few who might still come out to visit the graves of their ancestors. This was not a problem, both men agreed: its position would make it hardly visible from what Murdo was already thinking of as his new home. McRae went on to assure his potential client that there were no interments inside the church itself – unless, down in the foundations, there were some remaining from the previous building – but he did point out the row of four large, deeply-engraved slabs standing upright against the base of the tower, facing the entrance to the burial ground. Robert Anderson, the builder of the present kirk, and his kin; Sir James, the displacer of the village; the following generation, headed by Malcolm; and finally Sir Colin, with a note recording the death and burial of the younger Malcolm in South Africa.

"The original Anderson family plot is the midst of yon cemetery, but it was a good way to being full when Robert built this, and they thought it best to put him here, next to what he had made. It was his wish, you see. But he still looks towards where his ancestors lie, just through that gate. The others followed him here, rather than being buried down at the new kirk in Inveravond. You need to be aware," McRae said, turning to face Murdo, "that there is a covenant, a legally binding condition, regarding the property, to which you would need to agree if you were to buy it. It requires the owner to keep access between the burial ground and the kirkyard open at all times, and to permit any who wish to visit the graves in the cemetery and outwith the kirk to do so freely. The only entrance to the burial ground is through that gate, you see. So you could not bar the gateway or fill it in. It would be important for you to remember that and keep to the terms of the covenant." As though realising he was being rather too serious, he smiled and added, "It is a common enough practice to have such conditions written in, especially with unusual properties such as this. It is that sometimes sellers want to perpetuate old customs, or preserve the character of what they leave behind, if you understand me."

Murdo was already familiar with the concept from his earlier experiences, and this restriction was less arduous than some, so he merely returned the smile for the briefest moment and nodded slightly.

"Nae problem."

"I wouldna worry about it – you'll hardly be seeing a soul out here."

Then through the heavy door set in a Norman-style arch with chevrons carved around the edge, and into the church itself: worn stone flags on the floor; walls plastered and whitewashed, now yellowed and flaking in places; a barrel vault of dark wood; two high windows flanking the door and three in the facing wall, in a simple Decorated style and filled with clear glass; a chancel raised up two steps, with an east window formed of three lancets containing stained-glass images of Saint Andrew, Saint Peter and Jesus in the middle, with backgrounds clearly showing Loch Avond, the church and the castle as it had been. Inscriptions on the bottom of them read across: "Dedicated to the memory of Sir James Anderson of Inveravond by his family. Semper uniter. 1858." Opposite this was an arch leading into the base of the tower. There was no sign of altar, pulpit, pews or any other fittings apart from at the west end, where there was a cast-iron stove, from which black-painted heating pipes ran around the foot of the walls, and a small gallery over the tower entrance, supported by four wooden posts and reached by a narrow staircase at the side. Feeling unaccustomed excitement and moving with more energy than was his wont, Murdo led the way up; the gallery was laid out with wide steps, serving as seating, and at the top of these was a door which led onto the wooden floor which provided an upper room in the tower. If Murdo had had any doubts at all about this place – which he didn't – this room would have dispelled them: windows in each wall gave excellent views across the loch, to either end of it, and back down the valley a little way – with mountains on all sides, some still capped with snow. A ladder in the corner gave access, through a trapdoor, to the roof. They stood up there for a while, Murdo taking in the view and McRae pointing out the good state of the roof, then went back down. Before they left, the lawyer took him into the bottom part of the tower, where there was a narrow door which led out, near the Anderson gravestones, to a small lean-to for the storage of fuel, and also a tap: the original village had been supplied by water piped from springs in the surrounding hills, and a similar arrangement still served the church.

When they had driven back to McRae's office, Murdo asked him to pass on his offer for the property, which was a little below the suggested price but amounted to almost all his savings plus a temporary loan which he had negotiated with his bank, using his

Edinburgh house as collateral; sale of that house would repay the loan and provide the funds for the conversion and fitting out of the new property. Acceptance of the offer almost beat him back to the capital, and two months before his retirement Murdo McCann became the owner of Inveravond church. With McRae's help, he engaged builders from Fort William to carry out the conversion, and secured temporary lodging at the post office, from which he could supervise the progress of the work. Which brings us to the end of Summer, and to the point at which I broke off at the end of my opening paragraph, some time ago.

When Murdo finally arrived in Inveravond for good, he had to write the contractor a first cheque immediately, for the upper floor of the tower was almost completed already: the glazing had been renewed, the floor sanded and restained, the walls replastered and painted, the room ceiled, and the ladder replaced by an iron spiral staircase. A radiator, fed from the stove, was being installed. This was to be his bedroom, and for a moment he seriously considered moving into it at once and letting the workmen carry on around him – or rather beneath him. However, the lack of basic amenities soon dissuaded him from this, and for the next two months he lived in a state somewhere between excitement and frustration, and promising to collapse into exhaustion at any minute. He would drive down to the church after his breakfast with the postmaster's family, and spend part of the day watching and pestering whichever men were working – joiners, decorators, plasterers, plumbers – until they could stand no more of his interference and exhortations and threatened to down tools and return to town; then he would pace about on the loch side or the surrounding slopes until he thought it safe to creep back in and check up on them again. If it rained, he stayed up in the tower room and made plans, browsing through catalogues and writing to shops in Inverness and Stirling to order furnishings. When the builders finished for the day, he would lock up, take a last look around with a feeling of pride and satisfaction, and reluctantly return to his little room and a book. Two or three times, he happened to meet with Alexander McRae in the village and accepted an invitation to have supper with him in the bar of the Loch Avond Hotel, which was the widowed lawyer's resort for most nights of the week – though for food and society rather than for the drink. McRae enjoyed having some new company, but Murdo was not used to having to hold a conversation while eating, or indeed to conversing at all, and the sessions did not last much above an hour, with the talk consisting mainly of repetitious monologues on, on the one hand, the progress of the conversion work and, on the other, local places of interest. By the time the house was ready, neither man felt particularly inclined to continue the practice.

We now lurch forward in time a little again, to a morning at the beginning of October. Murdo McCann has just spent his first night in his new home, and has slept very soundly in his four-poster bed; in fact, he has slept soundly and dreamlessly all his life, but his slumber last night was particularly long and deep, as closure to the period of anticipation and stress through which he has just lived – and aided by the vapours of paint, glue and woodstain lingering in the air. Yesterday, the remaining tools, ladders and scaffolding went back to Fort William, a wagon from Stirling made its way cautiously down the road from the village of Inveravond with the last of his new furniture, and he said goodbye to the postmaster and his family. The day of his moving in, however, was not quite as momentous as Murdo had expected: he had already seen everything take shape day by day, so there was no surprise involved, and he was suddenly alone again, after getting accustomed to having the postmaster's family in the background and across the table. And so alone: despite the solitary nature of his existence, he has lived and worked all his life in a busy office in a great city, and even for the last few weeks he has lived in another's house and spent most of his time talking with the builders and listening to their noise; now he is two miles from his nearest neighbour, with only the lapping of the water of the loch to relieve the total silence. Nevertheless, he is now lying in his own bed, in the tower of his Gothic hall in the Highlands, and his dream is fulfilled. There is nothing pressing for which he needs to get up, so we shall not disturb him, but tiptoe downstairs to see what has been done.

Passing through the door, we go down a few wooden steps with a short but ornate balustrade, onto the gallery. The wooden tiers have gone; in their place is a richly carpeted space with armchairs, a writing desk and bookcases built against the walls. This is where Murdo will spend much of his time, reading or simply looking down into the main body of the building to admire his property. Downstairs again, and we find that the area under the gallery (to the front of which have been affixed three stags' heads) has been enclosed, and it and part of the base of the tower have been cleverly transformed into a small kitchen, scullery and pantry, with a corner becoming a bathroom, or rather a closet containing a galvanized tin tub. Turning to look to the east end, where the stained-glass windows are lit by the early morning light, we see an imposing dining room with the same carpet and a long table flanked by chairs and a fine carver at the end nearest us – Murdo's seat, and the only one which will be used more than occasionally. Along and mounted on the walls are various pieces of furniture and decoration which Murdo considers appropriate – a longcase clock, a carved oak chest, a pair of crossed basket-hilt swords, a suit of armour, a huge dresser filled with the blue and white Spode crockery of which only a handful of pieces will ever be used. At the far end, on the raised area under the windows, couches upholstered with a heraldic tapestry design are arranged around the walls, with a low table in the middle. Some twenty oil lamps, mostly attached to the walls in the form of sconces, provide the artificial light, with several three-armed candelabras placed strategically around the house for journeys between rooms in the dark. Such is what is now, according to the sign on the porch, "Inveravond House"; and now we can let Murdo continue to play out his story.

He soon settled into a routine. In the morning, he would attend to any necessary domestic chores, such as his washing or the cleaning out and relighting of the stove. In the afternoon, if it was fine, he would go for a walk, or, if it was wet, he would take to his armchair with one of the hundred leather-bound volumes, including complete sets of Scott and Dickens, which he had purchased from a second-hand bookshop in Edinburgh before his departure, to furnish his new shelves appropriately. In the evening, he would prepare his meal and read again – but not for long, as his habitual thriftiness had returned, with regard to the use of oil. Every few days he would drive down to the village for provisions; otherwise, he saw and spoke to no-one. By this point in the year, even the occasional tourist had gone home, and none of the locals bothered to look at the loch, for no-one but a newcomer bothers to enjoy whatever is on his own doorstep, no matter how grand.

His walks took him to different points from which to view his 'kingdom' – for, although he owned only a few square yards of it, he regarded the loch and the surrounding slopes as his property, and the absence of others encouraged the illusion. He would walk up one of the hills and look down on his house, or round the loch and view it from across the water. Sometimes he would poke about amidst the tumbled and blackened stones of the old castle – so called, though judging by the antique pictures he had seen of it, it had been more of a fortified manor house. He hoped to find some overlooked relic, but the site had been thoroughly worked over by the locals for years. The huge fire and subsequent toppling of the walls had been devastating; the estate had salvaged anything of value; in the period of neglect which had followed, the masonry had been pillaged by the villagers. In Inveravond, Murdo had seen a weathered stone carved with a coat of arms above a faded motto (a mysterious 'mper unit' was visible in the middle of the line, but the edges were worn), set incongruously in the wall in front of a cottage, and a battered statue of a heraldic beast decorating a garden, and had guessed their origin. He did find one thing of interest in the ruins: the broken stone jambs of a doorway, fallen in a rough rectangle; the lintel, presumably an intact carved piece, had been removed, but the parts that remained were some eight inches wide and six deep, with a twisted barley-sugar shaft standing proud of a right-angled section. The longest piece was perhaps two feet long, and Murdo decided that, although there was no way in which he could carry it, he could just about get it in and out of his car to take it home. He was dubious about driving round the loch: the rough road from the village to his house had caused him a puncture already, though it had been given some attention over the years, and the continuation of it round to the ruins, never intended for motor vehicles, had been totally neglected since before the fire and was now little more than a potholed track. However, taking it slowly and carefully he managed the short journey without mishap and with some effort manhandled the stone aboard. He set it up as a short column by his front door, and felt absurdly pleased with his achievement, partly because he felt that in some vague way it linked him to the castle; certainly, the fragment was older than the fabric of his house and, in his mind, gave more substance to the air of antiquity about the place.

The curious thing was, though, that it would not stay upright as he left it. The morning after he had brought it, he found it fallen over, presumably because its base was not straight; he used a couple of smaller stones to wedge it in place. The next morning the same thing, so he leaned it against the wall of the house. The next morning, it was lying a couple of feet away on the path, and Murdo began to suspect that someone was moving it – someone who was coming into his garden. But he had heard nothing, and nothing else had been interfered with. Nevertheless, the thought disturbed him: the church windows were too high up for him to keep watch out of them, or he would have mounted guard. But he left the stone piece lying on its back on the grass and nothing further happened.

Visitors to Inveravond House were almost non-existent, as I have said, but one morning nearly two weeks after his arrival Murdo opened his door to a man whom he did not know but had seen tending the new churchyard in the village. In the road there was a small cart containing tools and drawn by a pony. In few words, the man explained that he had come to cut the grass in the burial ground and that he would need to cross back and forth through Murdo's garden with his barrow. This necessitated Murdo moving his car from where he parked it between the cemetery gate and the tower; he had removed the farm gate from his wall to widen the entrance, replacing it with a chain, and had put more gravel down, widening the footpath at that point. As he backed out, in his mirror he noticed the man frowning and shaking his head as he watched him.

"What's the matter, man? Is there something wrang wi' the car?"

The gardener shook his head again, but instead of replying took out his scythe and walked past him. Murdo was put out by this rudeness, but he was unused to hard words and avoided confrontation, so he went indoors until the work should be finished. Peering out a couple of hours later, he saw that the cart had gone, and went to put the motor back – but before he did so he was suddenly moved to look inside the burial ground, which he had not done so far in anything but a very cursory way. Now the long grass and great clumps of nettles and brambles had been cut down and carted away for the minister's compost, so that he could walk around freely and the stones were clearly visible, though many were too worn to be deciphered. He read the tragedy of Archibald McLeish, 1835, and his wife Margaret, 1838, and their five children, all dead before the age of five; of Sarah McInnes, drowned in the loch in 1824; of James McPherson, accidentally shot in 1842. But his main interest was the tomb in the very centre of the plot, a rectangle a little over three yards by five marked out with a kerb with a stone urn on a plinth at each corner. There were five great slabs on the ground inside this enclosure, and at their head a Celtic-style cross seven feet high, flanked by the stone image of a lamp with a flame and a small marble obelisk. All except the cross carried inscriptions, though weathering and the moss which had spread over much of the site made these hard to read. The exception to this was the central slab, which bore just the name 'Anderson' across the middle, in very large, square letters, deeply cut, and across the bottom in smaller script 'Semper uniter', which Murdo recalled seeing elsewhere. He put on his reading glasses and, with one foot on the kerb, leaned over to examine one of the outer stones more closely. All he could make out was part of the name 'Anderson', possibly a 'Donald', and the date 'Oct.1768'; below this were several lines of what appeared to be verse, containing the rhyme 'together/forever' and the word 'Avond'. But clouds were gathering ominously and a breeze was blowing off the loch, and Murdo stayed no longer.

It was a couple of days later – around the middle of October – that the first incident to upset seriously the quiet routine of Murdo's life at Inveravond occurred, on one of his visits to the castle ruins. He was picking his way through the stones as usual, when he chanced to look across to his house on the far shore. It was a bright early afternoon, so he could see as clearly as his eyes would allow at that distance after four decades in the counting house; but he rubbed them in astonishment at what he saw. There seemed to be people in his garden – perhaps four or five dark shapes moving against the green of the grass and the pale grey of the building; he could not be sure what they were, but people intruding seemed the only possibility. They were around the west side of the house, where his motor car was parked, and he was suddenly fearful that they might be intent on stealing it, as well as outraged that they were on his property. However, he tried to calm his emotions by telling himself that they were not acting furtively and were perhaps just tourists under the illusion that it was still a church and looking around. Nevertheless, he set off back around the loch as quickly as he could – too quickly, given his age, the state of the road and the fact that he had never gone at more than a moderately brisk walking pace before in his life. He was confused by all the thoughts in his head – what they might be doing, whether he had locked up securely, what he would say to them, how he needed to have signs saying "private property: keep out" put up – and soon exhaustion added to his burden. Less than halfway home he was staggering and gasping; he turned his ankle on a stone; several times he had to stop and bend double to catch his breath. The house was in view most of the way, except where the road ran behind a low hillock or a few stunted trees, but he could not focus on it to see what was happening. Not until he arrived at his garden wall did he stop and try to compose himself. The car was still there; the doors and windows of the house were closed and intact; there was no-one about. Panting and steadying himself against the stones, he looked down the road to Inveravond and then scanned the slopes around: no walkers. Not a sign of anyone having been there, or travelling away.

Murdo tried to think no more of it, but he ate his supper listlessly that night, he could not concentrate on the Walter Scott he was re-reading, *Guy Mannering*, and it took him longer than usual to get to sleep – which he put down to a strong wind, intermingled with rainy squalls. But when he awoke quite late the following morning, the storm had blown the clouds away and refreshed the landscape, the sun was shining and it felt warmer than it had done since he had arrived: the house was colder than he had expected, and the old heating system had to be on much of the time to make a difference. He went into the village after breakfast, contrary to his practice, and stayed there longer than normal. He went into every business and, struggling with his inability to engage in small talk, tried to make discreet enquiries about what groups of visitors there might be in the area, without finding much out. It was in the bar of the Loch Avond Hotel, where he puzzled the barman with his strange questions but learnt that only a handful of individual travelers or couples were in residence at this unseasonal time, that he ran into Alexander McRae, whom he had not seen since moving into his house. For once in his life, Murdo felt that he needed to talk to someone, but as they sat at a table with a sandwich and a glass each, he could not bring himself to express his unease, and instead merely said that the house was "mair than satisfactory" – high praise indeed from Murdo, as McRae guessed. As they left the hotel, he invited the lawyer to visit him, as soon as he liked, he positively insisted on it – and it was not mere politeness on his part.

"By the way, Mr. McRae, you would be knowing Latin, I suppose; an educated man such as yourself."

"A little, though I have not used it since my college days."

"Would you know what 'semper uniter' meant?" He pronounced it as the English 'unite-er'.

"Well now, 'semper' is 'forever', and what was the second word?"

"Uniter."

"I don't know that one. How would you be spelling it?" McCann obliged. "Oh, 'uniter'"; he stressed the first syllable. "That would be an adverb formed from 'unus', meaning 'one'; so something like 'as one', 'in one'."

"'Together', perhaps?"

"Yes indeed."

"So, 'together forever'?"

"Just so. 'Together forever'; a pretty enough little motto."

Murdo fell back into his routine, but with a difference: whereas before the highlight of his daily constitutional had been viewing his house from different vantage points and with different backdrops, now he purposely avoided looking towards it from a distance. Even as he walked back homewards, he kept his eyes firmly on his feet or the path, lest he should catch sight of something which might upset him. Indeed, he gave up taking his favourite routes – the one around the loch and the one up the slope facing him, which afforded a fine view of the building with the ruins and the water behind it – and instead took to walking back down the valley or over the passes which led away from the loch. Once he deliberately set out late so as to return after sunset and so avoid having to see the outside of the house altogether, thus avoiding the risk of seeing, as he put it to himself, the hallucination again; but there was something about the place in the dark which disturbed him even more and he did not repeat the experiment. More than once when he was preparing his evening meal or washing up after it he thought he heard a bumping against the back door into the tower – which he now kept locked – but was in sufficient doubt about it not to investigate. But it was not so much the groundless fear of something intangible which plagued him as the feeling of disappointment that his lifetime dream, into which he had put the fruits of decades of humble labour, was not living up to expectations. He could have come to terms with the fact that simply buying this property had not transformed his life into that of a feudal lord, and the emptiness of his existence compared with the comradeship of the clan and the cloister hardly occurred to him, given the way he had lived his life; but he regretted and resented the fact that so much expense had resulted in so little enjoyment – and that was Murdo all over.

After one lengthy walk into the hills, he was feeling very tired, and it seemed to be dark very early. He tried to get on with *Guy Mannering*, but could not concentrate and found himself rereading the same page and drifting away. His usual practice was to reach the end of a chapter before stopping and then return the book to the shelf until the next day, but tonight he abandoned it mid-chapter and put it face-down open on the table, next to his reading glasses, so as not to lose his place. He had another restless night. Next morning, as he was crossing the gallery to go downstairs, he was alarmed to find that the book had been tampered with: it was closed, and two pages lay on the floor by the table. Murdo froze: someone had been in during the night, within a few feet of his bedroom door, and had done this malicious thing. He hurried down to check the doors: both were firmly locked and bolted, as usual. The windows were all closed and unbroken. Trembling lest the malefactor should still be in the house, he checked every room, making loud, threatening noises, mainly to encourage himself, before he opened a door or cupboard. Nothing. He returned to the gallery to see what had been done; nothing appeared to have been taken or damaged except the book. He picked up the loose sheets and examined them. They had been ripped out and torn – not torn up, but curiously torn into, so that two small holes had been made, very precisely, within the text. He reached for his glasses, put them on – but pulled them off again immediately: there was something on the lenses; paper with printed words on it. It was obviously the two missing fragments of the pages, stuck, one in the middle of each lens, apparently just by moisture. He had to pull the scraps off and put them in the palm of his hand so that he could use the glasses to read them. Turned one way, one was blank and the other contained an 'and' and part of a word, but turned the other way one read 'together' and the other 'forever'.

He recalled where he had last seen those two words side by side, and wished he did not. He sat and thought for some time; eventually, he almost convinced himself that, as plainly no-one else had been in the house, he must have done this bizarre thing himself, in his sleep. He had read of people doing such things unconsciously, remembering nothing of it on waking. He remembered a scene in the only Shakespeare play he had ever seen, because it dealt with Scottish history: Lady Macbeth had acted out the writing and reading of a letter which she had previously received, while sleepwalking. Why should he not do something similar with words he had recently read? There was no other explanation for a rational mind – if he still had a rational mind; there were thoughts in his head now which he would not have entertained for a moment in Edinburgh; he was ashamed of them, but they would not go away.

It was in the last full week of October that Alexander McRae finally took up the invitation to Inveravond House and arranged to come for lunch. It would be the first time he had been there since the restoration, and to be honest he was more interested in seeing what had been done to the place than he was about spending much time with the owner. McCann was not an unpleasant fellow, but he not particularly interesting or forthcoming either, and the lawyer was not looking forward to the inevitable awkward silences which he would feel obliged to break with some inane comment or question. Murdo went out when he heard the car pulling up, but found his visitor standing just inside the wall at the front, where he had replaced the gate with a chain and widened the gravel path to make a parking space between the Anderson gravestones and the entrance to the burial ground. Murdo stepped forward to greet him, but his ability as a reader of mood and character was so limited that he failed to notice the perturbation in his face and his tense stance, and he was completely taken aback by his stern words.

"Man, this is not good at all – not good at all. The covenant is quite specific: you have to leave that way clear, and there is scarcely room to half-open the gate and squeeze in past your car." Murdo frowned; this was taking his professional duties too seriously and too personally; McRae was here as a friend, not a judge. His attitude served only to reinforce Murdo's growing feelings of resentment and unease at his situation; the lawyer sensed the unspoken anger and modified his manner. "I dinna want to interfere in what you do in your own place and all, but the agreement is legally binding, you know. The Andersons were very insistent on the point, and it is for your own good too. I mean, you wouldna want that fine motor being scratched by the gate, would you?"

"Very well, Mr. McRae, I'll park further over in future." The tone was not as civil as the words.

"I dinna think that would be so good either. You are practically on top of those graves already. You could always make a parking place across the way if you wanted to get the motor off the road – no-one would object – and in any case there is hardly any traffic along here for you to be worrying about."

"I'll be parking my own car on my own property as I see fit, if you please, and I'd be obliged if you'd stop lecturing me about what I can and canna do in my own place." Even Murdo realized that they were on the verge of a row, and he could feel a rising queasiness inside him at the prospect of unfamiliar conflict. He backed down as far as he could. "I'll have that gate hung to swing the other way, if you want."

"Aye, or just park a wee bit further in."

"In the loch, perhaps? Would that suit you?"

"Och, man, I'm just trying to make sure that there is no trouble for you about it. It's none of my business after all."

"You're right there. I'm obliged to you, I'm sure, but let's say nae mair about it. Now would you care to come inside, which is what you're here for?"

Murdo was annoyed not only at McRae's criticism but also at the fact that it was now impossible for him to confide in the man – which would not have been easy for him in the best of circumstances. In place of the anticipated tour of the house, the visitor was simply left seated in the hall while Murdo disappeared into the kitchen to fetch the soup, which they ate in silence. Over the poached salmon, McRae ventured a few compliments about the decoration, to which Murdo replied politely but briefly. They finished their lunch as quickly as was decent; as he drove away, McRae noted in his mirror that Murdo walked straight back into the house without waving and without a glance at the parked car.

 A couple of days later, on a Saturday, Murdo made one of his regular trips into the village to get provisions, and as usual he left the car parked near the end of the high street, by a row of four terraced houses, where he would not be in the way of any deliveries. As he returned and was about to open the door on the passenger side to put his bag inside, he noticed the damage – a cluster of small dents and chips, numerous but quite close together, as though something had crashed into it repeatedly at the same height. He was horrified at the harm done to his cherished motor, and looked up and down the street. There was no-one nearby who might have seen it done, let alone do it, and he had not observed anyone moving away as he had approached it; but he had been away for over half an hour. The feeling of helplessness which he had felt after the incident with the intruders returned, a feeling close to panic. Agitated, he tried at the houses, getting answers from two. At one, an old lady was put out at being disturbed and questioned abruptly and told him nothing, but it was clear that she heard and saw little that was not immediately next to and relevant to her; at the other, where he modified his tone a little, the housewife was sorry that she had been doing the washing all morning and hadn't so much as looked out of the house to see who might be passing. Calming down, he reflected that he did not know when it had actually happened, as he habitually got in and out of the driver's side and parked at home with the passenger's door against the garden wall; he could not remember when he had last seen that side of the vehicle – possibly a couple of weeks. Yet he had not left it anywhere where it might have been scraped on that side by another vehicle, and it seemed that it could only have been the result of malicious vandalism or of an attempt to break into it – neither of which was at all a common crime at that time and place. There were so few cars around that anyone stealing one would be apprehended at once, and he had left nothing in it that anyone might want to take. He was left with the sickening conclusion that someone had deliberately damaged the car – perhaps the people he had glimpsed on his property. Someone in this place had a grudge against him, perhaps for taking over the church; his sinking feeling of bitter disappointment, coupled with that of isolation, returned, stronger than ever.

As he pulled into his parking place by Inveravond House, he

recalled what McRae had said about the motor getting scratched. He got out, walked round to the passenger side and tried partially opening the gate to the burial ground. Yes, the marks on the vehicle were at exactly the right height for them to have been caused by the handle and latch banging against the door. He put on his glasses and peered at the projecting metal. Yes, there seemed to be flecks of paint from the car caught in the rust. So there had been people visiting the graves, unknown to him; perhaps he had been out, or he would surely have heard them damaging his car. He remembered his promise to have the gate hung the other way; he would have to attend to that, but in the meantime he was certainly not going to let this continue, covenant or no covenant. After a moment's thought, he took the keys from the glove compartment and removed the padlock which held the fixed end of the chain which could be used to shut off the parking place. He backed the car out into the road so that he could get through the gate, then looped the chain under the arms of a cross-shaped stone just inside it. Stepping back and closing the gate behind him, he threaded the chain through its bars and pulled the ends tight, before fastening them with the padlock. He tested it: the gate could not be opened as much as an inch. He moved the car back into its space. He felt ridiculously pleased with himself at his ingenuity, and at having struck back at the insecurities which had beset him; and indeed, apart from the move from Edinburgh it was probably the most daring and affirmative thing he had done in his life.

"If they are that keen to get in, then they can be climbing over the wall."

But he later relented to the extent of making a cardboard notice and hanging it on the gate, advising visitors to apply to the house for the key to the padlock. And that, he felt, was quite enough – covenant or no covenant.

But it was far from the end of the matter. That night, he was awoken by a great crash, which seemed to come from a distance, perhaps down in the nave of the church, or outwith the house altogether. For a moment he wondered if it could have been another dream – he had read of people being awoken by frights or noises in their dreams – but then, recalling the intruders, he pulled back the curtain on one side of the bed, got out cautiously and peered out of each window in turn. It was a dark night because of clouds and he could see nothing, not even the usual reflections of starlight on the loch, but at least he assured himself that there were no lights from strangers' lanterns. He went quietly out onto the gallery, and lit an oil lamp, then another and another. Squinting into the gloom, he could still see nothing untoward: the suit of armour was still in place; the windows appeared unbroken – for that was the kind of noise he had heard. It must have been in his unremembered dream; nevertheless, he slept only fitfully for the rest of the night, and as soon as it was light enough he got up, dressed and went round the house, inside and then out.

His horror at finding his beloved car scratched was nothing compared to what he felt now. The passenger window was smashed in and the chain was hanging out of it. The other end was still padlocked round the bars of the gate, which had been pulled open so hard that the latch was stuck into the car door. For a moment, Murdo stared at the spectacle in comprehension; then, still open-mouthed, he lifted his eyes and turned round and round, several times, scanning the hills, the surface of the loch, the clouds overhead, as though looking not so much for the perpetrators as for some kind of explanation etched in the landscape. Struggling to function despite the sickness in his stomach, he edged the vehicle forward slowly to release it and began mechanically to clear up the broken glass. Closing the gate, he looked into the burial ground and was even more disturbed to see how that end of the chain, caught tightly under the arms of the cross, had been freed: the cross had been thrown over so that the loop could be slid off the bottom of the shaft. It had, moreover, been broken off its plinth to enable this to be done – and it was a solid piece of stone weighing, well, Murdo knew it was a good deal: had he been familiar with such things, he would have realized that it was about four hundred pounds. Why they had laboured to do this he could not understand: they had clearly climbed over the gate to gain access to the cemetery before demolishing the cross, so why bother trying to open it? If they just wanted to damage the car, out of spite or anger, it could have been done much more easily, and more effectively. They were making some kind of point, taking some kind of revenge, showing him that what he did would rebound on him. He understood enough about the size of the cross to realise that there must have been more than one of them, strong and determined men. What would they do next? What had he done to merit it? And why had he left the mundane security of Edinburgh for this place, this Eden after the Fall?

He sat in the car for some time, oblivious of the breeze cutting through the broken window. Eventually he roused himself, and as soon as it was sensible to do so he drove down to the garage. It was only when he got to the village that he remembered it was Sunday. The garage was shut up, and the Robertsons were not in their cottage, which was next door. Of course, they would be at church. Murdo sat outside, in his car, for almost an hour before they returned; then he accosted the proprietor on his own doorstep, and made his point about the urgency with which he needed the car back so strongly that the man almost feared for his own safety. If you had asked Murdo why there was such urgency about the matter, he probably would not have had a sensible answer. Perhaps at the back of his mind there was some idea that the car was a means of getting away, almost of escape, as a last resort, and so he was loathe to lack it. However, a broken window and some dents would not prevent him from using it thus, and the real, unconscious reason was perhaps a need to return things as far as possible to what they had been before they had gone wrong, coupled with a desperate desire to assert his authority over at least some small area of his life.

Murdo's responses to Mr. Robertson's questions were brief and unconvincing – he said he had accidentally clipped a wall and an overhanging branch had caught the window – but their tone indicated strongly that he should mind his own business, which was beating out the dents, repainting the door and getting new glass to fit. The first two were easy enough: he had to service the doctor's car first thing on Monday – obviously, nothing could be done on the Sabbath, regardless of Mr. McCann's pleading – but then he could get on with it, if Mr. McCann brought it back in, mid-morning; allowing for the paint to dry, it would be ready early on Wednesday. Getting the glass would take longer, perhaps a week, as he would have to order it, but in the meantime – and he could do this straightaway; it was the Sabbath, but he wouldn't charge, so it would be all right and not count as working – he could stick some film over the hole as a temporary measure.

"Of course, you'll nae be able to open it or see to the side as you could, but if you're just driving careful-like to and frae your house you should get awa' wi' it – as lang as you dinna run intae ony mair walls."

Murdo did not much want to go home – had it come to this, that the house which he had worked and planned for for so many years had become something to avoid? – and he almost went to Fort William to spend the day there. However, he did not want to risk driving far with restricted vision, especially as his nerves were not at their best, and it occurred to him that if stayed out too long he ran what seemed a greater risk, that of returning in the dark. He thought for a while of calling the police – rather later than this would occur to you or me, as he had never had involvement with them and they did not feature in his picture of the world. But there was no policeman in Inveravond and he would have to go to Fort William or else telephone to report the criminal damage. There were a few telephones which he could use – a public one in the post office (closed on a Sunday) and ones in the garage and the hotel bars which customers could use for a fee – but in all cases it would mean describing what had happened in front of the proprietor, and he had already given a different version to Robertson, which he knew would soon be all round the village. In any case, it was unlikely that the police would be able to do anything, and their presence might simply aggravate whatever grievance against him one of his neighbours had; the police themselves in this place might not be too sympathetic to an outsider who had taken over the church. He stopped a short way outside the village and walked about a little before driving back to Inveravond House in the afternoon. He locked himself in, then realized he had not eaten all day and got some bread and cheese. As it grew dark he put on some lamps and sat on the gallery with a bottle of whisky; he was not what is called a drinking man, but he had an occasional dram when he felt cold, and today he had more than his usual measure in the hope that it would help him sleep. The whisky began to take effect, and he went to bed without drawing the curtains, though leaving one lamp in his room lit to burn itself out, which it did.

Again he woke up suddenly, in a panic and with the image of a dream still in his brain – the more startling because he never remembered his dreams. He found himself sitting upright, gasping, grasping his sheets and staring into the darkness, fearing to see what he had just been imagining. But there was nothing there, and his heartbeat gradually slowed. He lay back, still clutching the bedclothes to his chest. Repelled but intrigued, he could not help but try to recall what he had dreamt, so vivid and coherent a few seconds before but already indistinct and rapidly fading. He had been standing in the burial ground, looking over the wall at his house; as is the way with dreams, the details were distorted or altered, so that the wall was now higher than himself and over it he could just glimpse a greatly magnified version of his tower. For some reason he had a desperate need to get out of the place – he seemed to have a fear of something behind him, but he could not recall what; he just knew he dared not turn round – and he rushed to the gate; but it had become the huge double door of a castle, bound with iron and locked and barred from the far side. He pushed it and pummeled it and cried out in his terror, but it would not budge. Looking up at the window of the tower, he saw himself looking down towards him with a ghastly expression and waving his hand in front of his face as though warding off the sight. It was then that he had awoken.

The rest of the night was a torment spread more thinly, but for so long that the eventual effect was worse. He was too fearful to get up and face the dark, too frightened of slipping back into his dream to go to sleep; he lay awake with his eyes screwed up tightly, or with his eyes open under the sheets. He could not even bring himself to sit up and close the bedcurtains – though he was in two minds about whether it would be better to have them as a screen or to leave them open and so forestall a nasty surprise. From time to time he would tell himself that this was ridiculous; that it was the nineteen-twenties and not the Middle Ages, despite his fantasy; that it was the age of motor cars and wireless and even aeroplanes, and that the light of science had been shone on things that went bump in the night. Nevertheless, in Inveravond House that night the oil lamp had burnt out and century-old joists creaked alarmingly as the wind cut down the passes and across the loch. When he got up next morning, having finally managed some sleep after dawn, he was so tired and so resigned that he scarcely noticed that the stone door-piece from the castle was lying on his threshold, two yards from where he had left it; he wearily accepted that the film which Robertson had firmly taped over the broken window had been ripped away, as by the wind, and drove into the village.

The garage was just opening when he arrived. Robertson looked at the hole but said nothing. Murdo asked him when it would be ready, stressing to the point of aggression how urgently he needed it back, and then felt a little embarrassed when he got the same reply as before and remembered it: he would start on it as soon as the doctor's car was finished. Murdo walked off with no clear idea of what to do next; it was certainly not a conscious decision that led him to the office of Alexander McRae, who was also just unlocking.

"I hope my manner the other day was not, did not strike you as, shall we say, rude at all. I was feeling a bit under the weather, you understand. Not too good. Things have not been going too well of late, if I am honest wi' you."

"Oh, I am sorry to hear that, McCann. What sort of thing would that be then, that is not going too well?"

McCann felt the need to have a friend, even if it meant apologizing, but he could not bring himself to confide things which now seemed so foolish, in this workplace full of neat files and orderly boxes of papers, with the light of a fresh Autumn morning coming in through the window.

"On, nothing very much, really. I have had some trouble with the car is all. I have just left it at Mr. Robertson's, in fact. It will need to be there for a few days, which is a wee bit inconvenient."

McRae saw how drawn and tired he looked, noted the way his

eyes avoided his and the hesitation before he spoke. The man might be a bore, but he was clearly worried about something.

"Well, you'll be needing a lift home, I'm thinking, at the very least."

"That would be very kind of you." He became evasive. "But I have a few things to do in Inveravond this morning, and you'll be wanting to get down to work, no doubt."

"I dinna have much scheduled for today. Would lunchtime be a good time, perhaps? Better still, shall we go to the hotel for lunch, and then I can take you home afterwards?"

"That would be very nice." At least that would delay the return by a few hours.

It was as well that it was a fine day, as Murdo spent the morning more or less hiding in the hills behind Inveravond again, sometimes pacing and sometimes sitting on a rock or a bank – but he was not thinking; his mind was blank with incomprehension and numb with weariness; he was simply staring ahead of him until the time should pass. When noon came he made his way to the bar of the Loch Avond Hotel where he and McRae had their formerly usual glass and sandwich; he was actually hungry but could do no more than pick at the food, through lack of concentration more than anything. He was glad to be with someone, though he could find even less to say than usual, and he resorted to inane grinning and nodding in an attempt to keep McRae's attention. The lawyer asked a few questions – was he sleeping well? what was wrong with the car? The answers he got lacked content, but they did not come from the angry and aggressive McCann: it was as though the man was trying, perhaps too hard, to be agreeable without actually giving anything away. When they got back to Inveravond House, Murdo hurried the lawyer into the house lest he should see the destruction in the burial ground and question him about what had been going on, and then tried to delay McRae's departure with a cup of tea.

"Mind now, dinna trip over yon stone in the doorway. I shall have to get it moved." Then, "Would you care to have a look around at what I've had done to the place? You didna see much of it last time."

"Thank you but no. I shall have to be going. I have a client to see at two o'clock. Another time perhaps."

"Yes, yes, you must. Supper, perhaps, to make up for last time. And soon."

McRae noted the tone and went along with the idea. "Well, if you are quite sure it wouldna be too much trouble."

"Not at all, man, not at all. Shall we say tonight then, or tomorrow?"

The insistence was becoming alarming. "Er, no, I am sorry; I have to be away to Stirling later, for a couple of nights. I shall not be back until quite late on Wednesday."

"Wednesday then; that'll be ideal – you'll nae be wanting to make yourself something to eat when you get back. Would seven o'clock suit? Or any time you like."

"Aye, all right, seven on Wednesday should be fine."

"That would be grand."

"And thank you," added McRae, as an afterthought; but why did he feel he was the one doing the favour? As he left, he did not notice, as Murdo did, that the carved piece of stone had moved off the threshold.

209

I have already mentioned that the custom of a lifetime had been ended at Inveravond, in that more than once Murdo had awoken in the night and been unable to get back to sleep. That night, it was even worse, as he could not get to sleep at all, despite being exhausted from a broken night and a morning of walking in the open. He thought he heard another bump at the door below him, but he could not be sure, and it did not recur. Part of him was straining to hear the sound of intruders; part was wondering what he had done to make an enemy in the vicinity; part was tortured by the misery of an idyll turned irredeemably sour; all seemed fearful, of the present moment and of the future. His past life had been uneventful to the point of tedium, so that now a few unfortunate, unexpected events weighed on his mind more than they would with most people. He felt the bedcurtains to be oppressive, so knelt up and pulled them back – cautiously; there were no clouds tonight and he could see well enough by the moonlight filling the room, for he had not bothered with the window curtains. Now it was that subdued light which he blamed for his inability to sleep; he was contemplating getting up to shut it out, when he sensed something down in the body of the church. I say 'sensed', because he did not exactly hear anything – there was near-perfect silence this calm night – but he was aware of something going on, beyond the stone wall of his bedroom; aware at some sensory level not to do with the normal processes of perception, effected perhaps by subtle movements of the air or frequencies beyond conscious hearing. It was the most extraordinary feeling. For a while, he sat half out of bed in the moonlight, wondering whether he should investigate. Suppose there had actually been a faint noise and intruders had broken into the house – how would he deal with them? He remembered the shattered cross. But eventually he decided that it would be better to find out what was happening than to wait until they found him, trapped in this room. He first had to see who they were and how many: if it was just a youth playing a prank, he would be able to storm down and see him off; if it was a gang of determined-looking burglars, then he would stay hidden and hope they soon left. A savage feeling somewhere between terror and excitement urged him on despite his trembling – he was not accustomed to adrenalin. He slipped out of bed and took down from a wall display of old weapons an antique dirk. Pulling on his slippers he went to the door with comically exaggerated slow strides in an attempt to minimise the sound he made; he opened it only enough to permit him to sidle through, then, crouching so as not to seen from he below, he inched his way across the gallery to peer down into the church, as St. Andrew, Jesus and St. Peter were looking down from the other end, dimly lit in the east window.

And then anything comical in the scene ended. Up to this point, he had been deeply worried about his suspected but unknown enemy, had felt threatened by acts of trespass and mindless vandalism, had even been disturbed by thoughts and fears for which he had no name in the daytime, but he had always been able to return to reason: a mechanic could fix the car, locks could secure the door. Now reason itself came to an end. As he looked over the balcony and down into what was supposedly his home and refuge, his vague fears turned in a heartbeat into a focussed extremity of terror. If he had been merely very frightened, he might have cried out and dropped the knife; as it was, he was seized by a sudden freezing of the nerves and muscles and a total numbing of the mind, confronted by something too awful even to acknowledge. He was beyond logical thought, and even beyond the fight or flight response of instinct.

There were two steps up from what had been the nave to what had been the chancel, where his couches stood in place of the altar. Along the lower of these was a line of upright figures, perhaps ten or a dozen of them, the size and shape of human beings but shrouded, and he understood that they were, thankfully, facing away from him, towards the east. They were motionless and dark, but the faint moonlight picked them out from the surrounding gloom and there was no denying that they were real, and not just bizarre shadows, even if they appeared as obscure images rather than as solid objects; the sensation of the hilt of the dirk digging into his hand as he gripped it fiercely proved that he was not dreaming. As you know, Murdo was not a superstitious man, but it was apparent to him that whatever these indistinct forms were, standing so inhumanly still and silent, they were not people as we generally understand the word. He closed his eyes tightly, either in the infant's belief that they would not exist if he did this or in the more common but even more irrational hope that they could not see him if he could not see them. There was a brief inner struggle – he did not want to look again, but he had to know what was happening – and he forced his eyes open. Fear gave way to a moment's elation: they were not there; perhaps they never had been there. Then caution took over: they could not have vanished; they must have moved, perhaps just out of his sight. He could not bring himself to stand up and look boldly straight down. Perhaps they had seen him and were at that very moment just below him and about to ascend the steps up to the gallery. He shuddered at the thought, and shuffled around to face the top of the stairs. That corner was in total darkness: the first he would know of their approach would be when they were almost halfway across the gallery and in the moonlight. He edged away to sit on the floor with his back against a bookcase, holding the dirk firmly in front of him – though really he knew that weapons would have no effect on them. A wild idea came into his head that he might leap from the balcony if they came at him, and make a dash for the door; if he should fall to his death it might be preferable to facing them, but to be lying paralysed and conscious as they surrounded and bent over him would be the worst of all. He stared intently into the darkness for ten minutes, twenty minutes, half an hour, then, almost incredibly, fell asleep, with the strain.

It took Murdo more than an hour to walk the two miles into the village. He was cold and stiff from sleeping hunched up on the gallery, and was only scarcely conscious of what he was doing; if asked, he would have been aware of what his actions were from moment to moment, but there was no plan or purpose behind them. His mind was wholly occupied by what had happened the night before – and in blanking it out rather than thinking about it. It was not until he was standing outside McRae's office that he remembered that he had gone away for a couple of days. He arrived at the garage as it was opening. Robertson was surprised to see him. No, he had told him, it would not be ready until Wednesday – tomorrow. The good news was that he had rung round and had been able to get hold of the glass, and it would be arriving later that day: if he came mid-morning tomorrow it should all be done. Murdo drifted away. For a while he sat on the bench outside the new church. He looked at the board: New Church of St. Andrew, Inveravond; Scottish Episcopal Church, Diocese of Argyll and the Isles; Reverend Duncan Campbell, M.A.. Was this what he needed? He shook his head. Had he known it, the Reverend Campbell had almost called on the new resident several times in the preceding weeks, but had decided to wait indefinitely: if Mr. McCann should appear in his church he would introduce himself, but otherwise he would leave him alone. The Reverend Campbell had a very clear idea of what was appropriate for a church building: it could either be a place of active Christian worship, preferably adhering to the principles of Protestantism, or else be a ruin venerated as a former place of such worship. The concept of a church converted to other, secular, uses appalled him, and he was suspicious to an unchristian degree of what kind of man this could be who would convert the house of God into a domestic residence. As far as he could ascertain from the taciturn McIver, there had been no trouble about access to the old burial ground for grass cutting, and it was unlikely in the extreme that he would ever have to preside over any new interments there, so he would leave Mr. McCann to find his own salvation in his own way – whatever that was.

Murdo could not go home, not yet; and not after dark either. When he had the motor back and could get away when he needed to, perhaps, but not yet. He walked up and down the high street, slowly; he had never known time to pass so slowly, except perhaps for some recent nighttime hours in Inveravond House. He sat outside the church again for a while, and then walked up and down again, until he became aware that people were looking at him – not just in passing, but standing in doorways and at windows to watch him. They recognized him, but not much more: he was the unsociable stranger who had moved into the old church and didn't go to the new one, and now he was behaving very oddly. He looked back at them blankly: some of them had to know what was going on, at least one of them had to be responsible for the damage to his car – but another part of his brain told him it was not necessarily so. Eventually, he made his way to the only place he could think to go to in McRae's absence.

At the Loch Avond Hotel, where he was known by sight and through gossip, he was met with surprise when, after a dram in the bar, he asked for a room for the night. It was not just the nature of his request, but his strange, abstracted manner, his disjointed speech and his inability to meet their eyes; there had been no smell of alcohol on him when he had come in, or they might have suspected that he had been drinking already. What was wrong with the place he had just converted and moved into? Nothing; no, that wasn't convincing; the heating had broken down and it was too cold to stay there. Then he would have to have someone come from Fort William, or further, to look at it, and he would probably need to stay several nights; perhaps the antiquated system needed replacing altogether. No, it was nothing so serious; had he said broken? No, he just meant not working: he had just forgotten to light it and it was a bit late now; he didn't fancy staying up there with no hot water, and would go back in the morning, when his car was ready. As it was still only lunchtime, this did not make a lot of sense, but it served to make further questioning seem impolite, and his order for another whisky ended the discussion.

After dinner alone in the hotel, Murdo slept more soundly than he had done for some days, and the following morning he felt strong enough to return to the house by the loch, despite the nasty change in the weather. Before leaving his room, he wrote a note for McRae reminding him that he was expecting him at seven, and he left this under the door of his office before going to collect the car.

As Alexander McRae drove up to Inveravond House, peering through the rain obscuring his windscreen, he noted that there was light evident at every window, suggesting that all the lamps were on. It briefly passed through his mind that this was out of character for the parsimonious McCann, but it was a cheering sight on such a dreadful night. Leaving the car on the roadside, he hurried to the porch, clutching his coat and hat against the squally wind. He had scarcely knocked twice before the man opened the door and all but pulled him in, bolting it behind them.

"Thank you; it is a foul night out there."

"Aye, a foul night it is, right enough."

He seemed preoccupied and nervous, even less of a host that he had been on the lawyer's previous visit, though without the hostility. Then he seemed to recall his duty, and conducted his guest to an armchair in the gallery; he gave him a dram 'for the cold' before going down to attend to their supper. All the lamps were indeed on. McRae noticed that there were three or four fingers in the other glass on the table, next to a near-empty bottle and a large open book. He could not resist leaning over to see what it was: a Bible, open at the Psalms. He did not have McCann down as a religious man at all, but then there was that large antique crucifix on the table at the top of the stairs; he did not attend the church, but maybe he was simply an adherent of a different denomination – a Presbyterian, perhaps, or even a Catholic.

Murdo soon reappeared, and informed him that he should come down. There was bread and soup on the great table, and a casserole of mutton and vegetables, Murdo's most adventurous dish, followed. The lawyer fell in with his host's near-silence and quite rapid eating, despite feeling very awkward; the man was very anxious, as though awaiting something unpleasant, and he seemed to be hurrying to get the meal over with in preparation for something else. Murdo eventually seemed to realise McRae's discomfort and reassured him – "I am very grateful to you for coming out on such a night; it gets quite lonely out here sometimes" – and then looked away in embarrassment. As they finished with apples and cheese, McRae finally asked him if there was something troubling him. McCann paused for a moment, then put his knife down very carefully and spoke with a new forcefulness.

"Aye, you may well ask. But I dinna blame you, you understand. I doubt you knew much about it. As you have scarcely been in here before, and no-one has even lived here afore me, you couldna have known much about it. But there is something wrang wi' this place you have sold me; something very – wrang."

"I didna actually sell it to you, you know. What do you mean, something wrong? Something the builders have done?"

"Nay, man, nothing like that – would that it were that simple. Listen – can you hear that?" McRae could hear only the wind outwith the house and the rain on the panes. "You will. Now we must get up into the gallery. Nay, leave the dishes. We must delay no longer."

Puzzled, McRae followed him back up, leaving the plates on the table and the lights on. Murdo topped up his glass and picked up his own, and then sat tensely, as if listening for something behind the noise of the squalls. For five minutes they did not speak; then the lawyer could hold back no longer: "What is it, man? What's the trouble? That's only the wind; you'll have to get used to a lot worse than that up here in the Winter – it's no Edinburgh."

"Och, it's nae the bit wind. It's mair than that – much mair."

He swallowed some of the whisky, and in a terse, disjointed way he proceeded to tell McRae something of what had been going on, while his listener strained to understand and to piece together the fragments without interrupting him. The noises; the dreams; the moving piece of stone; the words torn from the book; the damage to the car. Murdo was not eloquent, but he then said more than he had ever said, at one time, in his life before. There was a howling squall which drowned him out; he paused for another drink; the wind paused too, and in the brief quiet they both heard a thump from below, from the back door, as though illustrating his tale.

"And that's nae the worst of it."

McRae had become aware that his host was both visibly tense and also trembling as he spoke, as though some mighty emotion, barely contained, was bound up with the act of speaking; his voice was strained and unnatural, the words being forced out as though reluctant to be heard. Shaking so that the whisky threatened to slop out of the tumbler, close to tears, he told of the broken cross, and finally he brought himself to describe the terrible shapes he had seen. His free hand clutched the arm of his chair like a drowning man clutching at a rescuer's hand, and his neck and jaw were so tight that the words would hardly come, and McRae could not quite make out from the jumble how many times it had happened and where. Captain McRae recognized all this, and the expression on McCann's face: he had last seen them in the trenches, when men had been under bombardment for some time. When he had finished, they both sat in silence for a moment – silence apart from another squall of rain at the windows, and more bumping sounds. McRae was not lacking in sympathy for his plight, but he was being very careful in his response. The man's state was such that if he claimed that it was merely someone playing pranks, he would dismiss him out of hand, and it would not be helpful to suggest that his neighbours could treat him in this way. In any case, the lawyer did not really believe that that was all there was to it: ridiculous as it might seem, the things that had happened – the link with the castle, the words of the Latin tag, the obvious significance of the gate into the burial ground – pointed to something much more precise, and brought the covenant on the property into his mind. But surely no distant Anderson relatives had come to Inveravond secretly simply to enforce a condition of which they were probably unaware; if not, who was doing all this?

"I am sorry to bring this up again, man; I know it upset you last time I mentioned it. But everything you have described indicates that there is a particular cause for the problems which you have been having. Everything seems to be about the gate to the – the next plot, the gate which is the subject of the covenant. I think you should be more careful about keeping it free, and show a bit more respect by moving the gravel off the graves by the back door. Certainly you shouldna have parked your motor there, in front of the gate, as I see you have done again."

Murdo looked up sharply, steadying himself in an instant, with something of the defensive aggression which McRae had seen before. "I'll thank you to remember that it's my property and I'll leave my motor where I see fit." The lawyer made a face like a shrug but said nothing. Then the wind died down for a moment, and they heard a thump at the back door and faintly in the distance the sound of metal striking on metal. Murdo's expression crumbled again and he bent forward in his chair as though in pain. "God help me, it was just my own stupid cussedness which made me put the motor back there again."

Again they sat for a while without speaking, as the wind picked up again, mercifully drowning out other sounds; Murdo was in the grip of his torment and McRae was struggling with all manner of speculation in his head, to make some sense of what was going on. Lamely he said, "It must be the wind blowing the gate open, and something banging into your back door," but when Murdo stood up and, in despair, announced his intention of seeing what it was, once and for all, something made the lawyer spring up and clutch his arm. "No man, I'll go. It's best if I look. I dinna have to live here afterwards."

He went up the stairs and into the bedroom. The sound of the rain on the window panes was suddenly increased for a moment, as though something harder was striking the glass; McRae thought of the gravel on the path below. He looked out of the west-facing window; it was dark, but there was intermittent moonlight between the scudding clouds and a little of the light from the house helped, though almost all of the windows were on the other three sides. He stood for a little longer than was strictly necessary to make out what he could from the gloom, as though fascinated. When he turned back, Murdo was just behind him. Again he caught his arm, now with a tight and rigid grip, and propelled him back towards the door. "It wouldna help you, trust me," was all he would say, with an unaccustomedly harsh tone, and he almost pushed him back into his seat. Murdo was past protesting.

The bumping at the tower door became insistent blows which echoed through the old building, and when these ceased they could more clearly hear the crashing of the gate into the side of the car. Murdo shuddered at each shock. The wind howled, and forced its way through gaps around doors and windows; hangings swayed, lamps flickered.

"We must do something! We must leave, drive to the village, get away!" McCann was almost hysterical.

McRae stood stiffly for a while, silent and frowning, trying to get working a brain almost frozen by what he had seen from the window. He tried to get himself back into the frame of mind he had needed to adopt before leading his men over the top or venturing into No Man's Land for a night raid, steeling himself to face death and horror themselves. He weighed his response carefully.

"I'm not sure that that would be – sufficient."

"We could use your car. You are parked down by the other end of the house, are you not? Away frae – away frae all that."

"I did not say it would not be possible: I said that it would not be sufficient; I doubt that that would be enough to put an end to it."

"What are you talking about, man?"

"You see, I do not think that this is about you being here; it's not about you at all. It's about where your motor car is, as I have been telling you. Nothing will do except moving it and clearing the way in frae the gate."

Silence and self-reproach on Murdo's part; more furious banging at the tower door distracting him. "It has never been as bad as this before."

McRae became more thoughtful. "Do you know what night this is?"

"What has that to do with anything, man? It is the last day of October, I ken, not that that helps at all."

"Indeed, it is All Hallows' Eve. Does that mean anything to you?"

Murdo looked up from his seat to face McRae and slowly focused on his face. "You mean bairns' stories about ghosts and witches and the like?"

"When you put it that way, I can understand your scepticism. But the belief among the old folk is – and it is a serious, ancient belief, far older than the Christian faith," the lawyer was addressing himself as much as he was Murdo, "the belief is that on this night, of all nights, on this night, the, well, the –"

"It's all right, man; I have seen and heard things since coming here that have changed my mind about superstitions, or at least made me realise the power of them. I ken that I dinna ken everything about the world."

"Very well. The belief is that on this night the division is lifted between this world and the next; those who were once in our world can come back into it, for a while. Do you understand what I am saying?"

"You would have me believe that the spirits of Sir James Anderson and his clan are swinging on that gate and beating on my back door!" Written down, the words look like an incredulous, sarcastic rebuke, but they were spoken in a measured and thoughtful way, such as might be employed by a man who has just taken on board remarkable new ideas and is repeating them in order to get them clear. But he was trembling too; his eyes were watering and his whole body was shaking.

"To be quite accurate, I believe Sir James to be amongst those knocking on the door, but it is his grandfather who is at the gate." Again, on the page, this looks like a sick joke, but there was no jollity in the grim humour. Murdo was buckling under the strain, visibly, but as the tension increased a terrible calm came over McRae. He had commanded a company of the Black Watch in the thick of the fighting at Arras in 1917, and now nothing could unsettle him for long, not even after several years of peace. But he saw the signs in his host, and knew that he could not hold out for much longer.

"Then why can we not just leave them to it?"

"Because the one thing they want is for the passage between the burial ground, the graves and the church to be open, as it says in the covenant. Which means they want your car moved. And, if I am right, they will not leave you alone until they have that."

"So you suggest that I stroll out there among them, in this storm, start up the car and drive away?" The tone was angry, sarcastic, desperate; pause.

"I am afraid that it comes down to that, in essence. But I agree with you that there is no way that you can stand there and crank up the motor. We need to make this as quick as possible. Now, we only need to move it back far enough for the gate to open fully, just a couple of yards or so. I think I am right in saying that the incline is upwards as you come in off the road, before it falls down into the loch on the other side. I assume that you are parked nose first, with the driver's door just a couple of strides frae the back door, yes? Good. And you haven't put that chain back across the gap? That's excellent. Are the lights in the kitchen on?"

"No."

"Well, I suggest that we put as much light on at the back of the house as we can before we open the door – even if the wind soon puts the lamps out – as it will cause a bit of a shock and give us a few seconds. Then we can rush out. You open the driver's door and get in, take the brake off, put the thing into reverse and steer it back out. And for God's sake make sure the passenger doors are all unlocked. Meanwhile I'll go round to the front and give it a push, then get in once it's moving – I might have to come round the driver's side and get in behind you, I don't know. Then as soon as we can, when we think it is safe to do so, we get out and run to my car and get it cranked up. What do you think of that as a plan?"

For the first time in a long time, Murdo thought of someone else before himself. "You have the harder task, standing out there."

"But I am not the one who has broken the covenant. Oh, and you might like to bring that with you." He indicated the crucifix on the table. "It might give them pause, though they are not such as have cause to be frightened of such a thing."

When they threw the door open and rushed out in a blaze of light, almost tripping over the carved piece from the castle, Murdo focused rigidly on the car door and getting it open. He was helped by the fact that his eyes were not attuned to the darkness and were half-blinded by the rain, and all he sensed around him were shadows dancing in the squally wind. The wind plucked strongly at his sleeves and dishevelled his hair roughly. Inside the car he looked only at the handbrake, the gearstick and the steering wheel as he prepared to freewheel into the road; he was aware of a shape looming ahead of the car, but knew it had to be McRae pushing him. He sensed a swift motion as McRae threw towards the gate the crucifix which he was carrying aloft; he felt the car edge backwards, but did not dare to look in the mirrors. The door behind him was pulled open: a moment's terror seized him, then he assured himself that it was the lawyer jumping in. The car came to a halt with the front level with the wall, just off his property.

For a while he sat with his eyes closed, then he felt McRae tapping his shoulder.

"Are you all right?"

He opened his eyes. In the fitful light he could see the gate swung open; there was only blackness where his back door was open, as the lamps must have been blown out. He could see nothing else. "Aye."

"Come on then. Do you want to try starting her up here? No, perhaps not. We'll go over to my car, down the way. What about your door?" Murdo shook his head. "It should be all right, if a bit cold in there tomorrow; I think the rain is stopping, and no-one is going to come out past here tonight."

They drove away from Inveravond House. Murdo began to recover a little of his former self, and tried to put behind him the weakness he had shown in the past hour, and all that he had learnt, with hard and practical words.

"I wish now I had closed that door. The swine who have been plaguing me will be in and causing havoc in the house. I should have called the police in a long time ago and got to the bottom of all this. What have I done to anyone here that they should want to give me such a fright, just for blocking a gate?"

"Och, man, have you learnt nothing at all frae all this? The covenant was never meant to be for the benefit of living people."

RE-ENACTMENT

"*On December 6, 1745, the Jacobites withdrew from Derby and began the long retreat north, reaching Inverness in February. The army was steadily reduced by desertions, and after it had crossed the border increasing numbers of Scots departed to return home and attempt to salvage the lives they had led before joining the rebellion. One of these was Alexander McGow, who returned to Kinlochavond with about twenty of his followers and occupied the tower which forms the main part of the present house. A portrait of Alexander hangs in the Red Room, to the right of the fireplace. The Duke of Cumberland was not content to leave pockets of resistance behind him as he marched north to Aberdeen, and despatched a company of infantry under Captain Robert Grant, a troop of horse and two cannons to capture Kinlochavond Castle. The Government force arrived in the middle of March, 1746, and called on McGow and his men to surrender; Alexander replied that he would never abandon the place which had been his family's home for twelve generations. During the siege, which lasted a week, the cannons battered the tower day and night, causing much damage. This was largely repaired during the renovation in the nineteenth century, but the lintel of a window in the Blue Room bears a deep impression believed to have been caused by a cannon ball. Eventually the door was broken down and there was savage hand-to-hand fighting as the soldiers forced their way in. Everyone in the tower was killed by bullet or bayonet, including the women and children of the McGow household. Alexander himself is said to have been run through with a sword by Captain Grant as he defended the staircase leading up to the room where his wife and baby were sheltering. This episode is known in the family history as The March Massacre, and is the subject of an old ballad. The pipe tune McGow's Lament is also supposed to have been composed in memory of these events.*'"

"And that's what we've come here to see? A re-enactment of that horrible story?"

He lowered the guidebook. "Well, some of it. I don't expect they'll come into the house, it wouldn't be allowed, 'health and safety' and all that, and possible damage to the exhibits. But they'll probably stage a battle outside."

"So it won't be anything like what really happened? No massacre of women and children?"

"It'll give you an impression of what it was like, what battles were like then."

"No it won't. There won't be any limbs cut off or dead babies."

"Don't be so ghoulish."

"I'm just saying, it'll be nothing like a real battle. And it's the women and children who are always the real victims of war anyway. This is just some people who haven't anything better to do dressing up and play-acting. Men in kilts and – what do they call them? – bonnets, running around, waving swords and shouting a lot."

"It's historical re-enactment. It's history."

"It's nonsense. It's like you wearing that kilt. You never wear a kilt in Boston, but as soon as we arrive in Edinburgh you have to have one, and you have to wear it. How many people do you see walking around Edinburgh, actual genuine Scottish people, wearing a kilt? It's like you went nuts as soon as we got over here! How many in a company of soldiers, anyway?"

"About a hundred, I guess."

"So there'll be about a hundred and twenty of them altogether?"

"Well, perhaps half that. There are about sixty or seventy in the 'Dirk and Dagger' society, I think. We saw them at Killiecrankie; do you remember?"

"Yes, I remember it well. It rained all day."

"Mind you, most of them play Highlanders rather than government troops. As you say, I suppose it's mostly about dressing up in plaid with swords and targes."

"?"

"Those little round shields. I don't know how they'll manage if most of them are supposed to be redcoats."

"People are not exactly breaking the door down to see it, are they? There's nobody here apart from us."

"It's not until this afternoon. Three o'clock, it said. I wanted to come early so we could see round the house first. I doubt we'll ever be here again."

"No, we won't. Back to Edinburgh the day after tomorrow?"

"Yeah. And the flight home next Friday."

She didn't look upset at the prospect. "She did say we should wait in here, didn't she?"

"Yeah. Wait for the tour guide in there, she said. The tour's supposed to start on the hour. Ten minutes to wait, if that old clock's right."

"Do you think we can sit on the chairs?"

"I wouldn't. They're exhibits. We don't want telling off like at Cawdor."

"You're telling me! And we had paid good money! Ah, here we go."

"He must be one of the re-enactors. He's not the guide," he said, taking his reading glasses off.

"He might be. He might be both."

A tall, bearded man wearing a plaid and a bonnet and with a basket handle sword at his side and a flintlock pistol in his belt had walked in through the door from the ticket office in the entrance hall. He paused in front of them in the middle of the sparsely-furnished room.

"Excuse me, are you our guide?"

The man cocked his head to one side slightly and frowned. "I dinna guide; I lead. If you're needing a guide on the road, then you must be asking one o' the serving men." His accent was thick; the man struggled to catch his words and the woman merely looked blank. The newcomer turned away from them and started to look at the two pictures on the wall of the antechamber. "That is the view of the castle frae the river. But all this behind the tower is new."

"He is the guide, but he's in character."

"More play-acting."

"I thought you would appreciate method acting. Haven't you done classes?"

"This isn't Broadway."

"Shush! He's playing an historical character for us, like that man at Bannockburn. We should go along with it."

"OK."

"Excuse me, are you by any chance Alexander McGow of Kinlochavond?"

"This is Kinlochavond Castle, and I am Alexander McGow. At your service, sir, madam." He bowed towards the woman.

"Told you so. And you were killed here in the siege in 1746, right?"

"Killed?" The man paused; his lips compressed and his eyes turned up. The couple automatically looked at the ceiling. "Yes, killed. Killed. All killed."

"He's milking it a bit."

"Shush! On the staircase?"

"Staircase? Staircase? What are ye talking about, man? No, down there, down in yon ditch." The man pointed to the window.

"It says the staircase in the guidebook," said the woman, aloud this time.

"It only says 'said to have been'. They don't know," said her husband, putting his glasses back on and glancing at the guidebook again. "It's a matter of interpretation."

"Well, it's a bit of a change from gallantly defending the staircase to being dead in a ditch, isn't it? He ought to stick to what's in the guidebook. What's the point of having a guide and a guidebook if they tell you different things?" This to her husband, but looking accusingly at the man.

"Shush! He's just doing his job."

"Well, he ought to do it properly and not go confusing people. Are you sure you read the book right? Did you have the right glasses on?"

"Shush! Look – I hope you haven't offended him."

The man had moved off and was walking through into the next room. A card on a stand said 'Red Room'. There were pieces of late Victorian furniture and fussy ornaments, and a ponderous fireplace of grey stone carved with caryatids down the sides and a coat of arms in the middle of the mantelpiece. Red and cream flock wallpaper, deep red curtains and rugs of the same colour on dark wooden floorboards explained the room's name. Portraits and landscapes dating from the eighteenth and nineteenth centuries crowded the walls.

"All is changed," said the guide sadly. "Nothing is as it was. This room had wooden panelling. Now they've ripped it out. Burnt it all to ashes. I remember watching them do it. I tried to stop them, but it was no use." The woman raised her eyebrows and looked questioningly at her husband, but he just shrugged and looked away. "Then they put up this – rubbish instead." The guide shook his head and walked over to the fireplace. "This is as it should be, at least."

"What period is he supposed to be in now?" The woman was reading the card. "*Originally panelled in oak, this room is named for the red furnishings which date from the eighteen-seventies. The furniture, which is of this period, has been collected from various rooms in the house and other properties on the estate.* He's got that right at least."

The guide was looking at a more than life-sized, full-length portrait of a man in a tartan jacket and trews holding the end of the barrel of a musket resting on the ground, to the right of the fireplace. The background was of generic parkland and impossibly fluffy clouds.

"This would be me, I think. Some time ago, of course, afore I grew the beard."

"He's right," said James, putting his glasses back on and bending to read the card on the wall. "*Alexander McGow, 1704-46. Painted by Thomas Whitely, c.1736.*"

"Not difficult, as it's all written there."

The man made a frantic gesture at the woman behind the guide's back. She turned her eyes up with a look of bored resignation. The guide was already walking towards the next door.

"He doesn't give you much time to look around, does he? Tell him to slow down!"

They followed him. He was leaning with his hands on the sill of one of the wide windows in the Blue Room. The visitors stood by him, looking out into the grounds also.

"That was where they had one of their big guns." They followed his gaze to a raised knoll on which stood a folly, a cupola resting on classical columns, dating from the end of the eighteenth century. "Where they have put yon fancy thing wi' the pillars." He leant with his forehead on the glass. "And down there is where they did it." They craned their necks, trying to look straight down. He seemed to be looking at the ditch which surrounded the tower, the remains of an ancient moat.

"Where you say they killed Alexander?"

"Where they killed me and everyone."

"So why were you fighting down in the ditch?"

"We were not fighting. We had surrendered and they took us out there."

"Surrendered? There's nothing in the book about surrendering."

"Book? What book would that be?"

James held up the guidebook. "It says you died fighting when the soldiers broke in."

The guide shook his head with an expression between sorrow and disapproval. "It would have been better to have done so. That book of yourn must have been written by the Butcher's men, to conceal their wicked sin of murder." He closed his eyes and sighed. "Or by the family, I suppose, afterwards. To make us seem nobler." He paused for a while, and then started again, as though with an effort. The woman poked her husband in the thigh and he pushed her hand away quickly. "The simple truth is that, after a week of being bombarded and sniped at, half o' my men were dead or badly wounded and our supplies were running out; the soldiers had been right behind us in our flight and we had had nae time to gather in provisions. There were holes and cracks in the tower, and, even if the soldiers did not get in, the walls were in danger of falling on us. I decided that I had to surrender, if only for the sake of my wife and child and the handful o' other women in the castle. The soldiers made us go outside, carrying the wounded, and line up in the ditch; they tied the hands of the men who could stand; then they shot us all, starting with Catriona and little Angus and ending with me. I'm not sure what happened after that." He straightened up. "It was a very long time ago. Much has happened since." He turned and walked across the room and through the next door.

"He's far too quick," said the woman. "Not that I can understand half of what he says. They should get someone in who speaks proper English. He hasn't told us anything about this room." She looked round at the eighteenth-century furnishings. "And this room is so much nicer than that last one."

Her husband had put his glasses back on and was leafing

through the guidebook. "I thought I saw something... yes, here it is. This must be where he got that story from. *During archaeological excavation of this ancient moat in the nineteen-fifties, the skeletons of some two dozen individuals, including four women and one male child, were uncovered. Most bore clear evidence of having been shot at close range. From artefacts discovered with the bones, their deaths have been dated to around the time of the Second Jacobite Rebellion, 1745-46, and they may have been the victims of the March Massacre (see page 5), hastily buried in the nearest convenient spot. The bones were re-interred in a vault in the chapel (see page 18) and some of the artefacts can be seen in a glass case in the Long Gallery (see page 14).*"

He took his glasses off and the couple prepared to follow the guide. They were stopped by the arrival of a stout middle-aged lady in a white blouse and tweed jacket and skirt, hurrying in from the Red Room.

"Ah, there you are! They said you were waiting in the antechamber. I am sorry if I am a wee bit late. We get so few visitors at this time of year."

"Sorry, who are you exactly?"

"Well, I'm your guide, dear. For the tour, you know."

"You are the guide?"

"Yes, of course."

"Oh, I'm sorry. We were just talking to one of the re-enactment people. We thought he was you, if you see what I mean. Thought he was the guide, you see."

"Re-enactment people? I think not. That is not until next Saturday."

"No, it's today. It was on the flyer: March 21."

"No, I'm afraid it is on March 27, next Saturday, although today is actually the date of the notorious Massacre, which you might have read about. They thought we would get more people on a Saturday, and it's more convenient. The notices were not very clearly printed, I know. Indeed, the re-enactment people are not coming until next weekend."

ROOM 18, KINLOCHAVOND LODGE

21 Church Lane,
King's Chapel,
Guildford,
Surrey
August 14th, 1956

The Manager,
Kinlochavond Lodge Hotel,
Kinlochavond,
Inverness-shire

Dear Sir,

My wife and I were guests at the Kinlochavond Lodge, in room 18, from August 4th to August 11th. While we enjoyed our stay and I find no fault with the accommodation and service provided during it, and despite not being accustomed to make complaints, I am writing to inform you that a problem came to light when we unpacked our luggage at home yesterday: I discovered that several of my shirts had been slashed, with long, parallel, vertical slits made as if by a razor, making them completely unusable. They were not in this condition when packed and, as the cases were undamaged, they must have been interfered with during the period when they were awaiting collection in your lobby prior to our departure, or, before that, when they were left in our room during breakfast.

I must ask you to look into this matter in order to ascertain how this came to happen and who was responsible. Please be so good as to let me know what you discover and what action you propose to take, as regards compensation for the loss and for the inconvenience caused.

Yours faithfully,
James Hamilton

21 Church Lane
August 28th, 1956

The Manager,
Kinlochavond Lodge Hotel

Dear Sir,

I note that I have received no reply to my letter of August 14th, concerning the damage caused to my property during our recent visit to the Kinlochavond Lodge, nor any offer of compensation. I am surprised that you have not yet responded, ample time having been given, and must assume that nothing has been done to discover who perpetrated this outrage, and that consequently no action has been taken.

I am afraid that I must point out that not only has our holiday been spoiled in retrospect but that criminal damage has been done. If I do not receive a reply to my original letter within ten days of the above date, I shall be obliged to make a formal complaint to the police. I trust that I do not have to tell you what harm could be done to your business if this matter were to become a matter of public record.

Yours faithfully,
James Hamilton

Kinlochavond Lodge Hotel
September 1st, 1956

Mr. James Hamilton,
21 Church Lane,
King's Chapel,
Guildford,
Surrey

Dear Mr. Hamilton,

I apologise for the delay in replying to you.

I am very sorry to hear that your visit to Scotland was marred in the way which you describe, and that you feel that the Kinlochavond Lodge was in some way involved. However, you will appreciate that the hotel cannot be held responsible for damage to a guest's property which comes to light only after that guest has returned home. I would suggest that the damage might have been caused by the garments coming into contact with a sharp object in the suitcase during the journey, or perhaps during the packing or unpacking process.

Yours sincerely,
Alasdair McKenzie (Manager)

21 Church Lane
September 3rd, 1956

Mr. Alasdair McKenzie,
Manager,
Kinlochavond Lodge Hotel

Dear Mr. McKenzie,

I thank you for your letter of September 1st, but I must reject entirely the explanation which you offer. There were only clothes in the suitcase involved, and not even buckles or anything else which might have caused the slashing. I packed the shirts myself on our last evening in the hotel, in order to save time before our departure, and I know that they were undamaged at that time; the cases were in the car with us throughout our journey home; I also unpacked them, and am certain that nothing happened then which might have caused the damage. The case was left unattended in our room in the hotel during dinner and breakfast, and briefly in the lobby thereafter, and I can only conclude that the outrage was committed during one of those periods. As we left the room locked whenever we went out, and while we were asleep, I have to conclude that it must have been carried out by a member of staff, rather than by a guest.

I must reiterate that I intend to take this matter further if you do not take immediate steps to investigate and take appropriate action.

Yours sincerely,
James Hamilton

Kinlochavond Lodge Hotel
September 5th, 1956

Mr. James Hamilton,
21 Church Lane,
King's Chapel,
Guildford,
Surrey

Dear Mr. Hamilton,

On behalf of the hotel, while not admitting responsibility, I offer our unreserved apology for any loss or inconvenience which you suppose you may have suffered as a result of your stay at the

Kinlochavond Lodge.

I enclose a cheque for ten pounds, by way of compensation, and trust that this matter will go no further.

Yours sincerely,
Alasdair McKenzie (Manager)

21 Church Lane
September 10th, 1956

Mr. Alasdair McKenzie,
Manager,
Kinlochavond Lodge Hotel

Dear Mr .McKenzie,

I thank you for your letter of September 5th and acknowledge receipt of your cheque as compensation for the material loss involved, but I am afraid that this does not end the matter as far as I am concerned. While I accept your grudging official apology on behalf of the hotel, I must insist that you take steps to identify the culprit, from whom I require a personal apology. In fact, since this correspondence commenced, the matter has become significantly more serious. My wife informs me belatedly that on at least two occasions during our stay, she awoke during the night, believing there to be someone in the room with us. At the time, she dismissed this as a dream, although she has not had such an experience before; however, since we have discussed this in connection with the damage to our property, we have become convinced that someone was entering our room during our occupancy. As I have already explained, we are also sure that it had to be a member of staff, with access to a key.

I must again insist that you look into this as a matter of urgency, as the security and possibly the safety of your guests may be at risk and I find your response to the situation so far to be lacking in the appropriate degree of seriousness. I expect your reply by return.

Yours sincerely,
James Hamilton

Kinlochavond Lodge Hotel
September 12th, 1956

Mr. James Hamilton,
21 Church Lane,
King's Chapel,
Guildford,
Surrey

Dear Mr. Hamilton,

With reference to your recent correspondence, I assure you that I have been taking your complaint seriously and have made extensive enquiries; unfortunately, what I know about the situation and what I have discovered recently do not assist me in making you an acceptable answer. While not wishing to appear to disbelieve what you have told me, I am convinced that no-one could have entered your room overnight and that no member of staff did so after the room was cleaned on the morning of the day before your departure, until after you had vacated it. There is only one set of room keys in addition to the keys issued to guests, and those keys are kept in my safe except during room cleaning, when they are temporarily issued to the staff involved, who have been with us for many years and have given us no cause to doubt their integrity. My records show that the keys were in my safe from half past eleven on the morning of August 10th until a quarter past nine on the morning of the 11th, while you departed at twenty-five past nine. The same register also shows that the keys were in the safe overnight throughout your stay, and indeed for several days before that.

I have questioned all the staff employed by the hotel and do not believe that any of them were involved in this matter.

I am sorry if you do not find this response satisfactory, but I am at a loss as to how I can make any other.

Yours sincerely,
Alasdair McKenzie (Manager)

21 Church Lane
September 15th, 1956

Mr. Alasdair McKenzie,
Manager,
Kinlochavond Lodge Hotel

Dear Mr. McKenzie,

I am afraid that I am totally unable to accept the interpretation which you put on the events of which I have informed you, and in fact the matter has again become much more serious. Since my last letter, we have finally had developed the photographs which we took during our holiday in Scotland and have been shocked to find concrete proof of the presence of an intruder in our room overnight. Three frames on one roll of film clearly show my wife and I asleep in bed; I enclose one of the prints. All the pictures show both of us, so it cannot be that they were taken by one of us sleepwalking. Before you suggest another simplistic explanation, to the effect that it was the result of a mechanical fault in the camera, I would point out that the camera and the flashgun were kept in separate cases on the bedside table when not in use. For these pictures to have been taken, the two devices would have to have been taken out and connected, even before the adjustment of the settings and the pressing of the button, and then disconnected and put back afterwards. Furthermore, we always took pains to check that the door to the room was locked while we were in, as is our invariable practice; the intruder must have had access to the spare keys you describe.

Needless to say, my wife has been, and is continuing to be, severely distressed by this revelation.

Re-reading your letter of September 12th, with its talk of what you know about the situation and of the acceptability of answers, I believe there may be a suggestion in it that you have not told us everything which you know about this matter. I insist on your full disclosure of whatever it is that you know or suspect, by return, or I shall be obliged to take my evidence to the police. If it concerns aberrant behaviour by a member of staff, I further insist that appropriate disciplinary measures be taken; if it involves a guest, then I shall require you to report the fact to the relevant authorities.

Yours sincerely,
James Hamilton

Kinlochavond Lodge Hotel
September 18th, 1956

Mr. James Hamilton,
21 Church Lane,
King's Chapel,
Guildford,
Surrey

Dear Mr. Hamilton,

I am expecting further correspondence from you with regard to the matters about which you have made complaints, so I am setting out some facts for you to consider, in anticipation – though you may not regard them as facts.

Shortly after being demobbed and joining the staff at the Kinlochavond Lodge as assistant manager in 1946, I first became aware of the reputation which the hotel has locally. The story appears to go back to the late seventeenth century or early eighteenth century, when the old part of the building, which includes room 18, was a hunting lodge of Kinlochavond Castle, some five miles away. The head of the McGow family, who held the castle, had had a poor day's hunting and had drunk too much in the hall, part of which is now the hotel lounge. The story goes that he then went up the stairs to a room where there was either a maid or the wife of his guest, according to which version of the story you hear – although it is unclear why either a maid or the unaccompanied wife of a guest would be staying in the lodge. Doubtless many of the details of the story are lost or distorted; I have in fact failed to identify precisely the characters in the tale from contemporary records. Whatever the truth of the matter, the story goes on to say that McGow tried to force himself on the woman; there was a struggle; she fell down the stairs and broke her neck. As you will recall, room 18 is in a turret which stands apart at the top of its own flight of stairs; it is generally believed that this is the setting for the story. Since then, the woman, and according to some the man also, has supposedly been seen in that part of the building.

Initially, I thought the tale mere superstitious nonsense, as indeed you probably view it, but within a year I began to change my mind, as a result of the unexplained experiences which were being reported by some of the guests. I would stress that most of those who stay in room 18 are not troubled in this way, but a minority do have experiences similar to yours. Why some should be affected and others not, I cannot say.

A couple staying in room 18, who had almost certainly not heard the story, claimed that they had seen a shadow moving across a wall in the room; one of the cleaners refused to enter 18 on her own; another guest in the room complained that there were noises on the stairs and that the door was tried during the night. Since that time, I have kept a journal of such occurrences in and around room 18 and its staircase; there are over a dozen entries, to which I shall be adding your report. The incidents include objects being moved and sometimes hidden or damaged, unexplained sounds as of people shouting, impressions in the bedclothes and a general sense of being watched by something unseen. Two occupants have complained about being touched while in bed, and on at least three occasions frightened guests have had to be found alternative rooms, one refusing to stay in the hotel at all. To my knowledge, no actual apparition has been seen, though unexpected shadows and movements glimpsed out of the corner of the eye have been reported.

I am now in receipt of your letter dated September 15th. I understand entirely your feelings of frustration and sympathise with Mrs. Hamilton's distress. While it will probably do nothing to allay these, I hope that the above will go some way to providing an explanation of your experiences. Should you so wish, I can make the record which I have compiled available for your perusal.

Yours sincerely,
Alasdair McKenzie (Manager)

21 Church Lane
September 24th, 1956

Mr. Alasdair McKenzie,
Manager,
Kinlochavond Lodge Hotel

Dear Mr. McKenzie,

With reference to your letter dated September 18th, while not wishing to doubt your integrity, I am afraid that I regard your explanation of events at the hotel as utter nonsense. The suggestion that shirts were slashed and photographs taken by ghosts or any other supernatural forces is completely ludicrous. This is the middle of the twentieth century, not the Middle Ages, and ascribing such things to fictitious creatures taken from myths and legends is simply the avoidance of an unpleasant truth, namely, that one or more of your staff is engaging in voyeuristic and malicious acts against your guests. I do not propose to waste further time on this fruitless correspondence, but do intend to take this matter up with the owners of the Kinlochavond Lodge, when my wife and I are celebrating the New Year at the house of friends near Inverness. I shall be in touch to arrange a meeting nearer the time and expect to hear something more credible than ridiculous tales about ghosts and goblins.

Yours sincerely,
James Hamilton

Kinlochavond Lodge Hotel
November 2nd, 1956

Mr. James Hamilton,
21 Church Lane,
King's Chapel,
Guildford,
Surrey

Dear Mr. Hamilton,

We are in receipt of your letter of September 24th, addressed to Mr. McKenzie. I note from our register that you were a guest here in August. I understand from your letter that there was some problem during your stay, which has not yet been resolved, apparently involving accusations of misconduct on the part of our staff, which we take very seriously. However, I have been unable to find any earlier letters, probably as a result of an unaccountable small fire in a cabinet in our office late last month, and so I do not know the details. Because you are clearly unhappy about the situation, I have to apologise that we are unable to reply to you about the matter at this time. Mr. McKenzie recently had an accident, falling down some stairs in the hotel and suffering a severe head injury. He has been unconscious in hospital since. Should he recover, I have no doubt that he will endeavour to answer you, but it will be some time before this is possible. I note that you will be visiting Kinlochavond at the end of the year, and would be obliged if you could inform me in advance of the nature of your complaint so that I can pursue the matter further prior to meeting with you.

Yours sincerely,
Ian Donaldson (Acting Manager)

THE EDDESDALE SCREAMING

One of the most curious, disappointing and frustrating features of the Eddesdale Screaming is the fact that it is never to be heard by those who actually want to hear it – certainly not by those who deliberately seek it out. But you will have seen that in what you have read already, yes? A team of researchers from the psychology department at Edinburgh University; a group of American psychic investigators, sponsored by a New York businessman whose great-great-great-grandfather left Eddesdale the year Walter Scott died; a television production company fronted by a well-known media astrologer – all have spent time at the castle with cameras, night-sights and a variety of sensors, detectors and recorders for sound, temperature and magnetic field, without witnessing anything which could be described as supernatural. As those who, on the other hand, definitely do not want to hear it tend to keep away from the situation in which they might do so, accounts of the Screaming invariably derive from parties who have heard it by chance, almost always not knowing at the time what it was and finding out only by subsequent enquiry. This might seem to lend credence to their stories, as being spontaneous, unpremeditated and disinterested, but in fact it has led to much scepticism: the Screaming is not attested by any "scientifically-based" evidence, but only by those who have subsequently read or heard of the old story and have perhaps, if unconsciously, moulded their own experience to fit the pattern and so made themselves part of the tradition – satisfying at once the triple deep-rooted desires for personal notoriety, a feeling of belonging and a sense of there being something beyond the tangible present.

Indeed, if one were to look for a spot which embodied a combination of eerie otherworldliness and romantic communion with a Gothic fantasy of the past, then Eddesdale Castle would be hard to beat. It stands in the dark heart of the Borders, a few miles from Hermitage Castle in Liddesdale, itself a place with a savage history embellished with bizarre tales, its remoteness being the sole feature which prevents its name from being wholly ironic. But whereas Hermitage now stands amid clipped lawns by the highway and is open to the public for the price of a ticket and according to a schedule of times, courtesy of Historic Scotland and the kilted gatekeeper, this castle is isolated, untended and hardly known – except for the Screaming, and few would venture so far for the sake of a footnote in a book of folklore. It stands on a low rise in the gap between two hills through which runs the path, not a road, into high Eddesdale; it is by this route that the occasional hikers come, who make up the majority of the recent witnesses to the Screaming. Now open to the sky and bereft of its floors and fittings, the tall tower of dark stone is punctuated by darker window-openings which look like empty eyesockets; nothing remains of the surrounding buildings except for grassed-over humps which may conceal the bases of walls. But it was the Screaming itself which you wanted to know about, though I may from time to time refer to something in the castle's history or topography.

I call it the Screaming because that is the word which you used, and it is the one which most accounts adopt, following the earliest, passing reference to the phenomenon which we have, in the ballad *The Raid of Eddesdale*, first printed in 1780 but relating events of more than two centuries earlier. However, for me the word is not quite satisfactory as a description, because it has such a range of meanings in common parlance. 'Screaming' might suggest a violent dispute, but the sound at Eddesdale is neither a response nor expecting of a response, and, though baleful, lacks the energy associated with positive anger. 'Screaming' can even be used of enthusiastic or excited sounds, and this is totally wrong here; only at the opposite end of the

248

spectrum of meaning for 'screaming' can the word be seen as at all appropriate – the scream of fear. But even that is not right, for the Eddesdale sound is not one provoked by any feeling of threat or danger: those who have heard it say it comes from a stage beyond fear, when no further harm can be done or injury inflicted, though continuing pain can still be felt, and does not diminish with time. This outcry is not the instantaneous, instinctive expression of fright at a passing situation, but a temporary eruption of the enduring emotion derived from a chronic vision of universal horror; it is the howl of acknowledged despair, regret for everything when everything is beyond recall, total self-loathing, a sickness of the soul. But I like the other term used locally – the Shrieking – even less, as it is a thin-sounding word and conveys nothing of the resonance of the Eddesdale noise, and I suggest that you use the more traditional Screaming, should this article ever be published.

I sense that already you are feeling a little uncomfortable, and I can understand that the language which I am using might seem rather extreme or theatrical for a retired schoolmaster with pretensions to being a serious, albeit amateur, local historian; but, unlike you, I have actually heard the sound, which is why you are here now, and I can assure you that it is quite unlike any other experience, auditory or otherwise. It has more than a passing effect on its hearers, which is why they tend to make inquiries afterwards, come back here, read about it, talk about it. Though those who hear it have not sought it, it is not heard casually, or remotely, but in extreme close-up. We are a small coterie sharing a rare experience not understood by outsiders, and so viewed with some suspicion; I suppose we may seem rather like those who claim to have been abducted by aliens, a phenomenon which has become very fashionable. Nevertheless, before we go any further I feel I must try to give you some description of what is ultimately indescribable in ordinary language, to set up some kind of context for what we are discussing. I shall be drawing mainly on what happened when I heard the Screaming, but also on what I have been told by other hearers in the past twenty years or so, and to a lesser extent on accounts I have read going back a century and more.

Not that the Screaming has been a feature of Border legend for very long, in fact, though this is not unusual with tales of hauntings and such phenomena: ghost stories may be populated with medieval monks and nuns, errant sixteenth-century gentry and occasionally an unfortunate Victorian maidservant, but they can rarely be traced back more than perhaps four centuries. There is the occasional Roman legion on the march, but Ancient Britons and Anglo-Saxons do not feature; perhaps the nature of ghosts is such that they fade over time. The ballad which contains the reference to the Eddesdale sound, however named, must have been handed down orally for generations before being printed in Edinburgh in 1780, with many additions and changes incorporating other folklore and anecdotes, some of them postdating the cattle-raid which is its theme. The Screaming is mentioned in passing as part of a stock description of the castle and plays no part in the story, whereas one might have expected the original narrator to have made more of it; this perhaps indicates that the Screaming was not part of the original, contemporary ballad, but was added later, perhaps as late as the eighteenth century, though the allusive nature of the reference suggests that the detail was common currency then. This would tie in with the earliest datable account of the Screaming, which comes from an English officer's report written on Candlemas Eve, 1746. Candlemas? An ancient feast, celebrated on the second day of February; it corresponds to Imbolc, the festival of light in the Celtic calendar. I am sorry; you seem to be losing interest – no? Well, I shall be brief and summarise the episode and its context, but I think it is useful because it shows how features of a hearing of the sound have remained constant over time, and it helps us to understand why it has so caught the imagination. The officer was a subaltern called Taylor, who was in command of a small force of Hanoverian troops patrolling Liddesdale up to Hermitage castle in the wake of the retreat of the rebel army from Derby to the north of Scotland, following the collapse of the second great Jacobite uprising.

You look puzzled. I see. Well, do you know anything about Bonnie Prince Charlie? Yes, something like that. The battle of Culloden? Even better. Well, this took place around that time. Prince Charlie's men have retreated back into Scotland and the Hanoverian forces are gathering to crush them. Hanoverian; the royalist forces; we can call them the English if you like, although many of them were Scottish. Taylor and his men are looking for stragglers from the Jacobite army in the Borders. It is Candlemas Eve – that's right, February – and there is terrible driving rain and sleet, making a march impossible and reducing visibility so much that there is no option but to take cover in whatever shelter they can find, the lee of a wall or a bank, say, and to pull their coats up around their ears. Suddenly, they see two Highlanders ploughing their way through the storm towards them, shouting and waving their weapons, as if in the dreaded Highland charge; with a mixture of reluctance and terror the soldiers struggle to their feet and attempt to prepare their muskets with frozen fingers. Fortunately, there are only the two Highlanders, and they immediately throw their weapons away and advance with hands held up, in surrender. They are able to tell Taylor that there are no other rebels (though they would not have called them so) in the area, whereupon the patrol retires to its makeshift camp, focussed on a barn. There the two prisoners are questioned and Taylor makes his record.

The Highlanders claimed to have deserted for fear of coming disaster in the north, immediately after the Jacobites had crossed the Esk back into Scotland, a few days previously. They were making their way to Edinburgh, where they had friends, by way of Liddesdale and Teviotdale. However, on attempting to cross into Eddesdale the evening before, they had had an experience which had forced them to give up their plans and made surrender to the English or death in the blizzard seem preferable to enduring it again. When questioned as to what exactly had happened, however, the two men became, in Taylor's words, "fearful and reluctant to speak, as if the mere mention of what had befallen them should bring it back upon them"; under pressure, however, this fear turned to "embarrassment, since it did appear that what had affrighted them so was no more than a noise, the which they heard under the walls of the old fortress which stands there, though I know said fortress to be unoccupied and scarce capable of habitation by even such as they". Taylor seems to have lost interest soon afterwards, and only comments on the potency of the locally-distilled spirit after hearing from one that the sound was "that of all the demons in hell shrieking for blood" and from the other that it was "the wailing of all the damned in their torment". We do not know what happened to the two Highlanders – though Jacobite prisoners generally did not fare well – but their story connects with the most well-known early occurrence of the phenomenon, which happened less than three months later but did not appear in print for a further twenty-five years, when it spread the tale and perhaps influenced the editor of the ballad of the *Raid*.

Are you still with me? All right. And that machine is still running? Good. It is as well that you brought it; it would have been a sore trial to you to have taken all this down on paper. But to continue. The story goes that in April 1746 a shepherd boy was brought to a local minister because he had been badly scared near Eddesdale castle and, although no-one else had been involved, he was too frightened to go back to his duties. The lad eventually admitted that he had been frightened by "the earth itself groaning sorely". It took some time for the minister to convince him that it was not a ghost or anything else that he should fear; it was a few more days before news from Inverness reached the remote spot and it was realised that the boy's experience had been during the evening of the day of the defeat of the Jacobites at Culloden, on April 17th. For several generations, the Eddesdale Screaming was also known as the Groaning of Scotland, but the connection was in time forgotten. The first detailed account of the story in print is in *Explorations of Edinburgh and the Graces of the Border Abbeys and Castles*, 1823, by Andrew James Hamilton, a Church of Scotland minister with a romantic view of the past closer to that of Walter Scott than to the Presbyterian norm.

So why does the Eddesdale Screaming have such a powerful effect? Firstly, there is the setting, which plays with the nerves in its mixture of tranquillity and tension. Have you actually visited the castle? No? It might have been an idea to have done so before starting your research. Never mind: too late now. Well, typically, the hearer, or possibly pair of hearers, is passing by with the sun setting behind the hills, or in the early dusk, hurrying on his way to the next inn or campsite. Although his focus is down the little valley ahead of him, he glances up at the dark tower silhouetted above him but close enough for him to make out the vacant holes and the jagged crenellations. He may be a little surprised, not expecting such an imposing monument here, but he has seen castles and towers all over the Borders so is not astonished to see the head of the dale so defended. Having looked, he pauses, suddenly conscious of the intense stillness and silence – certainly no traffic, and none even of the normal noises of the countryside, such as birdsong, running water or sheep bleating – and overawed for a moment by the dark, dead stone sentinel. Did it sway then, or was it just the interrupted light of the setting sun? He shivers, not only because the temperature has just gone down a couple of degrees, disturbing his tired and delicate sensibilities even more, and is about to move on – when he hears it.

And yet again, nothing about the Screaming is simple or clearcut, and to present the moment of hearing it as uniform and predictable is an error. It is indeed literally true that most who hear it have come to it in the same way, along the same track through the hills; but in another sense, no two people come here by the same route, or bring to it the same combination of experiences, knowledge and attitudes. You see those folders stacked on that table? Those are the first-hand accounts of the Screaming which I have collected, with notes about the witnesses. You can look at them later; they all have names and addresses appended, with permission, for authenticity, and in many cases written authorisations for the people concerned to be contacted by parties whom I consider suitable, with a view to discussing their experience. You may like to follow some of them up. There we have a black Liberal Arts teacher from Madison, Wisconsin; an Israeli chemical engineer; a couple of middle-aged schoolteachers from Surrey – lesbians, I think; a Lutheran pastor from Saxony; a Danish photographer and her West Indian boyfriend; a future member of the Scottish Parliament – in short, all kinds of people from all over the world; but it's not just the range that's the point – it's the fact that they all converged here, to this precise, out of the way spot, though coming with a multiplicity of beliefs and values; they all heard the Screaming, but they all heard it differently; it made a lasting impression on each of them, but to a different effect in each case.

It is that variety which makes it so hard to describe the Screaming, or even give it a satisfactory name. It would be easy for me to say that it is like a lone wolf howling at the full moon in an icy northern forest, or whatever; and easy for you to write it down, or rather copy it when you play that tape back; and easy for your readers to understand. But it would be a deception: every description of the Screaming in those files is quite different, so much so that it cannot have been the same sound in every case – perhaps not in any two cases. To use of it a word such as shriek, howl, wail, cry or whatever is to ascribe to it particular qualities of pitch, volume, intensity, emotional force which might have been present on every occasion; of course, each of us has also a slightly different understanding of every such word, taking us yet another step away from the reality of the original experience. I listen to the account of a hearer's faulty, biased, subjective memory, couched in approximate language which is at best a shadowy reflection of the event, and attach my own meaning to the words; I summarise that up in a term such as 'scream' and pass it on to you, who have your own, different notion of what a scream is like. What I am getting at is that there is no single account of the sound; either it is purely a subjective experience and different every time, or there is an objective reality which each listener hears or interprets or describes differently. Do you understand me? You might need to listen to that bit of tape more than once, if you choose to make use of it. So what do you understand of what happened?

I see. What did I hear? Well, I suppose that's an easy way to cut through the speculation – but remember that it's just one example, you understand. To me it seemed like a great cliff of sound, with many voices at different pitches from the lowest to the highest range, all on the same indistinct syllable. The oddest thing was that they all started and ended at the exact same moment, and had the same volume throughout. Not shouting – each voice was quite restrained, and there was only one voice on each note – but the overall effect was overwhelming. But that was just what I heard, remember. In those files, you'll find descriptions of high, discordant wailing, gentle undulations like sobbing, and, from one musical lady, a protracted bass groan in a

D minor chord. Of course, if it had been recorded, we might have a better idea of what it sounded like, on at least those particular occasions –as long as we accept that we all have much the same impression created in our minds by a given auditory stimulus. But it has never been recorded, and that little machine of yours would not have been up to the task; you would probably need to set up a whole outdoor recording studio to do it justice, and then of course it would not reveal itself. That leads me to my own theory about the Screaming; I apologise if the route is a little lengthy.

A member of one of the teams of investigators who have been here played me some recordings they had made in a long-abandoned psychiatric hospital of the old type, in Ohio. Some had been made with the machine running in an empty room, and some with the investigators present; the people could be heard at times. Now, these recordings had picked up sounds like distorted voices – voices which could not be heard by those in the room at the same time. Apparently such recordings are common enough these days. He reckoned they were the voices of spirits of the dead, no longer capable of causing the physical effects which lead to what I may call biological hearing but still capable of being detected electronically or magnetically. I don't know about that, and in fact I wasn't sure they were voices at all, though I understand that there is a lot of research into such things: some were gruff sounds like coughs or drawn-out ones like rusty hinges, but some did sound like distant whispers and one very menacing rasping could be heard as "get out of here" – though whether that is what I would have heard if the researcher had not interpreted it for me I do not know. Yes, there is a point to this story, a relevance to the Screaming: assuming the American was telling me the truth about those recordings, they were good evidence for there being a class of physical effects without recognisable physical causes – and here is the parallel with the Eddesdale phenomenon.

Do you not see?

Look, look at it this way. Usually, it is individuals who hear the Screaming, and even when it is a couple they seem to hear very different things. No-one hears it accidentally, at a distance – only people actually standing under the walls of the castle, always at the end of the day. And all accounts of it stress the strangeness of the sound, the way it seems to be universal, so that no-one can tell from which direction it comes. Normal sounds come from a particular direction; even with stereo recordings, one can tell, say, that the 'cellos are on your right and the horns on your left. When I heard the Screaming, the entire sound seemed to surround me completely, from all sides, up from the earth and down from the sky. Perhaps that just means that it is inside the head, originating at one spot deep in the brain and taking total control of its auditory mechanism from within.

Exactly! You have it! I believe the Screaming to come from within, not from outwith the hearer, and to be drawn from what might be termed the subconscious by a particular set of circumstances of time and place. It may be that this is true of many or even all of what are called ghosts. No, how the idea or sound or image gets inside the subconscious mind in the first place I do not know. But we have made some progress in our understanding, perhaps. What's that? What are you doing? Oh, you need to turn the tape over; I see. Is that all right so far?

RESTORATION

"I expect you've had quite a lot of work done to the place since you first came here, when was it, about four years ago?"

"About that. Oh yes, a very great deal. It was pretty dilapidated when we moved in; it hadn't been lived in properly for years, you see. We had to put in modern bathrooms and central heating; we ripped out the kitchen completely; repairs and redecoration were needed in every room. It took two years to get it really habitable. It cost me nearly as much to do it up as it cost to buy. And you wouldn't believe the paperwork."

"And the experiences you described to me started when exactly?"

"Around the time the work was finished. Though it was a few months before we realised that there was something wrong – that it wasn't just tricks of the light or random co-incidences."

"I see. That is a bit unusual."

"Why's that?"

"We often find that these sorts of phenomena start or intensify when work is being done on a place. I would have expected you to have noticed something a lot sooner. Which part of the building did you start with, when you were doing all this renovation?"

"The rooms we needed for living here, I suppose; the master bedroom suite, the kitchen, the lounge. Then we started staying here for periods while the rest of the work was done, until we could move from Edinburgh completely. Though I still have a small flat in the city."

"And those rooms would be over here, in the newer part of the castle?"

"Aye. We didn't do as much in the tower. Not as radical, as it were. There it was more about preserving the existing features, as the surveyor and the architect put it. And we don't use the rooms over there much, except for the studio. I didn't need that until we left Edinburgh."

"The studio being the old hall?"

"Aye, that's right. So what was that about ghosts and building work?"

I should explain a bit about the topography of the place before I go any further, so you the reader can understand what is going on. Castle Merleston was built in two main phases, according to what I've read. First came a fifteenth-century tower house with three storeys, topped by battlements and corbie-steps: the great hall in the middle, with storerooms and animal shelters below and private chambers above. The rectangular two-storey wing was attached to it two hundred years later, in a similar but more fancy style. Latterly, the Merles used the tower only for special occasions, the hall serving as a ballroom and the chambers as guest bedrooms, until the last of them left about fifteen years ago; with his death ten years later, the building came up for sale just at the time when James Sinclair had become sufficiently established and sufficiently rich to look for a suitably impressive house outwith his native Edinburgh. According to an interview I remember seeing on STV, he wanted new sources of inspiration and thought that mountains and lochs might do the trick. Not that I know much about art; I only remember it because I thought at the time it was an odd thing for him to say, seeing as how his paintings never include anything you might call realistic, let alone mountains and lochs.

"If you believe that the spirits of the departed stay around the places they knew in life," I said, "then perhaps they are angered by them being changed, even try to protect them. Or if you believe that traces of emotionally-charged deeds in some way linger in the fabric of the places where they occurred, then perhaps disturbances trigger a shadowy rerun of events."

Even before I knew he was there, Donald's trademark snort signalled his appearance behind me.

"The 'stone tape' theory?" suggested Sinclair.

"You know about that?"

"Aye, I started reading up about ghosts and haunted houses when things started happening here. I never had any time for such matters before; thought it was all superstitious nonsense, really. Strange how first-hand experience can change your mind so quickly."

"Perhaps too quickly sometimes," Donald chipped in, with his usual brusqueness. "When you start altering things in an old, settled building like this, it's bound to disturb other parts of it. You knock a hole through a wall, the doorframe above moves and suddenly the door starts sticking or swinging open. You move a heavy piece of furniture that's been there for decades and the loose floorboards beneath start creaking. You – "

"Thank you, Donald. My colleague is pointing out that sometimes there are purely physical causes for apparently strange phenomena, and we have to be very careful to rule them out before we come to any conclusions."

"I wasn't expecting one of you to be a sceptic!" Sinclair was surprised, disappointed even. I needed to shift the focus back onto the matter in hand.

"It's no bad thing to have someone on the team who ensures we keep a proper balance. Now, when we spoke on the 'phone you said that you had seen things?"

"That's right; not just me either. But I'm not sure that I'd call it 'seeing' exactly."

"Either you saw things or you didn't." I hadn't succeeded in suppressing Donald. Don't get me wrong: Donald is a useful member of the group. I wasn't lying when I said it helps our credibility to have an obvious sceptic amongst us, and he can be a valuable brake on the excesses of our more imaginative and romantic members. I just wish sometimes he didn't have to force a black-and-white dichotomy, a clear-cut simplicity, on absolutely everything. Things just aren't like that, at least outwith pure mathematics – but there again, he is a maths lecturer. And I wish he would be a little more tactful with the clients at times.

"It's hard to explain." Sinclair was uncharacteristically struggling to express himself – though in his case the problem came from a desire to be as precise as possible, rather than from a simple lack of words. "I – not just I; others who have had the experience say the same thing. I am aware of something, and I am aware of it visually, through my eyes, but it is not like seeing something in the normal way."

"How so?" I was interested; the man was an artist, and knew about looking at things.

"With most things, the more directly and the longer you look at them, the clearer they become, the more detail you see, the more they stand out from the background. With this, it's just the opposite. You glimpse it at the edge of sight, out of the corner of your eye as they say, but when you turn to look straight at it, it fades away – quickly, so that you're never sure what it is you've seen."

"If anything," snorted Donald. I winced, but Sinclair didn't seem to be offended.

"Oh, it was there, right enough; I'm sure of that. In my business, you learn to see more than others. But this happens when it's quite dark, and it gets lost in the shadows very quickly."

"Well, I'm not unfamiliar with the kind of phenomenon you describe." I wasn't sure what I was going to say, but I had to stop Donald from having another go at him, in case he began to think we were only there to mock. "And it's in this part of the house that you usually see them?"

"Well, no. Actually it's usually in the tower."

"In the hall?"

"The studio."

"Aye, the studio." I needed to get as much information as possible from him about what he had experienced, because there was no other source. Usually when we do an investigation, it is in a place with a long history of happenings and we read up on it beforehand; even if it is only an old legend, there is invariably a starting point. But there was nothing about Castle Merleston: no sinister traditions, no earlier records of sightings, no family stories. Before the Sinclairs moved in, it seemed, it was one of the few castles in Scotland without a resident ghost, brownie or other supernatural being – allegedly.

"There, and in the rooms above. Most of the guest bedrooms are up there. That's where other people have seen things."

"It begins to make sense: the work on the tower was done more recently, which is when the phenomena started. That is clearly where we need to concentrate the investigation."

Mrs. Sinclair reappeared, followed by the maid, Janet, with a tray.

There were a half a dozen varied glasses on it, with a variety of drinks in them. Mrs. Sinclair was already half-way down a large red wine; it was just as well she wasn't carrying the tray. "Here we are! At last! G. and T. for James. White wine for – "

"Seonaid. Thank you. Would you mind me asking?" I said. "You said you see it in the dark: why would you be in the hall, the studio, in the dark?"

"And beer for – quite." Donald raised his glass and winked at her mischievously.

Sinclair grimaced at him and smiled at me. "We had to put in a lot of lighting, especially in there, as the windows aren't very large. There's a switchboard, but it's a few steps from the door. It's when I've just put the lights out, or before I put them on, that it happens. You see, I often work very late, or even get up in the night to go to the studio."

"Yes, too often. He wakes me up, doesn't he? Don't you? Blundering about in the dark. As always." Mrs. Sinclair drained her glass and took another from the tray.

"I never developed a disciplined work-habit; I just paint whenever the spirit moves me."

Not the best choice of words, I thought. Mrs. Sinclair was steering Janet towards the door.

"I see. Perhaps it's time I had a look at the studio, and see how Dave and Moira are getting on," I suggested.

We followed them out into a white-washed, stone-flagged corridor which led to a broad flight of stone steps, at the top of which was an impressive double door of dark wood inside a pointed arch and flanked by two suits of armour. To the side, at ground level, was a smaller, though equally ancient, door. I asked Sinclair what

264

was through it.

"The crypt!" he said, with a comic air of menace. I assumed he meant the old cellars I had read about; they would certainly need investigating. Outsiders tend to think people in our line of investigation only work in grand rooms full of antiques or in echoing chapels; in fact, we spend a lot of time poking around damp basements and cobwebbed attics, examining ancient plumbing and old electricity cables for sources of unexplained noise and magnetic anomalies. And you'd be surprised how many of the reports we get in are about bathrooms and toilets – often installed in what were once very different types of rooms.

Mrs. Sinclair was making a grand gesture of pulling open one leaf of the double door to let Janet through with her tray – almost pitching herself back down the steps in the process. I hung back, not wanting red wine splashed on my new jacket; Sinclair insisted on holding the door open, which Donald assumed was for his benefit. The artist hardly seemed to notice his wife's behaviour; either he was so used to it that he really didn't notice, or else his way of dealing with the embarrassment was to pretend it wasn't happening. Neither scenario said much about their marriage of some fifteen years, dating from about the time when Sinclair had first gained international recognition.

Inside the hall, or studio, David and Moira had been taking preliminary magnetic field readings and setting up cameras and recording equipment. "We're about done here," said David; he's a professional photographer and she's an IT wizard, both invaluable skills for the group in collecting and analysing data.

I don't know if you have an image of an artist's studio in your mind, but I suppose I always thought it would be like a Vermeer interior, with light streaming into a spotless, uncluttered room and an elegant, even foppish figure dabbing with a brush at a canvas on an easel. So James Sinclair's workplace was a bit of a disappointment, disillusionment even. The hall was evidently intended to be used occasionally as a dining room, though it would have taken quite an effort to get it into a state fit for a formal dinner party of the sort I imagined Mrs. Sinclair expected to give, when sober. The chairs were lined up against the walls, with the long table pushed against one side; that was apparently of dark oak, massive with bulbous legs which I could see below the old blankets draped over the top to protect it from the jars of tinted water, tubes and pots of paint, brushes and palette knives which were scattered across it haphazardly. Stained and splashed sheets also covered much of the wooden floor. And the room was quite dark, though it was still broad daylight; the windows were not plentiful or large for such a large space, and it didn't help that the walls were wood-panelled, apart from the chimney-breast of dressed stone. The fire-surround was of massive grey stone blocks, simply and shallowly carved with armorial designs, and in the fireplace, which could have taken bunk beds comfortably, was a great iron rack for burning logs in. Either side of the fireplace hung abstract paintings, mainly in purple and orange, the size of double mattresses.

The one feature which fitted my preconception was the easel, though it was a chipped, paint-marked, plain piece of wooden geometry rather than the classically ornate antique I envisaged. On it was a canvas nearing completion – if the amount of surface covered with paint was a guide, as I didn't know what it was supposed to represent. It was basically irregular vertical bands of colour, arranged like a rainbow though far more solid-looking, being laid on thickly and roughly, and with a deepening of the shade across each band. A jagged red line cut down through the middle of the yellow and blue strips.

"The latest – creation?" I nearly said "masterpiece", but stopped myself in time, in case it sounded sarcastic. As perhaps it would have been.

"What is it?" asked Donald, without my qualms and caution.

"Modern art," I hissed.

"It will be *Red Shift in Spectrum Number Two* when it's finished."

"I see." I looked at it in silence for a while. It was the silence of astonishment and ignorance, but I hoped the artist would take it for awe and reverence. Donald wandered over to a stack of canvases propped against the wall and began pulling the tops of them back individually, like someone leafing through prints in a shop. I wished he would leave things alone.

"What will you get for that?"

"Fifty thousand."

Donald promptly let the canvases fall back into place gently, realising that he was casually flicking through half a million pounds' worth.

"Really? It'll fetch as much as that?"

"Yes. In fact it's been paid for already. It's a commission from a banker in Edinburgh. He already has *Red Shift in Spectrum Number One.* He bought it at auction for thirty last year and he wants this to go on the other side of the fireplace in his holiday villa." There was a tone of disgust in his voice.

"But you must be pleased about it?"

"Not entirely. I only got two grand for *Number One* originally. That was some time ago. I have very different things to say about the subject now. They're not really going to look like a pair."

We looked back at the unfinished painting, then at the door as

Janet closed it behind her. It was hard to imagine what would have been the other half of such a pair.

"Are those yours too?" I asked, indicating the huge pictures on the wall.

"Good heavens no! That's an Alexander Patterson and that's a St. John Stewart. Nothing like mine. But they're not bad, and I needed two pieces of the same size to fill the spaces. In any case, I couldn't afford to put a hundred grand or more of my own stuff up on the wall, not with this place to keep up. I picked up those for five grand apiece from a dealer in Edinburgh who was going out of business."

"I never realised art was so much about money," said Donald, gloomily. Really, I could kick him sometimes.

Sinclair just shrugged. "It's a business. It's my trade." So much for Vermeer.

Mrs. Sinclair had given out the drinks and engaged in some conversation with David and Moira which involved a good deal of laughter tinged with hysteria on her part. She was now leaning over a recorder which they had set up, and looking disappointed. "It's very small, isn't it?" She turned away and moved over to face me, still bent forward with her glass at an alarming angle. "Seonaid." She drew the "sh" out to a ridiculous length. "Don't you have any of those vacuum-cleaner things?"

I didn't know what to say.

"You must excuse my wife. When she heard that you were coming, she imagined it would be like a cross between *Ghostbusters* and *The Exorcist*."

"Excuse me, excuse me; I am talking to Seonaid." Mrs. Sinclair drained the glass again. "Seonaid." Then she began to giggle, shaking; it was just as well her glass was empty. I recall someone telling me she had been an actress before marrying Sinclair; she had even been in films, apparently, though I've never seen her in anything. I wondered what sort of films. Then she stopped giggling, and the shaking turned to a shiver.

"But this place is too cold for hell." She looked around her. "Look at it! I hate this place. Why did we have to come here?" This to her husband, with venom. "Oh yes, James has to have his place in the country, his castle, so that he can have all his Edinburgh friends over and play the laird. Where does that leave me?" Then to me, with a pleading tone: "Seonaid, can you make them go away?"

"Your friends?"

"No, no, no. Those – things. Those things that aren't really there. Can you make them go away? Seonaid."

"Well, I'm afraid we are only here to study phenomena, not really to get rid of them. We're not Rentokil."

My attempt at lightening the tone didn't work: she burst into tears. Sinclair finally intervened, taking her by the arm and pulling her gently towards the door. "Come along, dear."

As she went, she turned to me again. "Please do your best, love. Do your best." Was there a hint of a Glaswegian accent in there, for an unguarded moment?

With the Sinclairs out of the room, there was an uneasy silence as we looked at each other, broken only by a sardonic snort from Donald. Suddenly, he didn't seem so much of a liability – not as embarrassing as the client's wife.

"Right, we've got work to do. We are going to be spending the time here in the tower where, as you know, the activity is concentrated. Mr. Sinclair is going to show us around the rest of the rooms and we'll have a tour of the grounds to see what external sources of interference there might be. By then it'll be starting to get dark. We'll have a bite to eat, and then the first vigil will be me and Donald in here, probably with Mr. Sinclair, and David and Moira upstairs. After that, we play it by ear according to what happens. If anything. OK?"

"What about the others?" asked Donald.

"Others?"

"The wife, and the maid?"

"Janet doesn't live in. She'll be going home after we've eaten. And I gather that Mrs. Sinclair won't be joining us."

"You mean she'll be wandering around the house? That will compromise the rules."

Donald meant the practice guidelines, the first and most important of which was that everyone present on site should be accounted for and observed by another group member, or through a camera, at all times. We had to eliminate the risk that clients were causing phenomena themselves, either intentionally or accidentally, and even that we might inadvertently do so ourselves.

"She will be keeping to the new wing. She won't affect what's happening over here."

"That's what they'll tell us. But you've seen what she's like. A loose cannon."

Pretty much like you, Donald. But I didn't say so. Nor did I mention aloud what I really expected to happen: that she would drink more wine and safely pass out for the rest of the night.

****

Now, in my experience spiral staircases in castles are nasty, narrow, dark wells, the medieval equivalent of the staircases at the sides of multi-storey car parks, but this was different: it was bright, with white walls, a red carpet and recessed lighting. There were handrails of white rope in brass rings, matching the brass stair rods and the surrounds of the lights.

"It goes down into the cellar and right up into the turret on the roof. There's a lift as well, down the other side: we would have had difficulty getting the furniture upstairs without it."

We stepped out through the arch on the first floor and Sinclair showed us the guest rooms, with the air of an unconvinced estate agent. In truth, there was little to be said. Two large double rooms with full en suite and dressing rooms, and two other double and two single rooms sharing two bathrooms. Each room had a set of matching furniture, but no two were identical; the carpets and curtains were the same throughout, and the decoration was all exposed masonry, white-painted plaster and dark brown woodwork, doors and beams. Only two questions occurred to me as we walked round, and I asked neither: did Janet have to clean all this on her own, and on what criteria did the Sinclairs allocate the rooms amongst their friends? What I said was, "Do you get many guests?"

"It doesn't happen very often – my work won't stand too much interruption – but when it does we have eight or nine down for the weekend." He paused for a moment. "That didn't sound very good, did it, interruption? The point is that the studio has to be dismantled and cleaned up so that we can use it for entertaining. A weekend is the equivalent of a week of the studio being out of action."

"And how many of them, the guests, have seen or heard things?"

"Well, at least one person almost every time we have had a party down – that would be nine or ten times in two and a half years. So around twenty people, I would say, that we know of. I started writing down their accounts after a while, and there are a dozen of those."

"Could we see those?"

"Of course."

"And can we have a look at the cellars?"

"No problem, but I ought to warn you that it's a bit of a mess down there. I plan to do something with it one day, but we haven't got round to it yet."

"What will you do with it?"

"I fancy a small cinema. A gym, perhaps, for guests; that wouldn't really interest me."

"We'll just keep an eye on it this time, but concentrate on this level and the hall. Studio. We'll give it a bit more attention if nothing happens up here."

We went down to the lower level, and Sinclair produced a key to the stout oak door: "I keep it locked because the safe's in here." The ceiling in the cellars was noticeably lower than in the rest of the house, and the rooms were even darker than the hall; a couple of the high windows had been enlarged at some point, but most were still the narrow slits intended to keep intruders out rather than let daylight in. They weren't really cellars, more a ground floor a couple of steps down from ground level, with the grand hall above being the real lowest level of living space. The Sinclairs had evidently dumped the debris of their move in this basement and never thought of it since. Apart from a safe in one corner free of clutter, there were old tea-chests; discarded wrapping paper and dust-sheets; empty five-litre paint tins; large cardboard boxes, some standing and some flattened. In one room, I noticed what were obviously a couple of large pictures propped against the wall and covered with sheets.

"More of yours?" I asked.

"No, certainly not. They were in the studio when we moved in – where those pieces that you asked about are hanging now."

"You took them down?"

"Yes. I couldn't work with them watching me. They had to go!"

"Did the last people leave much behind?"

"No, not really." He frowned. "Now you come to mention it, hardly anything at all. Just those two canvases and some mouldy old rubbish in bags and boxes down here and in the attic. Odd, now I think about it – that they should leave two pictures. We got the rest of it taken away."

"But not these?"

"No. One day I'll get someone down from Edinburgh to value them. I'm sure someone'll pay good money for them. Genuine early nineteenth-century Scottish kitsch – good market for that amongst the émigré element in the States. I just keep forgetting to do anything about it."

"Oh, right." I went over and pulled one back, dragging off the sheet, so that I could look at them as far as the partial view and the gloom would allow. They were full-length, near life-size portraits in oils, in heavy, tarnished gilt frames and darkened with age. One showed a middle-aged man with a determined expression on his tilted face, dressed in an early nineteenth-century idea of Scottish, or rather Walter Scottish, costume: a vast plaid worn like a toga, a shortish kilt, a huge fur sporran and an enormously tall feather bonnet. One hand was on his hip and the other held the tip of the barrel of a long, ornate musket with its butt resting on the ground, where the corpse of a stag, disproportionately small for the great size of its antlers, was curled. It reminded me of the pictures of George IV in the fancy-dress version of Highland dress he wore on his Scottish visit. Everything that could be tartan was, from the plaid and kilt down to the long hose and hackle. And what a tartan: scarlet and a garish yellow, which was echoed in the sash of the pale Regency dress worn by the haughty woman with piled-up red hair who was the subject of the second painting. I could see that Sinclair might be distracted by them. Both of them were pictured against a menacing background of gathering clouds, bending trees with bunches of dark-blue foliage and a distant stretch of grey water.

****

We left Castle Merleston after a late breakfast. We had seen and heard nothing all night, but David and Moira took the films and recordings away to analyse; it's not unusual for something unobserved during the vigil to make an appearance afterwards, captured on the media. I drove Donald back to his flat in town before carrying on to the village where I stay. Even before I got the front door of the cottage open, I could hear my cat, coincidentally called Merlin, howling for food: the battery-powered carousel which had had four meals in it when I left was empty. After feeding him hurriedly, I went up and lay on the bed, feeling drained and fell asleep almost at once. I knew that David and Moira would be spending the rest of the day analysing the material, and would be at it until late for the next two or three evenings. The all-nighters have really started to take it out of me, though; age, I suppose. When I was a psychology student, I often left an essay or seminar paper until the evening before it was due, and then stayed up until the early hours to write it, even after a session in the union bar. I couldn't do it now; I couldn't even manage the bar now.

It wasn't the proverbial dreamless sleep. I was back at the castle, watching Sinclair dabbing away at his canvas, though we seemed to be in the cellars rather than the studio. He was getting frustrated, because he was trying to paint with red wine and it wasn't working. Even worse, Mrs. Sinclair was trying to drink it as he worked; the angrier he got, the more she giggled hysterically. But we weren't alone: the noise aroused a figure which stepped slowly out of the shadows under the small, high windows, growing and becoming more distinct as it came forward into the light. A figure in an overblown version of Highland dress, almost as far removed as it could be from the traditional working clothes of the Gael. An absurdly tall and bushy bearskin hat and an equally voluminous cloak of the most garish yellow and red tartan made him look gigantic, and even more intimidating was the stern, rigid expression above his slightly raised chin. We cowered, but felt relieved when he stopped his measured approach; however, our panic returned when he raised the long musket he was carrying and took aim at us.

Then he fired. Not just one shot, but bursts of fire, like a machine gun; surely old muskets couldn't do that? No, it wasn't gunfire: it was the 'phone, the mobile which I use mostly for group business, which had woken me up. I checked to see who it was: there was no name, but I recognised the number as being Castle Merleston. I glanced at the time as I answered it: I had been asleep less than half an hour. What was he playing at? I had told him that we would be back in touch when we had processed the material and met to discuss it, in a week's time at the earliest. But it was him doing the telling off.

"Outrageous..... thought you were professionals..... let you into my house in good faith..... behaving like hooligans..... good mind to call the police....." And so on. I was tired, annoyed and unable to concentrate: he was furious, loud and scarcely coherent. I couldn't take it in or deal with him. No, I couldn't call him back later; he was going to the police if I refused to do something about it immediately. All right, if I came in person to see it he would wait. Aye, after dinner then. Good - that gave me a couple of hours. I set the alarm on the mobile before falling back on the bed.

I was still yawning as I drove up to the castle. I hadn't been able to sleep; it wasn't until I had lain back that it had sunk in. Something had happened while we had been doing our investigation, some damage had been done, and Sinclair was blaming us for it. Exactly what, I didn't know: Sinclair hadn't been explicit – he had seemed to imagine that I knew what he was talking about – and I hadn't been sufficiently with it to ask the pertinent question. Well, I was soon about to face his wrath and find out. The important thing was to prevent anything happening which might destroy the group's reputation, and if feasible keep the client happy; I was discounting the possibility of us having actually done something reprehensible. I got out of the car, shook myself down and braced myself to meet his accusations with dignity and politeness; I had thought of bringing Donald for support, possibly even as a witness, but had decided that he was more likely to inflame the situation.

"Right, what have you to say for yourself?" This on the doorstep. He wasn't the suave, well-mannered character we had seen earlier; he stood solidly, arms folded and legs apart, filling the open half of the entrance. He had, though, had time to calm down since the 'phone call.

"I'm sorry, Mr. Sinclair, but I am struggling to understand the precise nature of your complaint."

A few more icy exchanges, in which he seemed to be doubting

my innocence, and he ordered me to follow him into the house. He went up the steps and into the studio, flicked on a battery of glaring lights and marched across to the easel. "There, now what have you to say to that?"

Red Shift was still there, and as far as I could see it was just as it had been. Mind you, it would have taken quite a lot of difference for me to have noticed any change to it: it wasn't the sort of picture you could disfigure with a comic moustache. I stared in silence, not knowing what to say; that much resembled my first encounter with it. "Well?"

"I, I am sorry, Mr. Sinclair, I don't see – "

"Look, woman, look there!"

In exasperation, he was waving his hand diagonally across the canvas. I edged closer and squinted. Yes, there was something: a cut through the thick ridges of paint from one corner to the other, a very fine, neat cut, as though done carefully and precisely with a razor or scalpel. The painting had in effect been slashed, but it was nothing like the brutal jagged tear one would expect from the use of that word. You had to look very closely to see it, and perhaps only then with a clue, but I refrained from saying that you'd hardly notice it.

"So what have you say about it now?"

"I really don't know what to say, except that it has nothing to do with our group being here. Which is what I think you are implying."

He had become less aggressive. "I'm not saying that you personally had anything to do with it, or even that you knew about it. You seemed pretty genuine just now, and you wouldn't have come alone like this if you had been guilty of such a dreadful act."

Thanks a lot. First-class honours in psychology, and as transparent as glass; fifteen years in the classroom, and frightened of a crazy painter. "But it had to have been one of your lot. My money's on that fat one: he didn't seem to have any respect for anyone or anything. Manners of a pig."

I fought back a desire to bring Mrs. Sinclair into the debate. "I am sorry but I have known Donald and worked with him for nearly ten years. We have been on twenty or more investigations together. His manner may be rough and ready at times, but it is ridiculous to imagine that he would do anything like this. What possible reason could he have?"

"Well, perhaps it was one of the others. They looked young and foolish enough."

"David is a professional photographer and as much an artist as anyone; it is absurd to think he could do this. And Moira is an IT manager with more to lose than the rest of us put together, as regards her professional reputation. So I am afraid that I cannot give any credence to your allegations."

He started to get angry again; I had the distinct feeling that he was unused to failing to get his own way and didn't know how to cope with frustration. "Well who the hell did this? You imagine I did it myself perhaps, threw away fifty grand in order to embarrass your little clique of weirdos? Or perhaps Janet crept in here and did it, risking losing a very comfortable little berth? Or perhaps my wife, eh?"

Actually, that wasn't so silly a suggestion, as I think Sinclair realised as soon as he had said it – hence his not elaborating the idea. She had been very agitated, had expressed a loathing for the place and had been very drunk when we left; she could have done anything in that state. Or perhaps not quite anything. That slice required a steady hand, a sustained pressure; it was almost dead straight and perfectly even.

"So who?" he roared.

Now, I've seen a toy car filmed apparently moving six inches across a flat surface in under half an hour; I've left a coin in the centre of a saucer and come back to find it near the rim; I've heard a book fall off a shelf from between other books and found it on the floor. But this was on a different scale altogether. Neither of us was looking in the right direction, so we couldn't say exactly what happened, but I caught a glimpse of movement out of the corner of my eye, in the direction of the fireplace, and a second later there was an almighty crash as the St. John Stewart canvas fell off the wall. Or rather it fell down the wall – straight down, not outwards, so that it came to rest upright. We were both watching it, horrified, as it slowly tilted forward from the top and finally passed its point of equilibrium and slammed flat onto the floor. Almost at once the Alexander Patterson performed the same trick.

****

"Now listen."

There was a brief silence; then we heard it. It wasn't as loud or as clear as the last time I had heard such a thing, but it was definitely a human voice, even if one unlike any voice you have ever heard, And I could recognise the tone, the deep, hollow tone; I couldn't make out the words, but it was the same voice. A strong brogue. It didn't last long; just long enough to disturb even Donald.

"Play it again," I said, "louder. So, this is the famous voice I have heard about, is it?"

"OK, but there's more." Moira rewound the tape a little.

"I need the bathroom." Then as an afterthought as he left the room, Donald muttered, "Excuse me".

The rest of us listened intently. It was tantalising: it was speech, but too indistinct for us to make out the words. Almost sotto voce; almost as though someone was talking to himself.

"Can you make it out?" I asked Moira.

"No. I've listened scores of time, but not a word. Now listen to this."

Dave played another tape. There was a short silence, then a faint rasping which became another voice. A much higher one; a woman's voice, again a brogue. This was a little clearer, in places, though at a distance and not directed to us. There was a possible "people", a definite "them", something which might have been "the chairs". Then it stopped, and Moira played it again.

"And that's not all." David was grinning his puckish grin and was plainly bursting to show us something. He fiddled with the equipment. The CCTV images disappeared and instead one of the monitors showed a patchwork of colours, mainly greyish. "You remember I left the thermal imaging camera on record while we were out of the room? OK. It was pointing at the fireplace, where he said most of the activity had been seen. You can see here: most of the room is pretty cold, and this great black area in the middle is the hole where the cold air comes in down the chimney. OK? You remember we left some of the lights on, for the cameras, including the strip lights above the paintings? OK. That's the very bright bars you see in the top corners. Then you get some brightness going down the image where the lights are heating up the tops of the pictures, fading into darkness as it becomes colder. OK? Now watch this. Remember that this is just after three o'clock, around the time those sounds were being recorded."

We watched intently.

"What are we supposed to be seeing?"

Then I became aware of it. The patch of brightness to the left of the fireplace was shrinking towards the light-source, as though cold was creeping up the painting. And it was not just the darkness of the room which was replacing it: it was the total blackness of the hearth. Donald returned, but sat down away from the screen. After a minute or so, only the horizontal line of the lamp was yellow, and the same thing was happening on the right-hand side. Finally, when both patches of light had been consumed, the strip lights themselves went out.

"The recording runs out shortly after this," said David, with a note of regret. "But I'm sure those lights were back on when we came back into the room."

"So what are we thinking?" I asked no-one in particular.

"We are thinking that we have good evidence of activity: EVP and thermals, to add to what you saw with the falling pictures."

"But no sightings, no unexplained movement, no clearly articulated auditory phenomena."

"We've had less at times in the past," Moira suggested.

"And we've had nothing, often enough," added Donald.

"So this is somewhere in between. So we go back to the client, show him what we have, and say that we think he is right in identifying unexplained activity in his house, but that we can't add really anything to his understanding of it. Right? I think he might have been expecting something a bit more definite than that."

****

We turned up at Castle Merlestone, just I and Moira, with the recordings. Sinclair opened the door and without speaking to us began to lead us quickly towards the studio; there was clearly something very wrong. Leaving the equipment, we followed.

"Is everything all right, Mr. Sinclair?"

"I know it can't be you. You haven't been here. I'm not blaming you – well, perhaps I am. We didn't get this until you came here. I don't know what you've done to cause this."

"Cause what? What is it, Mr. Sinclair?"

He didn't reply, but he didn't need to; when we entered the studio, it was clear what he was talking about. The damaged *Red Shift* had been taken off the easel and another canvas put in its place, with apparently a few strokes of a new painting on it – but that was not all: there was scoring across the face of it, not deep but extensive. The rest of the room bore signs of vandalism – an overturned pot of paint on the dining table, oozing red; brushes scattered across the floor; a palette knife stuck into the panelling of the wall. Sinclair was plainly very upset at the violation of his studio, but to my eye it looked curiously limited, disturbing rather than shocking, as though someone had been making a point but not wanting to do much real damage; I suppose to the artist any damage to his work was a serious outrage. I didn't say what I was thinking, and I squeezed Moira's arm before she could speak.

"So have you called the police?"

"No. What am I going to say to them? That a ghost has taken against my artwork?"

"No, but has anyone broken in?"

"No. All the outside doors and windows of the castle have been checked, and there is no sign of anything being disturbed outwith this room."

"I have to ask this," and it felt like the sort of thing the police say in crime dramas, "but do you think it could have been anyone inside the house?"

He looked puzzled. "Margaret," Mrs. Sinclair, "or one of the servants you mean? There was no-one else here. No, it can't have been one of them. Janet and Megan," the cook; I haven't mentioned her before, and in fact I hadn't even met her, "don't live in, and they don't have keys to the house. It can't have been Margaret; she has been in her room all night. Trust me, she couldn't have got up to do this." He didn't have to spell out what he meant.

"And you haven't noticed anything amiss in the rest of the castle?"

"No, nothing."

"Even here in the tower?"

"No, I've been upstairs to check."

Then the moment of inspiration, or rather the result of the experience of several dozen investigations. "OK. What about the cellar?"

"What do you mean?"

"Have you checked the cellar?"

He hadn't been down there since our first visit. Brushing aside his objections – there couldn't be anyone down there; he kept it locked – I made my way determinedly down the staircase so that he had to follow, and stood by the door until he unlocked it. It was pretty much as I remembered it, with one exception; I waited for

Sinclair to spot it for himself.

"Someone has moved them!"

"How could anyone have moved them, if you have the key?"

The two old portraits, the man in faux-Highland costume and the woman in the Regency dress, were propped, unwrapped, against the wall just inside the door instead of being in the inner room.

"Do you know who they were?"

Sinclair shrugged and made an equivalent facial expression. I got him to help me pull the painting of the man forward and to hold it up while I stooped and looked at the back. "There's a label. We need a torch." There was one on a table by the door. The writing was flowery and faded after two hundred years, but I could make out 'Eòghan Merle of Merleston, Baron of Glen Merle. 1823'. The year after the visit of George IV to Scotland. Euan, the noble-born. The portrait of the woman, done the same year, was of his wife, Iseabail. I shone the torch onto each face in turn, and Sinclair and I studied them closely; no-one had really looked at them before, to get past the outlandish clothes and settings. The man's face, below the ridiculous hat, was firm and determined; the woman's showed the same bold spirit, and shone with a glow complementing the bright red of her hair. I looked at Sinclair; the artist's expression was one I had not seen so far – compassionate and almost sorrowful.

"What do you think?" I asked.

"I think they don't deserve to be down here."

"Nor to be sent away from their home?"

"No. I suppose I shall have to get used to their company; perhaps on the stairs."